THE MOTHER'S SECRET

CLARE SWATMAN

ISIS
LARGE
PRINT

First published in Great Britain 2018
by
Pan Books
an imprint of Pan Macmillan

First Isis Edition
published 2018
by arrangement with
Pan Macmillan

A catalogue record for this book is available
from the British Library.

ISBN 978–1–78541–622–4 (hb)
ISBN 978–1–78541–628–6 (pb)

Published by
F. A. Thorpe (Publishing)
Anstey, Leicestershire

Set by Words & Graphics Ltd.
Anstey, Leicestershire
Printed and bound in Great Britain by
T. J. International Ltd., Padstow, Cornwall

For Andrew, Lisa, Will and Megan

Prologue

Something feels wrong as soon as I turn the corner. The house is in complete darkness, which is unusual. Light glows through the curtains of the other houses either side, making my home appear lonely and forlorn.

Standing on the stone step, I slide the key into the lock. It turns effortlessly and the door opens with a click. Silence spills down the stairs and pushes past me, surrounding me as I step into the cool hallway. The radiator ticks familiarly and I shrug my coat away before hanging it on the hook. There are no other coats there, which is odd. There are no other shoes lined up along the wall either. I shake each boot off, and leave them standing guard all alone. My ears listen for familiar noise — footsteps, someone breathing, a kettle boiling. Anything. But there's nothing but quietness.

My footsteps are muffled on the carpeted floor as I walk towards the door of the living room, which stands ajar. I give it a little push and it opens slowly; it's dark in there too, just a faint orange glow from the streetlight outside giving the furniture some form and shape through the heavy net curtains. The grate of the fire is completely dark, not even the smallest ember glowing

1

to suggest someone has been there recently. I shiver as I walk down the hallway. Ahead of me, the door to the kitchen stands open but I can see as I approach that there's no one there. I walk quietly across the tiles, my feet tapping gently with every step, and lay my hand on the kettle, the stove, the pan that sits on the side. Stone cold. There's a single cup on the table, a rim of coffee staining the inside and a red heart shape on the outside where lipstick has marked it. Half a biscuit sits on a china plate, a small bite taken out of it, the crumbs scattered round as though the person eating it had suddenly remembered they had something more important to do and just got up and left.

As I walk up the stairs, my breath hitches in my chest as a noise comes from the loft hatch. I stop, not daring to look up, listening for more signs of life. But there's nothing except the quiet hum of silence pressing heavily on my eardrums. I cover my ears with my hands and move on, pushing open the door of Mum's bedroom. The covers on her bed are neatly tucked in, hospital corners perfectly folded, a pink cushion propped up in front of the pillow. Her hairbrush with a few grey hairs caught in the bristles lies neatly in front of the mirror, next to a modest collection of make-up, face creams and pills. Mum's always so well put together, her room is always neat and tidy, but as I run my finger slowly along the wooden top of the dressing table there's a thick layer of dust on the end of it. Every surface is covered in thick dust. It looks as though the room's been abandoned for years, and yet we were all here this morning, together. Weren't we?

My body starts to shake as I walk quickly to the next room, the bedroom I share with my sister Kate, and push the door open. I'm not sure what I expected but my heart almost stops when I look in here. Instead of the two beds pressed tightly against the walls with a tiny table squeezed in the middle, the room is almost empty, as though nobody has been in here for years. Thick dust covers this room too; there's a pasting table in the middle with a roll of wallpaper hanging over it, the brush sitting on top, dried out. Pots of paint are piled in the corner and a cot, in pieces, is propped up against the wall. I stumble as I step towards the table and lift up the corner of the wallpaper. It's brittle and almost snaps in my hand, but I can see that the pattern is the same as the one that's been on my bedroom wall for as long as I can remember.

My knees feel weak and I'm not sure they'll be able to hold my weight for much longer so I crouch down and hold my head, pressing the palms of my hands hard into my eyes until I see stars.

But when I look up, nothing has changed.

I slowly walk back out of the room and tread down the stairs, clinging to the banister as I do. Each step makes my legs shake and my heart is pounding a hole in my ribcage as I try to swallow down the panic that threatens to overwhelm me. When I reach the bottom of the stairs I glance back at the kitchen and my heart stops again. I scurry closer, my eyes surely deceiving me, and stop dead in the doorway. It's as if the house has gone back in time to the 1970s, the cupboards painted a pale blue and an ashtray on the side with a cigarette propped on the edge, a trail of smoke rising from it and dissipating into the freezing cold air.

My heart is in my mouth and my breath comes in panicky bursts as I walk towards the back door, which is now wide open to the dark winter night, and out into the back garden. As I step out into the freezing air, I shiver. Slowly I tread forwards, each socked foot sinking into the cold, damp grass. But I don't stop. I'm pulled almost magnetically towards the end of the garden, where the shed stands, its door open and swinging in the breeze, squeaking with every back turn. When I reach the shed and look down, there's a patch of ground just in front of it where the earth looks disturbed, as though someone has been digging there, the soil turned over and patted down. What's been planted there? Or buried? I turn back to the house, seeing it in darkness, its windows like black eyes staring into the night. Why is no one else here? Where have they all gone?

What the hell is going on?

My mouth opens and I draw in a deep breath and try to scream but nothing comes out. Here I stand in the middle of the garden screaming silently into the world, a soundless voice unheard by everyone, desperate for someone to come and save me . . .

My sheet is tangled round my body like a straitjacket, constricting my movement, and I'm covered in sweat. My whole body pounds to the rhythm of my heart and I pull air into my lungs, waiting for it to slow down so I can breathe normally again. Pulling my arms out of the

4

sheet, I untwist myself from its confines and drag myself into a sitting position to wait for the world to right itself again.

Beside me Matt sleeps on, his face pressed into the pillow. The clock glowing next to me on the bedside table says 3 a.m.; it's the middle of the night.

My heart is pounding and I try to calm myself by drawing in deep breaths. It was only a dream. But it's a dream I've had several times over the last few years and the panic had felt very real.

Part One

Georgie

CHAPTER
ONE

20 October 2016

Georgie kicks a stone and watches it roll away across the wet sand, bouncing off rocks and pebbles until it comes to a halt just out of reach of a wave. She stops and looks out to sea, the flat grey expanse interrupted only by the occasional rise of white foam, stretching on forever, or to nowhere, the horizon a smudgy, indistinct line far in the distance. She closes her eyes and lifts her face so all she can hear is the wind pushing its way across the sand. It's whipping the sea into a frenzy, sending waves crashing as they hit the shore and shooting spray into the already-damp air. It pulls flags taut on their poles and drags empty crisp packets and dropped tissues with it indiscriminately as it races across the almost-empty beach.

She opens her eyes again and looks down at her feet, studying the footprints she's left in the sand, creeping up behind her like a stalker she can't outrun. A hand slips through the crook of her arm and she turns to find her big sister Kate next to her, smiling.

"Hey, you."

"Hey."

They turn and walk a few steps in silence. The sun is weak behind the gathering clouds and the wind's getting stronger, blowing their hair round their faces and making their eyes water. Georgie leans into the wind until she's almost at a forty-five-degree angle, at tipping point, daring the wind to stop. Next to her Kate shivers in her too-thin coat.

"God, it's cold isn't it?" Georgie straightens up and hugs her arm in tighter to Kate's.

"It is — but if you insist on wearing those clothes what do you expect?"

"Hey!"

"Hey nothing — that's nothing more than a cardigan masquerading as a coat, and your tights are practically useless."

Georgie glances down at her outfit and grins. She loves her patterned tights; oversized cardigans and finding bargains in second-hand shops is her mishmash style. Kate prefers sensible shoes, patterned tops and boot-cut jeans and just doesn't get Georgie's love of the quirky.

"Good point — but you can't really talk, you're shivering like a jellyfish too."

"This is true."

Without realizing it they've stopped again and are both staring out to sea, watching the froth on the tops of the waves gather and wane, over and over, never-ending. Kate plants her feet firmly in the sand to stop herself blowing away, and Georgie holds on tight.

"I wish Dad was here."

The words come out of nowhere and, unsure whether she's heard them right, Georgie leans in closer to Kate. "What did you say?"

Kate brings her mouth closer to Georgie's ear. "I wish Dad was here. Don't you?"

The words skitter and dance in the air between them, trying to find their place. Finally they settle, and Georgie frowns. "Where has *that* come from?"

Kate keeps her eyes trained on the sea and shrugs. "I don't know. Not really. I've just been thinking about him more and more recently."

Georgie follows her sister's gaze out to sea without speaking. She thinks about her father from time to time, of course she does. Naturally she's wondered what life would have been like if they'd grown up knowing him, if he hadn't been taken away from them before she'd even been born. She wonders what she'd be like too, whether she'd be different. Braver, stronger, tougher. Whether she'd have been as close to her mother, and her sister, if she'd had him there to dilute the love. But this question from Kate has still come out of the blue.

Before she gets the chance for an answer to form in her throat, Kate speaks again. "I know I can't miss him exactly. I don't even remember him, but — well, I suppose I do really. Miss him, that is. Especially now with — well, with Mum the way she is."

Georgie nods beside her. "Me too." Her voice is barely more than a whisper and Kate struggles to hear her. They stand in silence a moment longer, letting their thoughts fill the space where their words should be, both thinking about the man in the photo on their mother's mantelpiece, the father they'd never known.

"Do you think he'd be proud? You know, of us?" Georgie pushes a stray hair out of her face and tucks it pointlessly behind her ear, as it blows straight back out again.

"Yes. I think he would." Kate sighs. "But I don't think we'd be us, not us as we are now, if he'd been here." She turns to face Georgie. "Do you?"

"Probably not, no."

"I mean, I bet you wouldn't have fallen in love with the first boy you kissed if you'd had Dad around —"

"Hey, hang on —"

"No, I don't mean it nastily, George, I really don't. I just mean — well, if Dad had been here he probably wouldn't have let Matt anywhere near you, at the age of thirteen anyway."

"Mum wasn't exactly keen."

"True. But it's still different. You probably wouldn't have needed Matt as much if Dad had been here." She stops, thinks for a minute. "And let's face it, George, I probably wouldn't have been such a saddo either."

"Oh Kate, don't say that."

"Why not? It's true. I didn't have any friends at school. I never had a boyfriend. You were my only friend, really, George."

"You were mine too, Kate."

"I know." She shrugs, looks away. "Maybe it could have been different, with Dad here. But then again, maybe not. Who knows? But either way I'd like to think

12

he'd be proud of us. Let's face it, he'd have two pretty different daughters to be proud of."

Georgie smiles. "He definitely would."

They stand for a moment, their words flying away with the wind. Then Kate turns to Georgie.

"Do you think things would have been any different for Mum if Dad hadn't died?"

Georgie feels a hard lump form in her chest and she holds her hand to it. She can feel the soft *tha-thump* of her heart against her palm. Beside her, Kate's eyes are on her, willing her to look round. And, finally, she does.

"I honestly don't know."

The words are barely a whisper, but Kate shakes her head and turns away. "No, me neither. I'd like to think so, though." There's a beat of silence. Then: "George, I'm really worried about her."

Georgie nods. She'd known this was coming from the moment Kate had suggested a walk on the beach this morning. Now the words have arrived and there's no taking them back.

"You know she's been getting much worse, don't you?"

Georgie nods again. "Yes. Yes, I do. She didn't seem to know what was going on when I saw her a few days ago. She thought she was going to meet Dad for a date that night. I kept telling her she'd got it wrong but she didn't even seem to be too sure who I was, and couldn't grasp what I was saying."

Kate nods and takes Georgie's arm.

"Come on, let's go for a coffee." She points to the cafe at the top of the beach which, despite the weather, looks open, the windows steamed up. They walk in silence together, arms linked as their feet tread over sand and pebbles, until the sand gets softer and softer. There are drops of rain in the wind now and Georgie pulls her hood up and holds it tightly against her face.

The cafe feels hot and stuffy in contrast to the cold of outside, and they strip off their layers, hanging them on the back of the chairs as they go.

A good ten minutes pass before they're settled at a table with coffee and hot chocolate and a slice of cake each.

"It's scaring me, Georgie, what's happening to Mum. She's getting so much worse, so quickly. Remember in the summer, the barbecue we had at mine?"

Georgie nods, thinking back.

They'd all been there — Kate and her husband Joe, Georgie, Matt and their eleven-year-old daughter Clementine, as well as Mum's best friend Sandy. It had been Jan's sixtieth birthday party, and they'd wanted it to be a surprise. Once Jan got over the shock, all was going well.

"I can't believe you've done this to me," Jan scolded as she turned on her stool to face her daughters. Then, smiling, she muttered, "You're both terrible. I told you I didn't want a fuss."

"You didn't really think we'd let you turn sixty without doing *something* to celebrate, did you?"

"Well yes, I did, actually, as that's what I said I wanted. And I thought you were such good girls . . ."

Georgie grinned. "Oh shush, Mum. Look." She swept her arm around. "All these people are here for you, because they love you. So stop being a misery guts and just enjoy it."

Jan took a sip of her drink and set it back down on the kitchen worktop.

"OK, OK, I'm sorry. It was just a shock, that's all. Thank you, girls, this is wonderful of you."

Georgie gave Jan a squeeze. "You're more than welcome, Mum."

"Anyway, why don't you come out into the garden and mingle with your public?" Kate held out her hand and helped her mother down from the stool. "People have travelled miles to come and see you, the least you can do is grace them with your presence."

"Well, of course," Jan smiled, as she walked arm in arm with her daughters through the bi-fold doors and out into the garden. The hazy sun was warm on their arms, a gentle breeze keeping it from feeling stifling. Smoke rose from the barbecue, and a few people stood in groups on the decking and lawn. A small child swung back and forth on the swing, and the odd squeal drifted from the sandpit. They walked towards the barbecue, where two men in aprons were chatting behind a wall of smoke.

One of them turned, barbecue tongs in hand, a smile spreading across his face. "Well hello, you." He wrapped his arm round Georgie's shoulder and gave her a squeeze, then leaned across to plant a kiss on Jan's cheek.

"Happy birthday. Are you having fun?"

"Thank you, Matthew, I am." She leaned over the barbecue. "Ooh, what are we having?"

"Well, we've got sausages, steaks and grilled prawns. Oh, and some halloumi over here for Clem, of course." He turned to his wife. "Is anyone else veggie, George?"

She shook her head. "No, I don't think so."

Jan turned away towards Kate's husband, Joe, who was sipping a beer. "Hello, I'm Jan. And you are?"

"Er . . ." Joe's face wrinkled as he tried to work out whether she was joking or not.

Kate and Georgie glanced at each other. "Mum, what are you talking about? It's Joe."

"Joe?" Her face was a question mark.

Kate gave a nervous laugh. "Ha ha, very funny. My husband Joe. You've known him for years!" She tried to keep her voice light but it sounded strained.

Jan shook her head, confused. "Don't be silly, Katie, I'd remember your *husband*." She turned to Matt and rolled her eyes. "Honestly, these two, what are they like, trying to trick their old mum?"

"Um, yes." Matt flicked his gaze to Georgie, who shrugged helplessly.

"Come on, Mum, let's get you another drink." She'd led Jan away then to talk to some other people across the other side of the garden. Leaving her mother chatting for a while, Georgie made a mental note to speak to Kate about it later, find out what on earth was going on. But she hadn't had a chance before the next strange thing happened.

Georgie had been chatting to a couple of their neighbours, people she'd known since she was a little

16

girl, when she heard shouting. She strained her ears to work out where it was coming from.

"Sorry, excuse me a moment," she said, and turned and marched towards the source of the noise. As she rounded the side of the house the shouting got louder, and she saw Jan, Kate and Sandy in a huddle at the garden gate.

"I told you, I just want to go for a little walk."

"But Mum, we're having a party for you and — well, you haven't got any shoes on."

Jan looked down at her feet, surprised to see her toe peeping out through a hole at the end of her tights.

"Oh. Yes. That's a good point. How did that happen?"

"Mum? Kate? Is everything OK?"

"Yes, yes, it's all fine, nothing to worry about; your sister's just making a fuss, that's all. I'm OK. I'm just going to get myself another drink. You coming, Sandy?"

Sandy glanced at Georgie and shrugged. Georgie gave a little nod and Sandy steered Jan away, back to her party. She seemed fine now. Calm, and happy. Whatever had been bothering her had passed.

Kate, however, looked far from happy. Her face was red, and she was close to tears.

"What on earth's happened, Kate? What was going on?"

"I've got no idea. I just saw Mum wandering off and I followed her to see where she was going, but she didn't really seem to know. She just wanted to get out and go for a walk. I was just telling her to stay here, see her friends, but she — she got really angry with me."

Georgie hugged her big sister.

"I'm really worried about her, Georgie."

Georgie nodded, because she was too.

Now here they sit beside the beach, just a few weeks later, and Jan's behaviour has deteriorated rapidly.

Kate sighs and rubs her eyes. "I went to see her yesterday. I made us a cup of tea, like I always do, and we sat in the front room together. Then out of the blue Mum started talking about a meeting she had at the village hall later, about how she needed to go and see Mr Clarke about getting the zebra crossing put in outside the school."

Georgie frowns. "But there's already a zebra crossing outside the school."

"I know. It's been there for years. Mr Clarke retired three years ago as well. But Mum thought the meeting was yesterday."

"So — what did you say?"

"Well, I told her I thought she'd made a mistake and — well, she completely lost her temper. She shouted at me, screaming that I was always interfering, that I didn't know anything and that she had to go. I just watched helplessly as she put on her coat and walked out of the house. Instinctively I followed her all the way round the block to the park and I went and sat next to her on a bench. She was much calmer but when I asked her if she was OK, she looked bewildered and wasn't sure why she was even sitting in the park. Of course I ushered her safely home, made another cup of tea and she seemed all right after that."

Georgie isn't sure what to say.

"God."

"I know. I'm scared, Georgie."

"I know. I am too."

Georgie takes a sip from her steaming mug and holds it in her hands so the steam rises before her eyes, blurring the edges of her sister's face. Kate traces the ring left behind on the Formica table with her neatly manicured nail.

"You will help me, won't you? With Mum, if she needs it?"

Georgie looks at her sister, at her pleading eyes. "Of course I will. I'll do anything you need."

"Thank you."

They sit in silence for a while, letting the sounds of the cafe wash over them: the hum of the fridge, the hiss and burr of the coffee machine, the ting of the bell every time the door opens, the buzz of people's conversations making the air in the stifling room feel even thicker.

An image flits into Georgie's mind. Her and Kate, a day similar to this, at home with Mum, just the three of them, the same as always.

Their childhood hadn't been exactly conventional, and not just because their father wasn't there. Even at the time she knew that things in their home weren't the same as for the other children at school who had a mother and a father. But sometimes it just seemed more different than others.

19

★ ★ ★

This particular day was wet outside, and they were stuck indoors. It must have been the school holidays. Georgie and Kate were sitting on the rug by the fire as it flickered, playing with a pack of cards that they'd found in the dresser drawer. Outside, rain poured down the windows and condensation dripped inside, landing in puddles that crept dangerously close to the edge of the windowsill. The air felt heavy and oppressive within their four walls, and the girls' hair stuck to their faces in the sticky heat.

Every now and then Georgie would glance at the mantel-piece, where, along with piles of clutter and half hidden behind grinning school photos of herself and Kate, was the black-and-white picture in a gold frame that she loved so much. It was of her mother and father, the only picture she'd ever seen of him, taken before Kate was born. They were standing on a bridge and the wind must have been blowing hard that day too because Mum's hair was all over the place. Dad was smiling — even his eyes were smiling, all happy and crinkled — and they were looking just past the camera as though something funny was going on behind the person taking the picture. They had their arms wrapped around each other. It was odd; Georgie had looked at this photo so many times she didn't really see it any more, but when it caught her eye, she loved trying to imagine what they'd been laughing at. What had they been doing that day, where were they going, what had they eaten for dinner? She'd filled in their whole lives around this picture. She'd asked her mum about it, of course, many times, but she hadn't told her much.

"What were you laughing at?"

"I can't remember."

"Was it something funny Daddy had said?"

"Yes, probably."

"What was he like?"

"He was kind. And a little bit wild."

"What does wild mean?"

"Crazy. A bit silly."

She liked that description of him. He sounded like fun.

"Did you love him?"

"Yes . . ." And this was when the tears always started and Georgie didn't like to ask her anything else in case she upset her even more.

Now Georgie tore her eyes away before her mum noticed her looking at it again, and looked over at her mum instead. She was standing behind the ironing board, where she always stood, her face blurry and indistinct behind the steam rising from the iron, which made the warm room even stuffier. Georgie watched as her mother smoothed down the starchy fabric, and ran the iron across it with a gentle puff. Then the fog cleared for a moment and Georgie could make out the frown that furrowed her mother's forehead: the frown that was imprinted on her mother's skin like a bad crease in the shirts she was constantly ironing. Jan would occasionally look up and catch Georgie's eye, her cheeks puffing out in a sigh, and then she'd smile a smile that almost reached her eyes but not quite.

"OK, sweetheart?"

"Yes, Mummy." Georgie smiled and turned back to Kate who was quietly playing patience on the flowery carpet whose pattern stretched on and on as far as the eye could see. But she hadn't been OK, not really. She'd actually been sad that day, because she'd really wanted to go to a birthday party but Mum had said she couldn't go. Not that she'd been surprised, because Mum never let them go anywhere. In fact, Georgie was pretty sure that if Mum had her way they'd never leave the house at all. It was only thanks to their Aunty Sandy, Mum's best friend, that they ever got to go anywhere. And it was Sandy who had come to the rescue that day as well.

The steam iron had puffed again and it had felt to seven-year-old Georgie as though the day was never going to come to an end. Then, thankfully, the boredom had been interrupted by a knock at the door and both girls had jumped up and followed Jan to see who was there. When the door opened a familiar face had greeted them.

"Aunty Sandy!" Georgie yelled, almost throwing herself at Sandy's legs as she stepped out of the rain and into the steamy house.

"Georgie, let Aunty Sandy in, you silly sausage, she can't move if you're clinging to her like a limpet."

Georgie reluctantly let go and Sandy stepped further into the room.

"Gosh, it's like a monsoon out there." Her hair was usually big and puffy but today it was plastered to her head, making her look as though she was wearing a nun's habit. Aunty Sandy wiped her face with her sleeve and pushed her hair back out of her eyes.

"Come and sit by the fire, I'll stick another log on."

Within minutes the fire was roaring again and, for the first time all day, Jan had switched off the iron and put the washing in the kitchen out of the way. Mum and Sandy sat drinking tea from mismatched teacups; Georgie and Kate had a plastic cup of squash each. Georgie eyed up the plate of biscuits on the coffee table in front of her and waited for someone else to take one first.

"So, what have you girls been up to in this rain? Bet you haven't been out in the garden today, have you?"

Georgie stuck out her bottom lip. "No, it's been really boring."

"Charming," Jan smiled, taking a sip from her cup. She turned to Sandy. "I've been working — I had a load of shirts to get through that're being picked up tomorrow so the girls have had a bit of a dull day, I'm afraid." She shrugged. "You know what it's like."

"Oh, you are silly. You should have rung me, I'd have taken them off your hands for the day." She turned to the girls and winked. "We'd have had fun, wouldn't we?"

"Yeah!" the two girls cried.

"I know, I know but — well, I don't like to always ask and — well, you know what I'm like . . ."

"About them going anywhere without you? Yes, I know, Jan, but —" She stopped, not wanting to say any more in front of the girls. But Georgie and Kate both knew that Sandy thought that Mum should let them go out *much* more often. All the other children at school had their friends round for tea now and then. They'd heard Aunty Sandy offer to look after them lots of times, but Mum never took any notice. At least, she didn't seem to, because nothing ever changed.

"Georgie's been invited to a party, Aunty Sandy, but Mum says she can't go," Kate piped up, and Georgie felt her face go red. Mum had already said no to this, she didn't know why Kate had to go and bring it up all over again.

"Oh, I see." Sandy took a sip from her cup and — at last! — reached for a biscuit from the plate. Georgie snatched up a bourbon almost immediately and bit the top biscuit off, exposing the layer of cream underneath. The crunching sounded loud in her ears.

Aunty Sandy didn't say anything else, and eventually Mum must have felt the need to say something, to explain herself. "I just think she's a bit young, that's all. And you understand, don't you, sweetheart?"

Georgie nodded, crumbs flying from her mouth and spraying on the carpet around her. She swallowed. "Yes. When I'm a big girl I can go."

Sandy nodded, her eyes on Georgie all the time. Georgie had felt uncomfortable with Aunty Sandy looking at her like that, but eventually Sandy pulled her gaze away and turned to Jan.

"Yes, when she's a big girl I'm sure she'll be able to go to parties, won't she, Jan?"

"Yes, one day soon. I promise."

But they all knew, deep down, that it was an empty promise. Jan was never going to change her mind.

"Earth to Georgie."

Georgie jumps. She'd been so lost in the memory of that day she'd forgotten where they were, and now she looks at Kate's face watching her with concern and forces a smile.

"Where on earth did you go just then?"

"I was just thinking — about me and you, as children."

"Ah."

"Remember during the holidays when we just used to stay in with Mum all the time, while she ironed and we had to amuse ourselves?"

Kate nods. "It wasn't always like that. We did go out sometimes."

"With Mum."

"Well, yes, usually." Kate lifts her fork and presses the last few crumbs against the plate with the back of it, then lifts it to her mouth.

"Why do you think she was so overprotective?" Georgie runs her finger through the buttercream left on her plate and licks it off. "Do you think it was just because she was on her own?"

"I don't know, Georgie. But let's face it, we're never likely to find out now, are we? It's not as though we can ask Mum. She can't remember what she did thirty seconds ago, let alone thirty years."

"But do you think she'd have been different, if Dad had been there?"

Kate shrugs. "I've really no idea. She might have been happier, I suppose."

"Mum *was* happy. Wasn't she?"

Kate pauses, inspecting her nails, then takes a deep breath. "Not really. I don't think she was ever happy. I think Mum spent most of our childhood mourning Dad's death. It's as though a little bit of her vanished the day he died."

"Oh." Georgie frowns and pushes her hair from her face. "I guess that's why she never met anyone else?"

"Probably."

Georgie rubs her temple. "God, it's so sad. And now she's losing herself completely."

"Don't."

"Has the doctor seen her?"

Kate nods. "Yes. I took her the other day. She hasn't been officially diagnosed yet, but it's just a matter of ticking the right boxes, I think. The doctor seems pretty sure but she's seeing a specialist in a few days' time and we'll get some answers then. But it's so awful, Georgie, watching her look confused when she's trying to do something she's done a million times before. It breaks my heart."

Georgie nods. She hasn't been to see her mother nearly enough recently because — well, to be honest she's also found it really hard, seeing her this way. But she realizes now how selfish she's been, letting Kate shoulder all the responsibility.

"When I rang her the other day she was rambling a bit. She kept saying weird things, like she didn't want *that* woman to know, and she had to keep it to herself. I don't know what she thought was happening, but when I rang her later she seemed fine again, hardly

26

remembered anything about it. But I think you're right. She's definitely getting worse. I'm sorry."

"What for?"

"For being so selfish. Pretending it's all fine that you go and see her more and look after her more. I think I've been in denial, to be honest."

"Don't be silly, George. It's fine, really. Anyway, Aunty Sandy's been helping out as much as she can. Once Mum's seen this specialist and we have a diagnosis I might need your help a bit more, mind you. You know, looking after her, making sure she has everything she needs. Watching out for signs she's getting worse. Because she will. Get worse, I mean."

"I know." Georgie feels a pressure building in her head and she presses her fingertips against her temples.

"We just need to make sure she's safe."

"OK. I'll do what I can, I promise. Just ask."

"I will. Thanks, George. I don't know how I'd cope with Mum being like she is without you."

Slowly the cafe empties, the only noise someone sweeping up around them, pushing crumbs into a pile. Every time the door opens the crumbs blow away again, cascading across the tiled floor.

"We should go." Kate pushes her arm through the sleeve of her coat and stands. "You coming?"

Georgie nods, shoving her hands in her cardigan. They pay and leave, and minutes later Kate has the windscreen wipers going and the fan on in the car, waiting for the windows to clear. As she pulls out of the car park and into the road Georgie speaks.

"I've decided something."

"What?"

"I want to go on holiday. Abroad."

"What?!" Kate swerves as she shoots a sharp look at Georgie, then pulls the steering wheel straight just in time before she hits a bollard. "What's brought this on?"

Georgie shrugs. "It's time to do something."

"OK." Kate turns the fan off and risks a glance at her sister. "But why now?"

"I'm not sure. Maybe it's seeing Mum like this. I just keep thinking, what if it happens to me too, and I've never even done anything? Never been anywhere. There's got to be more to life than Norfolk, and I'd always regret it if I didn't see any of it because I was too damn scared."

The words hang in the air for a moment, the only sounds the rain hammering on the windscreen and the wipers swooshing desperately back and forth. Then Kate clicks on the indicator and pulls over to the side of the road and cuts the engine. Cars whoosh by leaving trails of spray in their wake as the world outside the windows becomes more and more smudged, obscured.

Kate leans across and wraps her arms round Georgie awkwardly, her coat snagging on the handbrake and tugging across her shoulders, restricting her reach. Georgie returns the hug, grateful for Kate's support.

They pull apart and tears shine in Kate's eyes. "Oh Georgie, this is brilliant news. Do you really think you can do it?"

Georgie nods. "I do. I have to, Kate. Don't you see? If I don't, I'll always wish I had."

"Are you — going to fly?"

Georgie's body visibly shudders. "I'd like to. I just — I can't really imagine it. Getting on a plane and being right up there." She looks up but can hardly see the flat, grey sky through the smeared water on the windscreen. She tries to picture a block of metal up there, suspended, with her in it. But she can't. "It just seems impossible. Terrifying. Like magic. It's hard to explain."

"But you know it's not, don't you? You know it's safer than being in this thing." She throws her arm in the air to take in the interior of the car.

Georgie nods. "I know. I do, in theory. But it doesn't mean I actually believe it."

"So how do you think you'll cope?"

Georgie shrugs. "I don't know. I need to think about it. But I'm determined this time. I know I've said it before, but I have to. It's not fair, on Matt, or Clementine. I just want us to be able to go somewhere lovely and warm and relax on the beach in the sun rather than huddle round a windbreak in Cromer." She pictures the look on Clementine's face when she tells her they're going abroad, and she knows that this time she really has to do it.

"Do you —" Kate stops, not wanting to upset Georgie. "Do you really think you can overcome your fear? I mean — you have tried it before, Georgie, and it — well, it hasn't exactly been a success."

"I know." The thought of being in the air was totally alien, but the truth was, she'd never really *wanted* to go anywhere else, because she felt safe at home. Kate had travelled the world, seen all kinds of places that Georgie had only ever read about. Kate had travelled on her own and later with her husband Joe, while Georgie had stayed at home to take care of their mother, who had always seemed too fragile to be left alone. Georgie could never have imagined leaving her as well. It would have felt too cruel. And so she'd stayed. And until now she hadn't minded too much. But now, she wanted to try.

"I have to do it this time. I can't end up like Mum. Trapped in my own mind and never even having been anywhere."

"I know."

"There is one thing, though."

Kate nods.

"I haven't got a passport."

"Well no, I don't suppose you have."

"And I don't have a clue where my birth certificate is."

"What do you mean? Don't you have it?"

Georgie shakes her head and takes her hat off, runs her hand through her hair. "No. I don't think I've ever even seen it."

"What? Really?"

"Really. I asked Mum for it once, I think, but it never materialized."

"Oh."

"I'm assuming you've got yours, then?"

"Well yes. I've always had a copy. Mum gave it to me years ago when I got my passport. And I needed it when I got married, of course."

"Exactly. Me and Matt never bothered, did we, so I've never actually needed it. I think Mum must still have mine. But I can't just ask her for it, not with her the way she is."

"No, you can't." Kate thinks a minute. "You're probably just going to have to go and look for it yourself."

"That's what I thought. Will you help me?" Georgie pleads.

"How?"

"Well, I'll need you to get Mum out of the house while I look for it. You know how upset she'll get if I start rummaging around in her things."

"But she hates leaving the house."

"I know. Sorry, Kate. I hate to ask but I need to do this before I change my mind. Will you help?"

Kate sighs and drums her nails on the steering wheel. "Of course I will. I'll take her for lunch, that should give you enough time, shouldn't it?"

"Hopefully."

"OK. I'll sort something and let you know."

"Thank you. But Kate?"

"Yes?"

"What happens if I can't find it? What do I do then?"

"Well, then I guess we'll just cross that bridge when we come to it. But if we can do it without upsetting Mum's routine, then that's better. Agreed?"

Georgie nods. "Definitely."

"Good." Kate turns to the front and starts the car, easing out into the flow of traffic, and Georgie leans back in her seat. Her palms feel warm. Now she's nervous because she's committed to doing this. To overcoming her fear. She has no choice.

There's no going back.

CHAPTER
TWO

24 October 2016

Georgie slides the key into the lock and it turns effortlessly, the door opening with a click. She glances around her nervously. She doesn't know why, but today she feels as though she's betraying her mum's trust just by being here.

"I just hope Mum doesn't freak out in the middle of lunch and we have to come home early," Kate had said on the phone that morning when she rang to confirm. "I'll text you if we do. Otherwise, you have two hours."

Georgie closes the front door behind her. Silence tumbles down the stairs and beside her the radiator ticks as it cools. She shrugs her coat from her shoulders and hangs it on the hook, shuddering as she remembers her dream, where nothing was here at all. Today, though, one other coat hangs here, looking lonely. A pair of shoes and some slippers are lined up against the wall, and she leaves her boots tucked neatly next to them. She strains her ears to listen for a sound — footsteps, someone breathing, a kettle boiling, anything. But there's nothing but silence filling the air.

Shadows dance on the wooden floor in front of her, a line from the door down to the kitchen a shade paler than the rest from years of footsteps wearing it down. Her footsteps sound loud as she follows the worn path halfway along then stops and turns left into the living room. The door stands slightly ajar and she gives it a little push. The room is silent apart from the clock ticking on the mantelpiece, marking time that no one is using. The room is so familiar, so ingrained in her memories, that she can almost picture herself and Kate kneeling on the rug in front of the fire, playing as the room filled with steam from Mum's iron, the iron that always seemed to be on, the hissing and steaming like a soundtrack to their childhood.

Quietly, as though someone might hear her, she pads across the room to the wooden sideboard. She's never really given much thought to what's in here, and as the drawer opens with a yawn she wonders what she'll find. There are some mismatched pieces of cutlery, a couple of coat hooks, a roll of Sellotape, one or two odd buttons, a small sewing kit that looks as though it came from a Christmas cracker, a bottle opener, a pack of cards and a few old receipts. She closes the drawer and opens the next one. Inside are piles of old envelopes and she pulls the whole lot out and sits down, placing the heap carefully on her knee. The weak winter sun strains itself through the net curtains that hang tidily at the window, creating diluted patterns on the sofa as Georgie shuffles through the papers as quickly as she can. It doesn't take long to realize there's nothing much she needs to see here, and she stuffs the envelopes back into the drawer and stands up. She opens the cupboards underneath but there's nothing but plates and cups in there, saved for best, which seem to be days that never actually arrive. A fine layer of dust covers the whole lot, and she shuts the cupboard doors again. She casts her eyes briefly round the room, although she knows it better than she knows her own house, just to make sure there's nowhere else she needs to check, then she moves efficiently to the door and back into the hall. The door to the kitchen stands open and she can see before she reaches it that there's no one there, just as in her dream. She walks quietly across the tiles, her feet tapping gently with every step. Then she lays her hand on the kettle, unsure why she's done it because she knows her mother isn't here. Everything feels cold. There's a single cup on the table, a rim of coffee staining the inside and a red heart shape on the outside where lipstick has marked it. Half a biscuit sits next to it, a small bite taken out of it, a few crumbs scattered round. She walks over to the drawers and looks carefully through them. Nothing.

Satisfied she's not missing anything, she goes back towards the front door and turns and walks up the stairs. It's darker up here, and she flicks the landing light on and tilts her neck upwards. She shudders as she remembers her dream, the noise that came from the loft, then shakes the thought from her head. There's nothing to be scared of up there.

Despite having lived here until she was eighteen, she still remembers her fear of the monster she'd always believed lived up there. When the loft stairs were first installed, she poked her head in to see what was up there. But it was just a load of boxes, a water tank and some cobwebs. Nothing to worry about, and she never thought about it again.

Now, though, she's hoping it will have exactly what she needs.

Pulling the hatch down with the long hook, she carefully unfolds the steps and starts to climb. The wooden steps are narrow and dig into her feet, and she looks up as she climbs into the gaping black square. Halfway up she stops. Is there a light up there? It occurs to her that a torch would have been useful. Soon her head is above the level of the ceiling, poking into the cavity. She realizes she's been holding her breath all the way up, and lets it out in one whoosh.

Slowly she swivels her head from side to side like a meerkat and spots a light switch at eye level. When she flicks it on, the dim light illuminates the immediate area, but fails to reach into the furthest corners, leaving dark, looming shadows. Georgie pulls herself completely into the loft and stands, her head bowed slightly to avoid hitting the apex of the roof. It's chilly up here and she pulls her fluffy cardigan tighter round her chest and turns slowly, peering into the dark recesses.

There are some suitcases piled in the front, and a couple of plastic boxes which she pulls towards her. This is as good a place to start as any. A quick glance inside the first one reveals it's not going to be any use, as it's filled with an odd assortment of shoes. The other is full of clothes — she can see a fluffy fleece and a waterproof jacket on the top and wonders briefly why they're up here and not being used.

Stooped over, she walks into the darker parts of the loft, trying not to block the light as she moves so she can still make out what's up there. "Gah!" she gasps and spits as she walks into a cobweb, and brushes her hand furiously up and down her face to remove any traces.

Peering into the darkness, she sighs. It's no good, she can't make out a thing. Perhaps the torch on the iPhone in her pocket will help. The beam that pours from it lights her path. Apart from the dust motes floating in the air that are making her nose tickle, she can see a few boxes piled up at the far end, almost hidden from sight. Maybe what she's looking for will be in one of those.

She pulls a blanket from the top of one of the bigger boxes and, placing it on the wooden boards, sits down cross-legged, her phone propped awkwardly on the floor next to her. There's nothing written on the first of the boxes to give a hint of what might be inside, but the top is loose and she pulls the flaps out easily, one by one. Dust flies into the air, making her cough, and she wafts it away with her hand and peers over the top. It's a pile of folders with faded black ink smudged along their sides with words like "Bills" and "House documents" and "Car insurance". She pulls one out and peers into it. The paperwork inside is clipped neatly into the folders but the most recent is at least three years old, explaining the dust on the top of the box. The other folders are all the same — neat, but out of date. A frown creases her forehead. Has her mother stored more up-to-date stuff somewhere else or has she simply forgotten to do it any more? Who knows, but that's a thought for another time. Right now, she needs to get a move on.

The next box is half empty, just a few old kitchen items and a couple of empty tins; the next one says "Christmas decorations" down the side in red marker pen, and sure enough it's crammed with tinsel, baubles and fairy lights. The next few boxes are pretty much the same — odds and ends from the house, things that her mother has apparently decided she might need one day or can't bear to throw away.

Georgie's becoming agitated; she yanks the last box towards her and claws open the top. Inside is a small box and it's Sellotaped shut this time, so she pulls the tape off carefully and opens the lid. On the top sit piles of photo albums and Georgie's heart thuds in her chest. Maybe there are some photos of her father here that she's never seen before. Her hands shaking, she pulls the top album from the box and opens it carefully. A loose picture falls out and she peers at it, holding it up to the light of the torch. It's a picture of two little girls and a woman and she recognizes immediately who the adult is — her mother. Kate, her curly blonde hair and chubby red cheeks shining in the sunlight, is with another darker little girl, so very different from her mother and sister, her hair in pigtails and a big grin plastered across her face. It's her, and although she doesn't remember the picture being taken — she only looks about two in the photo — it makes her happy. Desperate to see more, she opens the album and gasps. There are dozens of photos of her and Kate, playing in the garden, on a beach in the sunshine, huddled under an umbrella, walking along a promenade somewhere, eating ice cream.

Memories stir in her mind as she flicks through a few more pages, some so strong they almost overwhelm her. Why has she never seen these albums before? Why would her mother hide them away to gather dust in the loft?

It would be easy to sit and stare at them all day, lost in memories of the past. But she has a job to do so she tears her eyes away, closes the album and picks up the next one. There are a few black-and-white pictures at the front, which slowly give way to colour pictures, the colours faded to pale orange and grey. She recognizes some of them as photographs of her mother, very young, and an equally young Aunty Sandy, and she smiles. Both women look so youthful and carefree; it was a time before Georgie was even in the world. They seem like different people with their big hair and miniskirts barely covering slim thighs. The first few pages are all similar — but then suddenly, a few pages on, she stops, her heart thudding. There's a photograph of her mother, holding hands with a man. The only other photo of him that she's ever seen is the one that sits on the mantelpiece in Mum's living room, but she knows him instantly. It's her father. The pair of them are standing in front of a motorbike and Jan is holding her hand to her eyes to shade them from the sun. Her father has his free hand on her mother's tummy, as though trying to protect whatever is inside. Georgie realizes with a jolt that her mother must be pregnant with her or Kate — probably Kate, as there's no evidence of another child anywhere. It's not taken at this house, the house where she's lived her whole life. Was it a house they lived in together, before here, before her father died? The torchlight picks out the details of the photo, as though seeing it more clearly might help her hold the image in her mind for longer, or learn more about the man in it. The photo isn't clear but she drinks in the details she can make out, of his dark hair, his high cheekbones, his leather jacket. If only she could take the photo with her, but she daren't. There must be a reason her mother didn't want her to see this, and it's bad enough she's found it at all; taking it away would betray her mother's trust completely.

Setting the torch down again, she reluctantly turns the page to see if there are any more photos, but the rest of the album is blank, just endless white pages devoid of any memories, as though the world stopped just after the last picture was taken.

Georgie allows herself one last look at the picture of her father, then closes the album. A glance at her watch shows that almost an hour has gone already.

There's not much else in the box, just a few ornaments and a couple of empty photo frames. As she lifts one of the frames, something makes her pause. There's another box under here; she almost missed it. Gently she kneels and puts both arms inside the cardboard box and pulls out the smaller metal box, flat and wide, which is wedged in the bottom. There's a pattern of flowers on the top, and a small catch holds it shut. It looks like something personal, private, something her mother wouldn't want anyone else to see. She's not here to snoop through her mum's things, and Georgie feels bad about some of the photos she's found. After all, the intention was just to find her birth certificate, nothing more. Best put this back, leave it here, untouched.

But then again, what if her birth certificate is in this box? And if it is and she doesn't even open it to have a quick look, she'll never find it. If it isn't, then no harm will have been done.

Her hand brushes over the top and sweeps the dust away. It's amazing how dust gets through even the tiniest cracks and covers everything. She prises open the catch. It flicks open easily and she slowly lifts the lid, careful not to let anything fall out onto the floor. Balancing the box cautiously on her legs, she looks inside. There's not much to see at first, just a small white envelope with nothing written on it. She picks it up. There's something inside, but it's not a piece of paper. Nothing she needs, then.

But better to check, just in case. Georgie unfolds the flap of the envelope and peers inside. There's a small piece of plastic. It's a tiny, baby-sized hospital wristband. She studies the name on it: *Kathryn Susan Wood. 12 March 1977.*

Ah, it's Kate's band from hospital, from when she was born. Her finger traces the edge of the plastic, trying to imagine her sister small enough to fit this round her wrist. She puts the band down carefully on the floor beside her and peers back into the envelope to find her own wristband. The envelope looks empty, so she puts her fingers inside and feels around, expecting them to catch on another piece of plastic almost the same, but with the name *Georgina Rae Wood* on it, and her birthdate, 23 November 1979. But she can't feel anything at all. That's strange. With a frown she peers inside the envelope again. There really isn't anything there.

Her hand drops into her lap. Why would her mother have Kate's hospital band and not hers? It doesn't make sense. Unless there is another envelope, for her? Yes, perhaps that's it. She glances back down at the metal box hopefully, but there's nothing else in it. Another quick look inside the envelope, just to make sure, as though something might have materialized in the few seconds since she last looked. But of course it hasn't.

There is something else, though: not a hospital band, but a piece of paper pressed up against the side of the envelope, folded neatly in half. Her heart stops. This could be what she's looking for. It could be her birth certificate.

But as she carefully slides the paper out of the envelope with her thumb and forefinger, a sense of foreboding washes over her. What if this isn't what she's looking for at all? Does she really want to find out that her mother hasn't kept anything of hers, as though she doesn't matter? As though she doesn't exist?

She pauses, torn. But she knows she has to find out one way or the other now. The paper feels fragile beneath her fingers, as though it might disintegrate under her touch, and she holds it gently at the edges, careful not to rip it, as she unfolds it and brings it closer to her face to read it in the dim light of the loft.

It's yellowed round the edges and faded, but it's clear enough to read; it's a photocopy of a birth certificate. She reads the name, knowing even before she looks what it's going to say: *Kathryn Susan Wood*.

There's a lump in her throat that she can't seem to get rid of and she swallows over and over again to try and clear it.

She turns again to look at the things she's already pulled out of the box, making sure one last time that she hasn't missed something; that she hasn't overlooked an envelope full of memories of her birth.

There has to be some sort of explanation for this, for the fact that her mother has kept mementos of her sister's birth but hasn't got any record of hers. Perhaps she's just lost it. Perhaps she keeps it somewhere else, safe, not festering away in the loft.

But there's something nagging away at the back of her mind, something telling her that there's more to this. She needs to think, to try and pin it down and work out what it is.

She thinks back to when they were little, her and Kate so close, always together, rarely with anyone else. She thinks about Kate going off travelling round the world, getting married. And then she thinks about her own life; how she and Matt had never bothered to get married, and how she had never even applied for a passport. Both things for which she would have needed a birth certificate.

Something's swimming to the surface now; she needs to grab hold of it and tether it down. Memories flash into her mind, then disappear, like subliminal messages on TV. Her mother suggesting marriage wasn't right for her . . . her mother talking about her fear of flying, telling her frightening stories about plane crashes, explosions, hijacks . . . her mother promising to find her birth certificate but never actually finding it . . . watching as Kate flew off to travel the world, her mother telling her she was glad she wasn't abandoning her, she was staying to look after her . . .

Image after image, memory after memory, flashing through her mind like a film trailer . . . she's trying to piece them together, work out what her mind is trying to tell her.

But she knows. She knows that, for whatever reason, her mother has never had her birth certificate, and she didn't want her to find out. It makes sense. She didn't want her to apply for a passport, so she scared her away from going anywhere. She put her off getting married so she'd never need it for that either.

But why?

She has no idea. But she knows she has to find out.

Suddenly the air in the stuffy loft seems to disappear and Georgie retreats on hands and knees towards the open hatch. She moves quickly now, desperate to get out, her breath coming in gasps.

Down the stairs, into the kitchen she stumbles to unlock the back door with the key hanging from the hook where it's always been. As the door swings open, cool autumn air hits her full on and she takes deep,

44

rasping breaths, trying to calm her hammering heart and quell the deep ache in her gut.

She crouches down and rocks backwards and forwards on the balls of her feet, staring at the grass between them, the blades pointing proudly towards the sky, uncrushed. Her hand smashes down onto them, then they slowly unfurl again, defiant against all the odds. She smashes them down again and again until they're totally crushed, lying flat and lifeless against the soft earth.

Unsteadily, Georgie walks across the small lawn, where she and Kate had spent so many hours playing, sunbathing and gossiping. The garden is quiet now, the plants inert, biding their time until spring lets them know it's time to flower again, time for colour and life. But for now, the palette of the garden is mostly browns, blacks and the dark tones of the evergreens. The shed is grey and lifeless at the end of the garden and she shivers as she remembers her dream, the disturbed earth, the strange feeling she had about it.

Her feet are cold, so she heads back inside the house and sits down at the kitchen table, her head resting on the palms of her hands. She stays there for a few minutes, waiting for her breath to steady, to return to its normal rhythm. Slowly it does and she lifts her head, feeling dizzy.

She can't believe she's never thought about any of this before, but she knows it's because she's never wanted to. It's amazing what the mind can block out when it tries. Now, though, the memories have forced their way to the surface, and she can't deny them any longer. The truth is, her mother has always been covering something up. There's some mystery, something odd about the way Georgie came into the world.

Her phone vibrates in her pocket and she pulls it out and squints at the screen. Kate.

We're just leaving, we'll be back in 20 mins or so. Hope you found what you were looking for. K xx

Oh God, they're on their way back. She doesn't have a clue whether her mother ever goes into these boxes any more, but she needs to tidy everything up, make it look as though she's never been here. She stands and walks back up the stairs, more slowly this time, and climbs the steps to the hatch. Her phone torch lights her way again as she walks to the back of the loft where the papers and envelopes are scattered just where she left them.

Trying to stay calm, she scoops everything up and shoves it roughly back into the metal box, then pushes the cardboard box back into the dark depths of the loft where she found it. Everything else is pushed back into place: the boxes, the suitcases, before Georgie stands back and admires her handiwork. It certainly *looks* just the same as when she found it. Before she knew the secrets the loft was hiding.

She makes her way back down the steps, folds them back up and closes the loft hatch with a gentle click, then glances at her phone. Ten minutes to go. It's probably not a good idea to hang around and speak to her mum, or Kate. What could she say to either of them right now? Especially her mother. She needs to find out more first.

It only takes a moment to tap out a reply to her sister.

Thanks. All done. Will see you later. G x

She watches the message send then goes back to the kitchen and locks the back door; she puts her boots back on, pulls her coat over her shoulders and, without even a backward glance, opens the front door, slamming it hard behind her as she walks away from the house as quickly as possible.

As she walks she realizes her whole body is tense, and she takes a deep breath and slowly lets it out. She ups her pace, walking briskly in the cool air until her breath comes in puffs and her legs ache. It's only a sheet of paper and a tiny piece of plastic, but she can't stop thinking about the implications of what she found — and, more importantly, what she didn't find — up in her mother's loft.

She has no idea what it means and she's not entirely sure she wants to discover the truth. But there's no choice.

The wheels are in motion now.

CHAPTER
THREE

25 October 2016

Georgie's been watching the same spider scuttle slowly backwards and forwards across the floor for fifteen minutes and she still can't bring herself to move from her position at the kitchen table.

When she got back from her mother's house yesterday afternoon she was all fired up and ready to find out more, to try and discover the secret her mother was clearly keeping from her. Now, though, she feels almost crippled with inertia, as though the fear of what she might find has left her limbs paralysed.

She pulls air in through her nose and holds her breath until her head starts to spin. She lets it seep out slowly through her lips, her lungs burning. As the last drop of breath leaves her, the spider finally runs underneath the skirting board and she gasps, her lungs desperate for air.

"How come you're so out of breath? Been Mum-dancing along to the radio again?" The voice of her daughter Clementine cuts through her reverie and she snaps her head up. Clem is standing at the worktop now, reaching into the cupboard and pulling out a box of Shreddies, pouring them into a bowl. Georgie sees her as though from miles away, through a murky film, her mind still elsewhere. She watches her daughter as she pours milk into the bowl, gets a spoon from the draining board and walks across the room to the table, where she sits down next to her, scooping spoonfuls of cereal into her mouth, chewing quickly.

Georgie realizes Clem's looking at her strangely and smiles, remembering she's meant to be answering her question.

"Oh, I'm not out of breath, I'm just — sitting here."

The spoon rattles against the side of the bowl as Clem scoops up another pile of Shreddies. Then it stops, hovering in the air between the bowl and her mouth.

"Mum, are you OK? You look weird."

"Yes, yes. Sorry, darling, I was miles away. Don't know what I was thinking about." She stands, the chair beneath her scraping across the lino floor and almost tipping over. There are drops of milk on the wooden tabletop and she reaches for a cloth and starts to wipe them away absent-mindedly. "Anyway, what are you up to today?"

"Er, I'm going to school?" Clem screws up her face in disdain. "What did you think I was doing?"

"Ha ha, yes, of course you are. But I meant what have you got on?"

Clem shrugs. "Just the usual. Maths. Boring. English. PE. Gross. Why do we have to do PE? It's so degrading."

"What's degrading?" Matt's come into the room, pulling his jacket on and running his fingers through his unruly hair.

"Oh, Clem's just telling me how it's unfair that they have to keep fit at school and that she thinks she should be allowed to be a lady and sit it out."

Matt smiles, ruffling Clem's hair as he passes. "Daaad! I've just spent ages doing my hair."

Georgie and Matt stare at their daughter, this strange creature who's suddenly turned from a sweet little girl into a demanding, preening almost-teen, her hair wild around her face, piled into a scruffy knot on the top of her head, and both let out bursts of laughter at the same time.

"What?" Clem's voice is indignant.

"Nothing, darling. Your hair looks lovely." Matt grins at Georgie as he sits down with a cup of coffee and she smiles weakly back. His forehead creases.

"What's up? You look — sad." He slurps from his cup and puts it down in front of him.

"Mum's being really weird this morning," Clementine says, flicking a stray hair from her shoulder.

"Oh? Weirder than usual?"

"Way weirder. She's been staring at me like I'm from another planet and she forgot I was going to school today. Like I'm ever allowed to do anything else."

Matt looks at Georgie and she shrugs. "I'm just tired, I guess."

Matt nods. "Not surprised, you kept me awake most of the night with your fidgeting. What were you dreaming about, anyway?"

Georgie shrugs again, aware she's not being very friendly. It wasn't what she was dreaming about that was the problem. It was the fact that the thoughts rolling around in her head, about what her mother might be hiding, were keeping her awake.

While these thoughts are in her own head, though, they can't hurt her. Once she says them out loud, they become real.

Matt looks at his watch, distracted. "I have to leave in a minute. Do either of you need a lift?"

Clem shakes her head. "Josie's calling for me."

Georgie shakes her head too. "I'm not going into work today. I've called in sick. I'm —" She pauses, unsure how to explain why she's taken the day off from her job at their local library, a job she loves. "You were right. I didn't have a great night. I just need to catch up on some sleep."

Matt frowns at her and she knows he's worried about what's going on. And she will tell him, of course she will. Once she discovers whether there's even anything to tell.

"Are you sure that's all that's wrong?"

Georgie nods. "Positive."

"OK." She knows Matt's not convinced by her story at all, but there's nothing she can do about it right now. She watches as he stands and walks to the sink, rinses his cup and places it upside down on the draining board. She watches the way he moves, the fluid, gentle way his body switches from one position to the next. She watches the curve of his cheekbone, the sprinkle of stubble on his chin which by the end of the day will be more of a beard, softer to the touch, and his hair which he's tried to flatten with water but which always sticks up wildly no matter what he does. She watches his shoulders rise and fall as they shrug themselves into his coat, and his hands as they reach for his keys, dropping them into his pocket, and she feels a surge of love for him that threatens to overwhelm her. She mustn't start crying, not now. She blinks and clears her throat, then looks up to find Matt's face level with hers.

He leans forward and plants a kiss on the end of her nose. "Are you sure you're OK? You look pale."

Georgie nods and Matt's eyes lock with hers a moment longer before he gives a quick nod, then stands and moves to kiss Clementine on the cheek. "Bye, squirt, have a good day."

"Bye, Dad."

And then he moves to the door, closes it gently behind him, and is gone. Georgie feels grateful that he didn't push it. What could she have told him? "Oh, I just found Kate's birth certificate and hospital wristband in Mum's loft but mine wasn't there and now I'm convinced there's something sinister going on"? Said like that it sounds crazy, unhinged. Who in their right mind wouldn't just assume that it was elsewhere, stored in another cupboard, another box, rather than jumping to wild conclusions? And despite what Matt knows about her family — and he's been around long enough — she knows he wouldn't have understood, not really.

A few minutes later Clem leaves in a flurry and the house is quiet, the only sounds the roar from the boiler, the gentle hum of the dishwasher and the odd rumble of tyres as cars drive slowly past outside the kitchen window. Georgie knows she needs to move, to do something; she can't sit here all day. There wasn't anything else in her mother's house, she's pretty sure of that, because she would have found it, somewhere. And she can't do an Internet search because, quite frankly, what would she be searching for?

So she's decided the library is the best place to start. She knows libraries, she understands them, the secrets that they hold and how to coax them out from their hiding places gently and with care. But the local library where she works is off limits — not only because she's called in sick, but because she needs more than it can offer her. She needs newspaper records dating back years.

This is going to be a long search.

The drive doesn't take long and just twenty minutes later she's parked the car and is walking briskly towards the library and through the sliding glass doors.

She loves working in her little local library, but this one, in Norwich city centre, is completely different. It's busy, with people milling around the ground floor, pushing buggies, reading stories aloud. It makes her feel safe, secure. Nothing bad could ever happen here, could it?

She makes her way up to the research department on the second floor, taking the stairs instead of the lift. It's almost empty when she gets there, and she heads to the bank of grey filing cabinets lined up along the wall like sentries, keeping a careful watch. It's quieter up here, the atmosphere hushed, more serious, and she's conscious of her footsteps across the thin grey carpet. She takes a pad of paper and a pen from her bag and shoves the bag in a locker, then pushes the metal gate open and heads towards the filing cabinets. On top of each one is a printed list in a plastic stand, with dates of the births, deaths and marriages contained within. Finally she reaches 1979 and stops. The year she was born. Hopefully this will be easy — she'll find her birth details, get a copy of her birth certificate, and go home and nothing will have changed.

The drawer slides open, as it has countless times before, and Georgie flicks through the dates until she finds the right microfiche. She walks to the machine, loads it in as she's done so many times for other people, and scrolls through the pages until she reaches the right date — 23 November 1979 — where she slows down, reading the names of the people born in Norwich on that date. Names flash up in front of her eyes but none of them are hers. She pauses when she sees two born on the same day with the same surname — Foster. Twins, she thinks, and gives a smile before moving on. But then her birthday has gone and it's the next day, and the day after that, and there's no sign of a Georgina Wood. She frowns, and checks the front of the cassette case she took this from. Yes, it's definitely the right date and the right place.

So why isn't she listed here?

There will be a simple explanation. Her hands shake as she returns the microfiche to its case, then places it carefully back in the drawer and closes it with a quiet shush. She takes a deep breath and then moves along to

54

where the newspapers are archived. She's not really sure what she's looking for, but maybe there will be something that might give her a clue about what's going on. At the very least it's got to be worth a go.

She scans the dates of the *Eastern Daily Press* until she comes to 1979 again, then stops. This seems like a good place to start.

As she pulls the drawer open she tries to keep her hands steady, takes a deep breath and rolls her shoulders. She flicks through to the film that covers November, the month she was born in, pulls it from its slot and heads back to the same microfiche machine. It's just as well she knows what she's doing; it makes the task less daunting as she slips the film onto the wheel and winds it onto the one next to it. She turns the switch and the screen lights up, then she winds the film on noisily until the front page of a newspaper appears on the screen. The papers scroll by one by one, revealing inconsequential stories about sport competitions and a strike at a printing factory, and all the while the sound of her heart roars in her ears, getting louder and louder the closer she gets to the date she's looking for, her eyes scanning greedily over the blurry black words until she feels dizzy.

And then, suddenly, she stops. A story has caught her eye.

BABY SNATCHED FROM LOCAL HOSPITAL

Georgie shuts her eyes and grips the edge of the table to stop herself falling off her chair as the walls of the library seem to close in on her. She already knows what's coming next, but she's still not sure she can bear to read it. She forces her eyes open and carries on.

A newborn baby girl was snatched from Norwich maternity hospital last night.

The baby, who had only that morning been named Louisa by her distraught mother, Kimberley Foster, was taken from her crib at the end of her mother's bed in the Norfolk and Norwich maternity hospital between the hours of 1630 and 1700 yesterday afternoon. Her other child, twin Samuel, was left alone in his cot.

Ms Foster, 17, of Colindale Avenue, Sprowston, was too distraught to tell us any more, and is being consoled at home by her mother, Margaret. But Pamela Newsome, another new mother on the same ward, said: "This is every mother's worst nightmare. I can't believe this has been allowed to happen, and I can't believe that nobody saw anything. Kim has to get her baby back."

Police are calling for any witnesses, or anyone who has any suspicions of who the perpetrator may be to call the number below or call into Norwich police station.

The date is 25 November 1979. Two days after her birthday. She stares at the picture accompanying the story. It's dark and grainy but the eyes of the young woman staring at the camera are filled with so much pain Georgie can hardly bear to look at her.

56

Her hands resting on the table are shaking, her whole body is trembling as she tries to absorb the information, to pin down the facts of the story she's just read and process what they could mean. What they could mean to her.

A sense of dread creeps up her spine and she scrolls quickly through to the newspaper for the following day. Her eyes scan wildly back and forth as her heart thump-thump-thumps against her ribcage and blood rushes to her head. She feels sick but she needs to find out what happened. She keeps scrolling but there's nothing, nothing, nothing. Then, finally, there it is. Two days later, an update.

NO NEW LEADS ON MISSING LOUISA

A region-wide search for a baby girl snatched from Norfolk and Norwich maternity hospital three days ago has so far led nowhere.

Police have conducted a thorough search of the hospital grounds and the surrounding area for baby Louisa, who was taken from her hospital crib last Wednesday, 24 November, but have so far found no leads.

Baby Foster was taken from her hospital crib on Wednesday afternoon just hours after being born at the hospital. Her twin brother Samuel was still in his cot when their mother Kimberley returned to her room.

Although police are still conducting their investigation, it appears that nobody from the maternity ward noticed anything unusual, and there were no witnesses.

Chief Inspector Henderson from Norwich City Police said: "We are asking anyone with any information to come forward. We must find this little girl and return her to her family as soon as possible."

There's a roaring sound in her ears and Georgie glances round, wondering if it's obvious to anyone else how sick she feels. Whether anyone else can tell that, at any minute, when she's properly processed what she's just read, her whole world will be tipped on its axis. That she won't be the same person that walked in through those sliding doors when she walks out again.

She sends the cutting to the printer, then scrolls back and does the same with the first one. She's going to need time to read these again, to absorb the details, to make sure she hasn't made any mistakes. She stands and hurries to the printer and snatches them off the moment they come through before anyone else sees them, then walks back to the table and puts them next to her, face down. Her heart thumps wildly as she scrolls on and finds the next story, a week after the snatch.

POLICE HAVE NEW LEAD ON SNATCHED BABY

Police are following a new lead in their search for a baby snatched from her cot at Norfolk and Norwich maternity hospital last week.

The baby's father has been questioned and cleared, but police say they are looking for another member of his family for questioning. No other evidence has come forward. If anyone has any further information please contact Norwich police station immediately.

And then this one, from the following January:

POLICE REFUSE TO GIVE UP HOPE IN SEARCH FOR BABY FOSTER

Baby Louisa Foster, who was snatched from hospital in Norwich in November last year just 24 hours after she was born, has still not been found, but police are refusing to give up hope in their search.

And later, this:

POLICE HAVE NO LEADS ON BABY FOSTER

Police have admitted they have no new leads on the baby Foster snatching.

Louisa Foster, who was taken from her hospital bed in Norwich and Norfolk maternity hospital in November last year, was believed to have been abducted by her aunt, Sheila Thomson, 22, the sister of Barry Thomson, the twins' estranged father.

But following an investigation the police have admitted they have no evidence against Miss Thomson.

Baby Foster and her brother, Samuel, who is still with his mother Kimberley and her mother Margaret at their home in Colindale Avenue, Sprowston, were the result of a brief relationship between Ms Foster and Mr Thomson. Mr Thomson, 18, has had nothing to do with the family since the babies' birth. However, he did cooperate with police during the investigation.

Mr Thomson said: "My sister has had some troubles recently including losing a baby of her own and police were worried she might have been involved. But I knew she would never have done anything like this and just wanted to help prove her innocence. I hope baby Louisa is found soon."

Georgie makes fists with her hands and presses them to her temples. She feels faint, her breath coming in such short bursts she's almost panting as the words on the microfiche machine swim in front of her eyes.

The names she's just read fill her mind until there's no room for anything else. Kimberley Foster. Louisa Foster. Twin Samuel. Sprowston. Baby's father, Thomson.

Baby snatched.

Snatched.

Snatched.

Snatched.

She shakes her head as though to dislodge the word, which is stuck on a loop like a needle stuck on a record, playing over and over and over.

A baby was snatched from the same hospital she was born in, at least the one she was born in according to her mother. But there was no record of anyone called Georgie Rae Wood being born there that day. Or anywhere else.

But there was a record of a baby called Louisa Foster.

And that baby was taken from the same hospital the very next day.

The facts swim round her mind, floating like torn pieces of paper, each one containing a different name, a different piece of information. All she needs to do is fit them together, like a jigsaw, and she'll have the answer.

Except she already knows what she's found. The trouble is, she just doesn't want it to be true. She so doesn't want it to be true.

Yet what other explanation could there be?

She is Louisa Foster. Kimberley Foster's daughter. And her mother took her from the hospital, the day after she was born.

She knows it *has* to be true.

She just needs to know *why*.

Minutes have passed and Georgie is still sitting here, numb. The quiet of the library hums around her head like flies. How can silence be so distracting?

She knows she has to move, to do something. Mechanically, she winds the film back, replaces it in its case and walks stiffly to return it to its rightful place in the drawer. How long will it be until someone else takes that film out of the drawer and reads it again? Days, weeks, months? Maybe they never will, and the thought of it lying there, unread, gives her a pang. All those words, all those people's lives, tucked away in this drawer for people to forget about all over again. It's heartbreaking.

She walks slowly along the bank of filing cabinets until she gets back to the births, deaths and marriages section. She doesn't need births this time, and it doesn't look as though she's going to need marriages either, at least not as far as her real mother and father are concerned. But she *can* check whether her mother is still alive. At least then she'll know what sort of search she's dealing with.

Numbly, she pulls the deaths film out of the drawer and walks back to the microfiche machine and repeats the same process as before. This time a long list of names appears on the screen and she starts to scroll slowly through them, her eyes aching after just a few minutes. She carries on for a while longer but when she doesn't find anything she has to give up. She decides to move on to marriages after all. It's at least worth checking whether her mother and father ever got married. But it soon becomes clear it's like searching for a needle in a haystack, and she gives up again.

Perhaps she'd have more luck if she looked online, so she vows to have a look tomorrow when she's at home, but for today she feels drained, as though she's done all she can, so she makes her way out of the library and back across the forum. It's raining outside now and people hurry across the square in front of the church with umbrellas up, battling to hold them against the wind. Georgie wishes she'd brought a warmer coat. She pulls her hood up and walks blindly back to her car, not registering the journey at all. The newspaper cuttings she's printed from the microfiche machine are burning a hole in her pocket, she's so desperate to read them again, to pore over them, piece together the facts.

But all she can think about is Kimberley Foster's face.

The face of a mother who has lost a baby.

And then she thinks of her own mother, of her childhood, of the way she was brought up, just herself, Kate and her mother. How her new-found knowledge helps to explain a lot of the things that went on, and the narrow, insular childhood they'd had.

And she questions the mind of someone who has taken a baby from another mother. What must have happened to them to make them do something like that, something so evil? And even then, whatever the reason, how could anyone live with the knowledge of what they'd done, with that guilt, that pain, and still get up every morning and keep on breathing? She pictures again Kimberley's stricken face, the pain etched into the furrows of her forehead and the lines that ran prematurely down her youthful face, and she rubs her hand across her own face, roughly.

And then she thinks about herself and feels her shoulders tighten. The truth is, she no longer really knows who she is.

She's Georgie, yes. But she's also Louisa.

And does the fact that she can't possibly be two people at the same time simply mean that she's neither?

Her mind reeling, she reaches her car and climbs in. Pulling the cuttings from her pocket again, she unfolds them and stares at the picture of Kimberley, at the face in the blurry, thirty-seven-year-old photo. It's hard to make out any features clearly, but Georgie is sure she can see a hint of herself in that picture, the way she was at that age: the dark hair that she'd always assumed had come from her father, so unlike her mother and Kate's pale hair and complexion; the furrowed forehead, the arch of an eyebrow. She's sure she's not imagining it.

This is her mother.

Kimberley Foster.

Her mother.

The realization makes her head spin and she slumps back in her seat, crushing the cutting in her hand.

She doesn't have the space in her head to think about what this might mean for the life she's led so far. She can only get as far as processing the information she's just discovered. She's going to need time to work out what she's going to do with it.

But first, she needs to speak to the woman who claims to be her mother.

CHAPTER
FOUR

25–27 October 2016

The printouts from the library cover the kitchen table, the dark eyes and prematurely deep lines of Kimberley's face staring out balefully. Georgie's studying the face she saw for the first time only a few short hours ago, fragments of her mind flying like moths around the room as she struggles to contain them, to keep them in place long enough to try and make some sense of it all.

The facts are this:

She's called Louisa, not Georgie.

Her real mother had twins; she's a twin.

She has a brother. Samuel.

Her real mother — Kimberley — fell pregnant by accident.

She, Georgie, was taken away from her real mother when she was less than a day old.

Her mother — Jan, she's not even sure she can bear to call her her mother at the moment; Jan, then — took her, and she never gave her back. Instead, she spent her whole life lying about who Georgie really was.

Kate isn't really her sister.

Jan isn't really her mother.

Her whole life is a lie.

How could Jan have done it? If she had acted on a whim, then why did she never admit it and hand her back, even secretly, before too much damage had been done? How different would Georgie's life have been then, if she had? And Kimberley's? But instead, she'd kept her. She'd left this woman always wondering whether her daughter was out there in the world, or whether she was dead. She'd left her utterly heartbroken.

How could you? she mutters to herself, as she draws in gulps of air.

Her thoughts are interrupted by the sound of a key in the lock and she gathers the papers together hurriedly, glancing up at the clock as she does. It's six o'clock already. She hadn't noticed it growing darker outside, the evening light fading and filling the room with smudgy grey. She holds the papers down under her arm and looks up, expecting her daughter to walk through the door. But it's Matt.

As he comes into the room he stops dead in the doorway.

"What's going on? Why are you sitting in the dark?"

He flicks the light on and Georgie squints against the sudden brightness. She stands and scurries over to the sink. She knows her face will give away everything she's feeling and she hasn't yet worked out how to articulate those feelings. Running a cloth under the tap, she squeezes it and turns to wipe down the worktop, rubbing furiously and pointlessly at non-existent stains.

"Will you just stop that for a minute, please."

Matt's voice is loud, shriller than usual, and it makes her stop and look up. His face is chiselled with concern and she knows she has to tell him what she's found. He'll know what to do. Or at least he'll listen to her, be someone to talk things through with.

She lets out a long breath of air, drops the cloth in the sink and stands staring out of the kitchen window into the almost-black of the garden. The trees are dark lumps against the sky, and the table and chairs huddle on the patio in the darkness. She feels Matt's hand on her shoulder and she jumps, then turns to look at him. His face is close, and he puts his other hand on her other shoulder and looks at her intently.

"Please, George. Tell me what's wrong. And don't say it's nothing."

She pauses, then before she can think about it any more, she starts to speak.

"I found something. In Mum's loft. Or rather, I didn't find something."

Matt doesn't reply, doesn't push, but waits for her to carry on.

"There was — an envelope. It had a baby's hospital wristband in it, with a name on. It was Kate's. Her birth certificate was there too. At least, a copy was."

She takes a deep, shaky breath. "But there was nothing of mine, Matt."

Matt's eyes look directly into her own and she wonders whether he can read what she's thinking, whether he understands how scared she is.

"And you're worried about this, right?"

Georgie nods.

"So what else has happened? Because this is obviously about more than just a missing birth certificate, George."

She nods again and with a shaky hand points at the kitchen table. Matt walks across and leans over, spreading the cuttings out and studying them one by one. While he reads them she watches him, to see what he's making of this bombshell.

He looks up, a deep frown on his handsome face, the face she's loved from the moment he walked into the room, the new boy at school, when she was just thirteen years old. "But I don't understand. You don't think — do you? You think this is you? This snatched baby?"

"Yes." The word comes out small.

"But George. Your mum would never do something like that. There's no way. She hasn't got it in her. You must have got the wrong end of the stick, love. You must have done." It's as though he's trying to convince himself as well as her.

Georgie shakes her head and speaks more loudly this time.

"Look at them, Matt." She picks one of the cuttings off the table. "Look at this face. Don't you think she looks like me?"

Matt peers at the grainy photo and shakes his head. "I can't really see what she looks like in this, love. She could be anyone."

Georgie can feel her frustration start to build. She jabs the paper with her finger. "This is me, Matt. Louisa Foster. I'm Louisa Foster. I'm absolutely sure of it. Why else doesn't Mum have any record of me being born?"

Matt shakes his head and sits down. Georgie stays on her feet, pacing up and down the kitchen floor.

"But there's more, Matt. I went to the library — that's where I found these. I also found out something else. Nobody with my name was born on the day of my birthday, or any time near it. According to the records, I don't exist. I was never born. And yet this baby was, on the same day, and she went missing, was never found. That's a pretty damn big coincidence, don't you think?"

She feels dizzy and reaches for a chair, sitting down opposite Matt, her chin resting on her hands.

Matt doesn't speak for a moment and she carries on, her voice shaky. "Plus, think about it, Matt. It explains so much. I mean look at me, for a start. I'm so dark — dark skin, dark hair, dark eyes. Mum and Kate are both fair — and yes, I know Mum's always said I've got Dad's colouring, but I just don't buy it. I look nothing like him."

Matt still doesn't seem convinced. Georgie carries on.

"It explains so much about my childhood, too. Think about it. Maybe she was just scared someone would realize who I was, or — I don't know. I can't begin to think what was going through her head to do something like this. But she must have been mad, to do it . . ." She trails off, her heart hammering, her hands clenched into fists. "And it explains some of the weird things she's been muttering about recently too — being scared about the woman finding out, about keeping it hidden. I thought she was just rambling, but there's clearly something more to it."

Matt's looking at the newspaper story, reading the words again, just as she's done so many times since she found it. She waits for him to finish and then she meets his gaze with a question.

"I'm right, aren't I?"

"I — I don't know, Georgie. I mean, yes, it does seem like a possibility, in theory. But really? Your *mum*? I mean, I just can't imagine it. It's so far-fetched."

Georgie shrugs. "You see, I don't think it is. I just think it explains so much that it can't *not* be true. I know I've told you what it was like growing up, being so smothered, never allowed to go anywhere. But you weren't there. You can't really understand it. Only Kate can. And it explains why Mum never wanted me to go abroad, why she always actively discouraged me from going anywhere. I always thought it was because Kate had gone away and she didn't want to be left alone, and like a fool I stayed, for her. And don't you remember how she was with us, about us getting married? Remember what she said when we mentioned it?"

Matt nods. "That it was pointless, that marriage ruins good relationships."

"Exactly. I didn't think much of it at the time because we weren't that bothered anyway. But you can see, can't you? It wasn't because she didn't want us to get married — it was because she actually didn't have my birth certificate, and she couldn't let me find that

70

out." She stops, runs her hands through her hair, unsure what else to say.

"Have you told your mum? About this, I mean?"

Georgie shakes her head.

"Why not?"

"I don't know, Matt. I just wasn't ready to tell anyone. It's too big. It changes everything — for her as well."

"It doesn't have to."

"What do you mean? Of course it does. It means our childhood was all a lie. It means — it means I'm not even me." Tears are falling down her face now and she wipes them away. Matt moves round the table to her, and runs his thumb gently down her wet cheek.

"You'll always be you, George. Nobody can ever change that."

She shakes her head and buries her face in his chest. "But it's too late. I've already changed. I mean — I've got a brother, Matt. Think about that."

Matt draws her closer and she sinks into his warm chest. "I think you should tell Kate."

"Tell Aunty Kate what?" Clementine has walked into the room behind them and is crunching down on an apple she's taken from the bowl on the side. Georgie pulls away from Matt and snatches up the newspaper printouts, gathering the other ones together into a pile quickly before her daughter sees them.

"Nothing. Just something about Grandma." Her voice is wobbly and she hopes Clem hasn't noticed anything. Clem adores her grandmother and she couldn't bear to see the pain in her eyes if she told her what she'd found. But Clem's looking at her and then back at her dad with a frown on her face.

"Why are you crying, Mum? What's going on? Is Grandma ill?"

"No, it's nothing, love. Honestly. I'm just being silly." Her fingers drum the pile of papers on the table and she shivers. She hates lying to her daughter but she doesn't need to know about this. At least, not yet.

She needs to talk to her sister first.

Clem looks at them for a moment longer then shrugs and throws herself on the sofa and starts flicking through her mobile.

Georgie lowers her voice to a whisper. "I will tell her. I'll speak to her tomorrow, I promise." Then she plants a kiss on Matt's nose and walks up to bed to spend the whole night wide awake.

Georgie has never been scared to tell Kate anything. But this morning, as she drives over to her house, she can feel her pulse hammering in her temples, her hands slipping on the steering wheel. She's exhausted and her eyes are puffy, but she has to do this.

She remembers Kate's surprise when she rang her this morning.

"I'm here this morning, George, but I'm planning lessons. I've got about half an hour if you want to pop over for a coffee."

It's not enough but it'll have to do, so Georgie had agreed to head over for eleven o'clock. Watching the minutes tick by on the clock in the kitchen all morning had been agony, as she tried not to think about what her sister would say when she told her what she'd found. She wasn't expecting it to go well.

Now, as she drives, she's trying to take her mind off what's about to happen and finds it drifting, thinking about the past. Mostly, unsurprisingly, about herself and Kate. Their childhood hadn't exactly been conventional — they'd got used to not having a father around, but it didn't mean they didn't question it. Even at the time she knew that things in their home weren't like most people's, yet when she tries to think back to an example, she struggles to put her finger on it. Mostly, it was a feeling of being so smothered by their mother's love that they felt trapped.

But Kate was always there, they were always together. Best friends, through choice as well as necessity.

Now, as she drives along the wet street, with the windscreen wipers squeaking occasionally as they try and push away the water spraying up from the road, she thinks back to one day in particular. The only other time she'd been worried about talking to her sister was when she was fourteen.

This particular day Georgie and Kate had been asked to make dinner while their mum finished some ironing, and it had started well enough. They'd watched Mum leave the kitchen and then Georgie had swung round to face the window over the sink. The sun was forcing its way through the gaps in the open blind and making stripes on the worktop that crept across the floor and up the wall.

"We don't need to start just yet, do we? Can't we go outside and sunbathe for a bit first?" Georgie held her hand up to her face, shielding her eyes as she looked longingly into the garden.

Kate sneaked a glance back towards the living room, where she could hear the slosh of the water from the new steam iron every time it was moved, the swoosh of the metal against fabric. There was canned laughter from the TV, Mum watching some terrible show like *Catchphrase* or whatever she found on TV at this time of day.

"It'll only take ten minutes if we do it together, then we can go outside for a bit. Deal?"

"Yeah, OK, boss."

"Good."

Kate pulled onions and carrots from the fridge and placed them carefully on the side.

"Right, you chop the onions, I'll peel the carrots."

"But onions make me cry."

"Don't be such a baby."

"I'm not, you always give me that job."

"Well, Mum said I was in charge."

"No, she didn't!"

"She did. She asked me to cook dinner, and said you had to help me. So that means I'm in charge and you're chopping the onions." She slung the bag of onions across the worktop.

"All right. Bossyboots."

The two girls worked in silence for a few minutes, the only sound that of knives hitting plastic chopping boards. Every now and then Georgie's head turned towards her sister, and her mouth curled into a shape as though she was about to say something important. But then she thought better of it and snapped her mouth shut, keeping the words trapped inside her head.

Finally, she couldn't keep them in any longer, and they flew like butterflies into the open air round their heads.

"Can I tell you a secret?"

Kate looked at her sister. Georgie's cheeks had turned pink and a smile teased the edges of her lips.

"Always." Kate had stopped chopping carrots and was watching Georgie's face carefully. It seemed to be lit up from the inside, and Kate stayed perfectly still as she waited for her sister to form the words she wanted to say.

"It's about Matt. And me."

Kate had waited, not saying anything.

"We . . . we want to sleep together."

Kate's cheeks reddened and she tore her eyes away from her sister's face immediately.

"Kate? Did you hear me?"

Kate nodded, watching the knife slice deftly through the carrots on the board in front of her.

"Yes." Her voice is croaky and she clears her throat.

"Well? Are you going to say anything?"

Kate shook her head and looked back at her little sister.

"Sorry, George, I just —" She stopped, unsure what to say.

At the time Georgie had just thought her sister was being a bit weird about it, but now, of course, she understands that her sister was jealous. Not of Matt, necessarily, but of Georgie, having a boyfriend. Of them being ready to sleep together. Poor old Kate was older than her and had never even been kissed by a boy.

A tear fell down Kate's cheek and she wiped it away quickly, but not before Georgie noticed.

"Are you OK?" Georgie peered more closely at her sister. "Are you crying?"

Kate shook her head. "No, of course not. Sorry. It must be the onions."

A crease troubled Georgie's forehead for a minute, and a shadow passed across the sun, turning the room a few shades darker. Then the moment was over and Kate pasted a smile on her face that didn't quite reach her eyes, glanced behind her to the living room where the TV was chuntering on, the iron still slipping quietly over cloth. "Let's shove everything in the pot and then we can go outside and talk."

They scraped onions and carrots into the pan, then tipped in mince and a tin of tomatoes and stuck the lid on.

"It'll be all right for a bit."

Kate grabbed the key from the hook above the door and let them out into the warm sunshine, closing the door behind them quietly so Mum didn't hear. The sun was still strong, but a breeze passed through the garden every now and then, making the leaves in the tops of the trees dance, and the hairs on their arms stand on end. They plonked themselves on the grass, in a small patch of sun not shaded by wall or fence or tree. They could hear the clip, clip, clip of secateurs as Mr

Pritchard from next door but one snipped at non-existent stray shoots of hedge. A dog barked somewhere a few streets away and a young child screamed with delight in the garden behind. Georgie lay right back, folding her arms under her head like a pillow, while Kate stayed sitting, tipping her face up towards the sun. An aeroplane weaved its way lazily across the pale-blue sky, leaving a fluffy trail behind it.

"OK, come on. Spill. Tell me you haven't already done it, George?"

Georgie glanced over to the back door.

"Don't worry, Mum can't hear us out here."

Georgie, reassured, looked at Kate with a smile on her face. Her cheeks were flushed.

"I — I know it's awkward, Katie, but — well, I can't talk to Mum about this, can I? She's not exactly thrilled that me and Matt are even going out. But — I need your help."

"My help? What for?"

Georgie shuffled into a sitting position and a breeze lifted her skirt for a moment, exposing tanned, slender legs. Kate stared at her own pale, chunky legs poking out of the bottom of her sensible school uniform.

"I need some —" Georgie stopped, her cheeks reddening even more.

"You want me to get you some condoms, don't you?"

Georgie nodded, staring at her toes.

"But Georgie, you're only fourteen!"

"I'm nearly fifteen! And anyway, that's why I need to ask you. I won't get them, but you're old enough."

"You're fourteen and a half, and I really don't think you've thought this through, Georgie."

"But Kate. Please. I'd do it for you if I could, you know I would."

Kate's face softened and Georgie knew she was going to agree to it. She'd do anything for her little sister.

Kate let out a huge sigh, her cheeks puffing out.

"OK. I'll do it."

"Oh, thank you, Kate. You're an angel." Georgie leaned over and threw her arms round her sister's neck.

"But —" Kate pulled away stiffly. "There's one condition."

Georgie nodded.

"Promise me you'll be careful. And don't tell anyone."

"That's two conditions."

"Georgie." Kate's voice was sharp.

"OK. I promise. I don't want to get you into trouble."

"I don't want Mum to find out either. She'd kill me for doing this. She'd probably disown me."

"I won't breathe a word. Thank you, Katie. You're the best."

"I know."

A loud cry pierced the air, and there was a bang as the back door flew open. "For goodness' sake, girls, I ask you to do one thing, and you can't even do that properly!"

They both leapt to their feet guiltily.

"We've put dinner on, we were just having a break."

"Well, I think you'd better come and see the state of the dinner before you tell me that. It's burnt to a crisp."

The two girls slunk back inside guiltily. At the time they'd been mortified but now, remembering it, Georgie can't help smiling. She loves thinking about the past, about the things they did together. But now, it hurts. Because now, it feels as though it was all a lie. As though it had happened to someone else.

As though it's all fading away like the images on an old photograph.

It's with these memories jostling for attention in her head that Georgie finds herself pulling up outside her sister's house. Her hands are shaking as she parks and glances at the familiar house, the roses climbing up the front, neatly pruned, the solid black front door, the dazzlingly white window frames surrounding immaculately clean windows. Kate loves to keep her home in order, and her garden is no exception. Today, though, Georgie sees it through different eyes. Today she's here to tell her sister something that could destroy everything they've ever known.

She draws in a lungful of air and lets it escape slowly through her lips, trying to quell the dizziness. She checks in her bag one more time for the folder of cuttings, and reads through the top one again, the words already so familiar that they barely register any more. She tries to see them the way her sister might see them, but fails. For the first time ever, she has no idea how Kate is going to react.

She takes a deep breath. She can't put it off any longer.

Shoving the papers back into the folder, Georgie unclips the seat belt and climbs out of the car. Her heart hammers as she walks up the garden path, and she shakes her head. This is ridiculous. This is *Kate*, the person she loves most in all the world — apart from Matt and Clem, of course. The person she's shared her closest secrets with, her darkest fears. There's nothing to be scared of.

She presses the bell and seconds later her sister's footsteps can be heard approaching the door. She can feel the panic rising in her chest and takes a gulp of air just as Kate flings the door open with a warm smile. It quickly becomes a frown when she sees Georgie's face, and Georgie's heart plummets.

"Georgie, what on earth's the matter? You look like you're about to be sick."

"I'm OK." She knows she's unconvincing but she needs to bide her time. She can't rush this and blurt it all out on the doorstep, it would be wrong and unfair.

Kate steps aside, her face folded into creases, and Georgie slips her shoes off and walks down the hallway to the kitchen. The patio doors are flung open and a cool breeze ripples through the room. The rain has stopped now but the edge of the tiled floor is speckled with raindrops and water runs down the glass. The smell of coffee wafts through the air from the expensive coffee machine, and two cups sit side by side on the gleaming marble worktop. There's not a crumb in sight or a plate out of place, just a neat pile of papers where

80

Kate's been working. Georgie pulls herself onto a stool at the island, aware of Kate's eyes watching her from the doorway, a puzzled look on her face.

For the first time since she arrived Georgie lets herself look at her sister properly. Her fair hair is cut into a neat bob round her face, her nose long and straight, her narrow lips pinched even tighter together so they're almost non-existent. She's on the plump side, her choice of sensible clothing not helping to disguise the growing thickness of her waist, the increasing appearance of a bosom rather than breasts. Her skin is pale, almost translucent, like their mother's — or rather, *Kate's* mother's, thinks Georgie bitterly. Georgie, on the other hand, is dark; her hair is so dark it's almost a shimmering black, her skin a shade lighter than olive. She's tiny, too, her frame dwarfed by Kate's solidity. It's so obvious they're not related she can't believe they never thought of it before. They'd just assumed she looked like their father who, from the one picture they'd seen, they knew was dark and mysterious. But maybe she doesn't look like him either.

So who on earth *does* she resemble? That woman in the photo, grief making her look old before her time? The random man her birth mother had a fling with? It's impossible to tell.

She tears her eyes away from her sister: the sister who's always been so familiar and who now looks like a stranger standing in front of her, their contrasting appearances almost taunting Georgie, and she looks down at her hands. They're shaking and she shoves them underneath her thighs to try and keep them still.

"So."

The one word rings out through the room and Georgie looks up, startled, as though she's forgotten why she's there. Kate is still looking at her, her expression unreadable. Georgie can't bring herself to say anything, the words not wanting to form on her tongue. Kate's the one who speaks next.

"Are you going to tell me what's happened or are you going to make me guess? Is it Matt?" She stops for a moment, then gasps. "Something hasn't happened to Clem, has it? Is she OK?"

"She's fine." The words come out louder than Georgie had expected them to and she makes herself jump. She shakes her head, trying to clear it.

"Sorry. I'm —" She stops, takes a deep breath. "I need to talk to you. About Mum."

"Mum?" Kate sounds surprised, as well she might. After all, it's Kate who sees their mother more; it's Kate who's been trying to find out what's wrong with Jan for the last few weeks, taking her backwards and forwards to her GP appointments; who's been worrying herself senseless about her mother's failing memory. And they'd only talked about it a few days ago. What could Georgie possibly have to say that Kate doesn't already know? Of course it isn't what she was expecting Georgie to say.

Georgie nods slowly, trying to work out where to start. In the end, she takes the folder of newspaper cuttings out of her bag and carefully unfolds them, spreading them out on the worktop. Kate's still standing in the doorway watching her, but when

Georgie pushes a piece of paper silently towards her, she walks into the room and picks it up.

She glances at it, then looks at Georgie and back at the newspaper cutting. She reads a bit more then puts it back down on the worktop.

"Georgie, why have you given me this?"

"Read it properly." Georgie doesn't want to have to explain, to have to say the words out loud to her sister. She wants her to work it out for herself, the same way she had to, even though she knows that she's being unfair. Kate doesn't even know about the things she found in the loft yet.

Or didn't find.

This time Kate leaves the paper on the table and leans over to read it, as though touching it might burn her skin. When she gets to the end of the story, her face is white. She looks at Georgie, waiting for her to say something.

"It's me. Do you see?" Georgie didn't mean to blurt it out, but it's out there now. Maybe it's better this way than beating around the bush, anyway.

"What? What are you talking about?" Her voice is sharp.

Georgie nods her head at the worktop. "The girl. It's me." Her voice is trembling but she doesn't care.

Kate's staring at her, her face a deepening shade of red.

"If this is a joke then it's not very bloody funny, Georgie." Kate spits the words out so angrily that, for the first time in her life, Georgie feels slightly scared of her big sister.

"It's not a joke, Kate." She stabs the newspaper cutting with her finger. "It's me. The baby. Mum took me."

"But —" Kate stops, rubs her neck and looks up. Her movements are stiff, as though the anger has taken over her body. "Don't be so bloody ridiculous. What the hell are you talking about?"

Georgie has never seen Kate so furious, and she sits down before she falls.

"I — I don't really know where to start."

"Well, you'd bloody better start somewhere. Come on, what's going on?" Her words are clipped, staccato, and Georgie fears she's going to lose her rag.

"OK. So, when I went into Mum's loft, I — well, I found your birth certificate and a hospital wristband. Yours. Not mine."

Kate nods stiffly, waiting.

"Well, I was worried. Confused, I mean. It didn't make any sense. And something — well, something told me that there was more to it, Kate. That Mum hadn't just lost them but that — well, that there was more."

Kate's neat nails drum on the worktop, her eyebrows raised.

"More?" The word is dripping with barely contained contempt.

Georgie nods weakly. She'd come in here so sure of what she was going to say, but Kate's reaction is beginning to make her lose her nerve.

"What, so because Mum doesn't have your birth certificate to hand, you automatically assume that this — this snatched baby — that it's you? That Mum did this? What sort of person would jump to that conclusion? Have you gone completely mad?"

The words hit Georgie in the stomach like bullets, making her feel sick. She'd known, really, that Kate would be like this. Why wouldn't she? She does sound mad. But she has to make Kate understand, make her believe that what she's telling her is true, because she simply can't get through something this tough without her.

"Listen, Kate. I know this sounds like I've lost it, but I promise you I haven't. I need you to listen to me. And while you're listening, think about all the things Mum's done to stop me from ever needing my birth certificate — scaring me about flying so I wouldn't go abroad, so I wouldn't need my birth certificate to get a passport; using emotional blackmail to make me stay behind when you went off travelling the world, telling me I didn't need to go anywhere else, that she needed me here —"

"Hey, hang on a minute —"

"No, Kate, it's true. You weren't there. She was so lost, so lonely when you left, and I was there. I never felt I could leave her after that, I felt as though I had to be there to protect her. Not to mention all her recent ramblings about some woman, and how she mustn't find out. Perhaps the illness is releasing something that's been locked away in her mind for years? And there's more: I went to the library to get a copy of my birth certificate. But it wasn't there, Kate."

"What wasn't there?"

"My birth certificate. I wasn't born at that hospital on that day. There was nobody registered with my name."

Georgie lets the words hang in the air a moment, waiting for them to settle. She watches her sister's face.

"But —" Kate stops, her eyes flicking wildly round the room. "But that could have just been an admin error. Of course you were born that day. Why would Mum have lied?"

Georgie points to the cuttings again.

"This could be a reason, Kate." Her voice is gentle this time. She wants her sister to understand, but she doesn't want to hurt her any more than she needs to. She watches as Kate scans the story again, takes in the details: the time, the date, the location, the same way Georgie has done countless times since she found it, trying to find a reason why it couldn't be her, trying desperately to find something she'd overlooked. But there's nothing written in those black-and-white paragraphs that might exonerate their mother.

Then Kate looks up at Georgie, her eyes searching her face desperately.

"But this could be anyone, George." Her eyes glance down at the paper and back to her sister.

"It could be. But you see it, don't you?"

Kate's whole body seems to slump then, as though she's given up the fight. "But you can't be sure this is you. That it's about Mum. There's just no way she could do this. I mean, it's *Mum*. It's ridiculous." Her voice has less conviction now, though, and Georgie knows she's starting to doubt herself, to believe what she's read.

"What else could it mean, though, Katie?"

Kate shrugs. "Anything. It could mean anything. There are all sorts of explanations for this, things we can't even imagine. You can't go round assuming Mum took a baby, Georgie. I mean, listen to what you're actually saying. She would never do anything like that."

Georgie nods. "I know. I'd have said the same a few days ago too."

Kate sits unsteadily on the stool opposite her sister, rests her elbows on the worktop and puts her head in her hands.

"Oh God." Her voice is a whisper, muffled behind the sleeve of her jumper. "I can't believe this. I just can't believe this can happen."

Georgie longs to go to her, to wrap her arms round her and tell her everything's going to be OK. But how can she, when she doesn't think for one minute that it is? So she sits perfectly still, and waits for Kate to speak.

Finally, Kate lifts her head and looks Georgie in the eye. "You haven't said anything to Mum about this, have you?"

"No. I only found all this out yesterday."

"Thank God. She can't cope with this kind of shock at the moment, not in her state."

"But I will have to speak to her, Kate. I can't pretend this hasn't happened. I need answers, and she's the only one who can give them to me."

"Don't you dare." The words come out as a hiss and Georgie jumps. "The shock will make her much worse. She's — she's so fragile, Georgie, I don't know what this will do to her."

"But I have to, Kate. Don't you see? This explains so much. It explains our childhood, why Mum was overprotective. But more than anything, it explains me. I mean — look at me. Look at you. We look nothing like each other. We *are* nothing like each other. I love you, Kate, and I always will, but I really, *really* need to know the truth. I need to hear it from Mum's mouth."

The colour drains from Kate's face and her body starts to shake. "It doesn't make any sense, Georgie. At all. None of this makes any sense. And if it *is* true, then that would mean — it would mean you wouldn't be —" her voice cracks — "my sister any more."

Georgie's thought about this already, and it breaks her heart. But now she gets up and walks towards her big sister and wraps her arms around her tightly, feeling the too-fast rhythm of Kate's heart thumping against her own chest. She pulls away and looks at her, at the pain chiselled into the lines of her face.

"Oh Kate, you'll always be my sister. Always. Nothing can ever change that. But I can't forget I've seen this, can I? I mean, I have to find out more, don't I?"

"I suppose so," she says, her voice flat. "But —" she pauses, pushes her hair behind her ear, and looks up at her sister — "Georgie, I can't help you. With Mum, or — or if you decide you want to go looking for your real family later, then — well, I just can't do it. I'm sorry."

88

Georgie nods, her lips pressed together. "I understand."

"Do you? Because it's not that I don't want to help you. I would. But I think you're making a huge mistake. I understand why you would feel you need to find them but you don't have a clue who these people are. It makes me feel sad just thinking about it and I can't be part of it. I just can't. And I can't do that to Mum. Even if she has done you wrong. I'm sorry." She looks down at the worktop again and runs her fingers across the well-polished granite.

Georgie picks up the clippings and puts them carefully back into her folder, her actions slow and deliberate. She feels heavy, as though her feet are made of lead.

"I am going to talk to Mum, though, even if you can't be there. Maybe Aunty Sandy could come, to cushion the blow, make sure she's OK. I'm — I'm not sure I want to hear what she's got to say anyway, but if I do find anything out, do you want to know?"

Kate shakes her head. "No. I don't think I do. Not yet."

Georgie nods, blinking back tears. "OK." She stands and hoists her bag onto her shoulder. "I'd better get going, then. I'll see you soon."

Kate nods, staring at something in the distance. "See you soon, Georgie."

Georgie turns and leaves her sister's kitchen and, for the first time in her life, she doesn't know when — or if — she'll be welcomed back. She feels further apart from her sister than she's ever felt before, and it's not a feeling she likes.

But she has to find out who she really is, even if it means losing her mum and her sister.

There's no other choice.

It was a strange little family tableau of sorts, Georgie supposed: her mother, Aunty Sandy, herself and Matt, all waiting patiently at the table for Kate to arrive and complete the line-up. The formidable five. Or something like that. She'd been wondering where Kate had got to for several minutes now. It was unlike her sister to be late for anything. In fact she was a stickler for punctuality, thought it the height of bad manners to be late. Unlike Georgie, who was always a little free and easy with timekeeping. With everything, really. And yet here she was, waiting for Kate.

Georgie turned her fork over, tines down, onto the starched white tablecloth, and then flipped it back over again, then back, and back, until the cloth started to pull. Voices murmured in the background, but all very quietly, politely. It was a polite kind of restaurant, really, all hushed tones and gleaming hairdos. She shuffled in her seat uncomfortably, adjusted the bra strap that was digging into the soft skin on her shoulder. She was feeling impatient. She had something important to say — *they* had something important to say, her and Matt — and she just wanted to say it and be done with it. And yet they were still waiting for Kate and she couldn't say it without Kate here. She sighed dramatically and her mother's head snapped up, the line between her eyebrows carved deeper than ever.

"You all right, darling?"

Georgie nodded. "Fine. Hungry." She smiled and Matt clutched her hand under the table and gave it a squeeze. She was fine. Just a little impatient.

A commotion at the front door made her turn her head, and she saw Kate shrugging her coat off her shoulders and handing it to the waiter. She looked different. It was her smile that Georgie noticed first; dark-red lipstick stained her mouth, something she rarely saw her sister wear. She looked radiant, Georgie thought, as she started to walk across the room towards them. Her skin glowed and her hair was tousled and she was grinning happily. Georgie glanced at her mother, who was watching her elder daughter's approach with a serious expression on her face. Neither of them could have been sure at what point they realized that the man behind Kate was walking with her, as opposed to following her on his way to the loo. But it happened, and then it was clear: the look on Kate's face, the smile, the lateness. Kate was in love.

She got to the table and looked at everyone sheepishly, the man stopping abruptly behind her.

"Hello, everyone, sorry I'm late." She turned her head and smiled at the man. "Sorry we're late." He stepped forward and gave a little nod, his smile awkward on his face.

"Everyone, this is Joe. Joe, this is everyone."

"Hello, Joe." It was Matt who stood first and thrust his hand out for Joe to shake firmly. "Lovely to meet you." Georgie saw Joe's face soften slightly, so she pushed her seat back and leaned forward to peck her sister's new man on the cheek.

A flurry of introductions followed, and as they all spoke over one another Georgie watched her mother, her gaze trained carefully on Kate and Joe. A smile played on her lips, but her eyes were grave. Georgie wondered what she was thinking.

It wasn't until later that Georgie had cornered Kate, and even then, stuck behind the plant by the toilets, she'd had to lower her voice to a hushed whisper. "Why on *earth* don't I know about *him*, then?"

Kate looked at the carpet beneath her feet. "I just wanted to keep it secret, you know, for a bit."

"Uh-huh." Georgie folded her arms sullenly.

Kate looked up. "Do you like him?" Her eyes searched her sister's, looking for approval.

"Of course I do. He seems lovely." Georgie glanced towards the table. "So, he's a teacher too?"

"Yes. He started last month. He teaches maths."

"What, and you got it on in the cleaning cupboard, pushing each other up against the bottles of bleach?"

"Georgie!"

"Oh come on, Kate, I'm only kidding. So —" she pushed her hair back behind her ear — "is it serious?"

Kate's face flushed. "Yes." Her voice was barely a whisper. "Yes, I think it is."

Georgie had never seen her sister like this. She'd never really had a boyfriend, not properly, and now here she was, twenty-five years old, and she'd finally fallen in love. Nobody knew then that two years later they'd marry, but spend the next five years trying and failing to have a baby. For now, for this moment, everything was perfect.

"Listen. I've got some news too, but I don't want to announce it now, take away from yours."

"What is it, George?"

It was Georgie's turn to blush now. She'd been dying to tell her sister this news since the moment she found out.

"I'm pregnant."

"Pregnant?!" Kate's voice was high, almost a squeal.

Georgie gave a small nod and before she could say anything more she was wrapped tightly in Kate's arms, crushed into her chest, Kate's chin resting reassuringly on the top of her head. She'd known Kate would be happy for her, but she'd also been worried that her happiness might be tinged with a hint of jealousy. It seemed she had underestimated her sister.

"Is this just for you two, or can your old mum join in?"

They turned to see Jan next to them, her blonde hair haloed round her face, backlit by the light from the restaurant.

"Oh hi, Mum."

Jan's eyes roamed from the face of one of her daughters to the other, searching for clues.

"So are you going to tell me what's going on, or do I have to guess?"

Kate and Georgie glanced at one another and grinned. "I'm — I'm having a baby."

Georgie wasn't sure what she'd expected. Hugs, maybe. Happy laughter. Perhaps, but unlikely. A smile. At the very least. She hadn't expected the long, stretched-out silence that followed, one that seemed as though it was never going to end. Kate broke it, at last.

"Mum? Are you going to say anything?"

"I —" Jan stopped and looked at them both again, as though she'd only just realized where she was and what she was meant to be doing. "I — I'm sorry, Georgie. It was just — it came as a bit of a shock. I'm —" she brushed her hand over her face, which had turned a deathly shade of grey — "I'm so happy for you." She stepped forward and wrapped her arms round her daughter, but it was without any of the warmth of Kate's hug. It was almost as though she was scared she was going to break her. And then she pulled away and wiped a tear from her cheek and turned and walked towards the bathroom, the door closing with a firm swoosh behind her.

Georgie looked at Kate. "Was that weird?"

Kate nodded. "Yes, it was a bit. It was probably just a shock." She sounded uncertain, though.

"Yes. Yes, I'm sure it was just that."

And without saying another word they went back to the table to carry on with dinner. Nobody ever spoke about Jan's strange reaction again.

It's been a few days since Georgie last saw her mum.

She yanks a dress over her head and tugs a brush through her hair, and she thinks about Clem and how she'd feel if she ever lost her. She just can't do it.

Clem used to follow her round everywhere like a little shadow, always wanting to be where her mum was. Now, of course, at eleven, Clem has a whole part of her life that Georgie knows nothing about, and it feels as though a piece of her heart is missing.

Georgie had promised herself, when Clem was born, that she was never going to give her a childhood like the one her mother had given her. She wanted her little girl to grow up with a sense of freedom, the kind she had never known. Even if Georgie did want to wrap her daughter up in cotton wool, and keep her in the house every single day of her life, she'd never actually do it. She smooths her hair down, takes one last glance in the mirror, then goes downstairs and snatches her keys from the side.

It doesn't take long to drive the familiar route to her mother's house and as she pulls up outside she feels a sense of dread descend over her like a veil. It feels as though the atmosphere has thickened, making it hard to pull the air into her lungs, and she gasps, telling herself to calm down.

She climbs out of the car and walks up the short path to rap lightly on the door. She has a key but she doesn't feel now is the time to let herself in. Seconds later the door swings open and Aunty Sandy is standing there, a soft, gentle smile playing on her lips.

"Hello, Georgie. Good to see you." She hugs her briefly and Georgie breathes in the familiar scent of her mother's oldest friend, then Sandy steps aside to let Georgie pass. As Georgie walks into the living room she almost gasps. Jan is perched on the hard edge of the sofa, her whole body tense, hands clenched in her lap, a stern expression painted onto her face. She looks tiny, frail, and Georgie looks at Sandy, who shrugs, then looks back at her mother. She has to get this over and done with, however hard it is.

"Mum, I need to talk to you about something." Georgie keeps her voice soft and watches her mother's face as she speaks. Jan's refusing to look her in the eye and Georgie wonders whether she's somehow worked out what she's going to say. But how could she have done? It's been thirty-seven years; surely she hasn't guessed today, of all days, that Georgie's found out the truth?

"Your mum's upset because you've ruined her plans for the day," Sandy says, her voice low.

"It's OK, Sandy, I don't need you to explain anything for me, I can speak for myself."

"I know you can, Jan, but Georgie looked confused. Why don't you tell her, then, why you're cross?"

Jan looks at her daughter and then shifts her gaze to slightly above Georgie's left shoulder and fixes it on the wall behind her. "You, young lady, have spoilt everything today. I was meant to be going out with your father but now I've had to cancel that to come here and see you." She almost spits this last word, as though seeing her younger daughter is the last thing in the world she wants to be doing. Georgie stares at her mother, shocked. She doesn't know what to say. She knew Jan had been going downhill recently; Kate had told her how she'd been behaving. But seeing it with her own eyes, Georgie's shocked at just how much worse Jan seems since the last time she saw her.

Sandy places her hand gently on top of her friend's. "You weren't meeting their father, Jan. He's dead, remember? We've talked about this."

Jan looks at Sandy, who's perched herself carefully next to her on the sofa. Jan's face is still angry. "Of course he's not dead, don't be ridiculous. I only saw him this morning. What a horrible thing to say." She snatches her hand away and cradles it in the other one on her lap. She turns back towards Georgie. "Now, what did you want to talk to me about? Let's get it over with."

Georgie looks at Sandy in desperation. She can't do this now, not with her mother in this state. Jan's agitation seems to be growing by the minute, her hands in her lap moving over each other again and again, round and round like a washing machine. Sandy shrugs. "I think it's probably best just to ask whatever it is you need to ask her, love."

"OK." Georgie takes a deep breath, wondering how to phrase it. She'd been so angry before she got here; she'd planned to come in here; today and blurt it out, shock her mother into telling her the truth. But now that she's seen her mother — Jan — her anger has softened into something else, and she's not sure it will get her anywhere. Instead, she plucks one of the newspaper clippings from her pocket where she's folded it neatly before she left, unfolds it and places it on the table in front of her mother and Jan, smoothing it flat, just like she'd done with Kate, and Matt before that. It seems to be the best way, to let people work it out for themselves. Jan's eyes flick down towards the cutting and she leans forward to read it. As she takes it in her eyes widen and her face turns ghostly white. Georgie looks at Sandy but she looks almost exactly the same, her eyes wide, her face white, staring at the words in front of her. Both women sit like that for a moment, as though time has stood still.

"Where did you get this?" Jan's voice is almost a shriek, and she snatches the cutting up, screws it into a ball and throws it across the room. Georgie gasps and, as though it's snapped Sandy out of her trance, she looks up at Georgie as well, her face painted with shock.

"I — I found it. At the library."

Jan stands suddenly, her legs shaking so much it looks as though she might fall straight back down again. "Why? Why did you feel the need to go poking your nose around things that don't concern you?" Sandy puts her hand softly on Jan's forearm, pulling her gently to make Jan sit back down again. As she does, Jan lands with a thump, and falls back into the cushions of the sofa.

Sandy speaks next, her voice shaky.

"I'm not sure this is a good time to talk about this with your mum. She's not having a great day," Sandy pleads, trying to catch Georgie's eye.

"It's never a good time," Georgie snaps. "But I want to know what my mother has to say about this."

She looks at Sandy defiantly, then back at Jan. Jan has wrapped her arms round her chest and is staring at a spot on the floor. She seems to have withdrawn into herself, to be utterly detached from everything, and Georgie's sure she's wasting her time. But then she realizes her mother's lips are moving and she leans forward to try and make out what she's saying.

And then she hears the words.

"I loved you, I loved you. You were mine."

Part Two

Jan

CHAPTER
FIVE

1975

I can always tell when someone new arrives in town. Cromer's only a small place and it's as though the air has shifted somehow to make room for an extra body.

And that's exactly what happened the day Ray Wood came into town, because he certainly made a big impact. On me, at least.

I saw him first. Shirley will tell you she did but I spotted him a good five minutes before she piped up, only I kept my mouth shut and just sat and watched him as he climbed off his motorbike and smoked a cigarette by the sea wall. I watched as he sucked in his cheeks, pulling the smoke deep into his lungs, then parting his lips to let it curl out into the air, to be swept away by the wind and across the sea. He smoked quickly, his leather jacket stretched tight across his shoulders, his dark hair unruly, ruffled by his helmet and the wind. A real life Elvis Presley, right here in Cromer.

He had his back to us at first so he hadn't seen us. We were sitting in our usual lunch break spot outside the Bluebird Café, sipping cold lemonade, gossiping, with our cardigans pulled tight round our shoulders.

Pamela was telling us about the date she'd been on the night before and laughter filled the sea air. I carried on pretending to listen, looking over and smiling every now and then so they didn't notice I was distracted.

Then Shirley's voice carried across the table and into my ears. "Hey, check him out." I knew she was looking at Ray — although I didn't know he was Ray then, of course — and I whipped my head round with the others to see where she was pointing, as though I didn't know who she was talking about. We all watched him for a few seconds in a kind of awed silence. He was looking in our direction now, although he was too far away for us to make out his features clearly. He was scanning the buildings along the seafront, his head moving slowly backwards and forwards as though searching for something. Then his head stopped moving and I realized he was looking at us, that he'd spotted us gawping at him, and I felt blood rush to my face.

"He's seen us," I hissed, and grabbed my cold glass and took a sip.

"So?" Sandy's voice was laughing.

"Oh God, he's walking over here." Pamela's voice.

I was dying to look up and watch him as he approached but I didn't want him or anyone else to think I was interested, so I kept my eyes trained on the tabletop, on the smudges of black on the stainless-steel surface, my eyes tracing the drops of lemonade that had spilled from my glass, and willed myself not to look up.

A few moments passed, then a dark shadow passed across the table and I was acutely aware that someone was standing just to my left, blocking the hazy sun.

"Hello, ladies." His voice was unexpectedly loud and deep, and I squinted up at him, shading my eyes with my hand. He was nothing more than a silhouette against the bright sky and I felt vulnerable knowing he could see my face but I couldn't see his.

"Hi." Pamela sounded silly and girly and I rolled my eyes.

"I —" He paused for a moment as though uncertain what to say next. "Do you all live here?"

The sound of nodding can be surprisingly loud, and it filled the air for a moment.

"Great." His voice was quieter now and I could detect a London accent, the edges of his words short and staccato next to our blurred Norfolk ones. "Don't suppose you could point me in the direction of the nearest garage? My bike's making a really strange noise."

It was ridiculous but I felt disappointed. This meant, surely, that he wasn't stopping here for long, that he was just passing through and that we'd probably never see him again. I wasn't sure why a lump formed in my chest at the thought of it, but it did, and I knew I had to say something before anyone else did.

"I'll show you." I jumped up and as I stood I saw his face properly for the first time. Soft stubble threaded its way across his chin and neck, and his eyes were dark, set deep in his head. His nose was straight and long and his lips full, slightly parted to reveal straight, even teeth. His hair was swept back from his face now, and he ran a hand through it.

"Oh thanks." He smiled and creases appeared at the corners of his eyes, softening his face. I knew the girls were all watching me, wondering what I was up to, but I refused to look at any of them and instead turned and walked purposefully away, across the road and towards the sea. I glanced behind me only once to make sure he was following, but I kept going until I reached the spot where his motorbike was parked by the seafront. Then I stopped, my heart thudding wildly. This was so unlike me. I wasn't sure why, but there was something about this stranger that was making me behave a little out of character. I watched him take the last few steps towards me and I smiled at him, holding my skirt down with one hand as the wind threatened to blow it up.

"So —" I stopped, unsure what to say, suddenly shy.

"So," he repeated, his eyes not leaving mine. "Where to?"

My mind raced with endless possibilities, of places I'd like to go with him. But I knew what he meant.

"Shall I come with you, show you? It's not easy to find." I nodded towards the motorbike. I'd never been on one before and the thought thrilled and terrified me at the same time.

He looked at the bike and back at me. "I haven't got another helmet, but . . ."

"It'll be OK. It's only just up the road."

He shrugged. "If you're sure?"

I nodded, trying not to show him how nervous I felt.

"Right then, hop on behind me."

I climbed onto the bike, hooking my leg over the seat, tucking my skirt under my thighs and wrapping my arms around his body. My face pressed against his leather jacket and I tried not to think about how close I was to this complete stranger. He swivelled his head.

"I'm Ray, by the way."

"I'm Jan."

"Pleased to meet you, Jan." Then he kick-started the bike and whisked me away, up the hill, and towards adventures unknown.

OK, so that was a bit dramatic. But Ray did sweep me off my feet that day, without even really trying. There was just something about the darkness of his eyes, the dimple that appeared in his cheek when he smiled — which he did, often — and the hint of danger about him, that hit me in the middle of my chest and left me feeling a bit winded.

He got his motorbike fixed that day, and we chatted as we waited. There was a cigarette constantly on the go, and Ray would blow smoke into my face, which I tried to bat away without him noticing. I couldn't bear the smell but I didn't want him to know that. He was twenty-two, three years older than me, but he seemed much older, with a wise head on his narrow shoulders.

"It's been very nice to meet you, Jan." He strapped his helmet on and climbed onto his bike. "Will you give me your phone number so I can ring you? I'd very much like to see you again."

As my head spun and my heart leapt into my throat, I somehow managed to find a pen to scribble down on the back of an old receipt my phone number at the clothes shop where I worked, and passed it to him with shaking hands.

He glanced at it. "I promise I'll call you, OK?"

I nodded. "OK."

And then he left. I watched him wind his way down the hill until he disappeared round the corner and out of sight, and then I let out the breath I hadn't even realized I'd been holding, in one big whoosh.

He did ring — it took him a good few days, mind you. Days when I moped around the flat I shared with my friend Sandy until I got on her nerves so much that she took me out to the pub one night and got me drunk on Babycham.

I cried, of course. Lost love, and all that.

"Don't be crazy, you only met the man for an hour. You've got to pull yourself together. Anyway, it's only been five minutes since you split up with Alan. You're just on the rebound."

Poor Alan. Safe, boring Alan from the office above the shop, who just nodded with resigned acceptance when I said I didn't think it was working between us. "We're better just being friends," I'd told him, although we both knew we probably wouldn't even be that, and he'd looked like a little lost dog who'd been abandoned on the side of the road as he'd accepted his fate. It wasn't as though we'd exactly set the world on fire, though: holding hands in the cinema and sharing milkshakes in the seafront cafe was as exciting as it had got. It was no great loss.

"I know, I'm sorry. I'm being pathetic . . ."

"A little."

108

I shook my head. I could always trust Sandy to be there for me, and I always knew she'd tell it to me straight. Sometimes, though, it wasn't what I wanted to hear.

So I think she was as relieved as I was — but for very different reasons — when the phone pealed out through the shop the following day and it turned out to be Ray. Sandy had answered and I knew from the smirk on her face as she handed over the receiver who it was. My hand shook as I took it from her.

"Hello?" The quiver was clear in my voice and I coughed to cover it up.

"Is that Jan?" His voice was tinny and distant.

"Uh-huh." Smooth.

"Jan, it's me. Ray. We met the other day." As if he needed to remind me who he was. The sound of his voice made me want to squeal, and I turned my face away from Sandy's stare to look at the wall.

"Hello, Ray."

"I'm sorry it's taken me so long to ring you. I wasn't trying to be mysterious. I've just — been busy. You know." I could almost hear the shrug down the phone. I nodded, then remembered he couldn't see me.

"It's OK."

The next few seconds of silence felt like days but I couldn't think of anything to say. I'd never been very good at this sort of thing, especially over the telephone. Phones made me a bit nervous. Instead we both stayed silent, listening to the crackle and hum of the telephone line, while I twirled the cable into knots round my finger. I could hear Sandy sighing loudly in the background and I turned and glared at her until she got the hint and walked slowly into the tiny kitchen at the back of the shop.

"So —"

"I just —" We both spoke at the same time and then laughed in unison. It felt like a bad script and I just wanted the conversation to be over.

"Go on, you go first."

He cleared his throat. "I was thinking. D'you fancy going out for a ride on the bike? I thought we could go up the coast?"

I nodded again. "I'd love that."

"Great, excellent."

Another silence. "I'm free tomorrow?"

"Tomorrow? I, er —" He paused. "Yes, tomorrow is good."

"Good."

"So shall I pick you up at, say, eleven?"

"Yes, great." My mind spun, desperate to find something else to say, but it only drew a blank. I had to hope words would reappear in the morning. "See you tomorrow, then."

I was about to hang up the phone when I heard him shouting, "Wait, wait, I need your address."

"Oh yes, sorry." I gave it to him and put the receiver down gently, letting out a huge breath of air as I did. I sat for a moment, staring at the phone. My heart was pounding so hard it made me feel dizzy. I wiped my palms on my skirt and walked into the kitchen. Sandy was leaning against the work-top, one leg bent, gently tapping the cupboard door with the toe of her shoe. There was a crooked smile on her face.

"So, someone looks like the cat who got the cream. I assume you've got a date with Mr Motorbike, then?"

"It would seem so, yes." I grinned, unable to hold it back any longer. "He's called Ray, and he's taking me out tomorrow."

"Ooh, exciting. Where are you going?"

"No idea. He just said up the coast."

"You should find out, you know. We don't know him from Adam; what if he's a murderer or something?"

"Oh thanks, Sandy, I feel much less nervous about it now."

"Sorry." She grinned mischievously and pushed herself away from the worktop and walked towards me, placing her hands firmly on my shoulders so I had no choice but to look her in the eye. "Just — I worry about you. You've only ever been out with two men, and you're — well, you're a bit too trusting, Janny, that's all. Promise me you'll be careful."

I nodded and looked away. "I will. I promise."

Her arms moved round me and she squeezed me in a hug. "Good. Now — go home and have a bath — I can hold the fort here. You need to get yourself looking your most beautiful for tomorrow. A girl can't go out on a first date with wild hair and bushy eyebrows."

I smiled. I didn't need telling twice.

"Thanks, Sandy."

And that was the last day of my life "Before Ray". Because although I didn't know it then, the next day would change the course of my life forever.

It was bright and sunny the following morning, which was a relief as I didn't fancy riding on the back of a motorbike in the rain. I hadn't slept much thinking about the day to come, and I felt tired but excited as I waited at the front window of the flat, pretending I wasn't listening for the roar of Ray's bike. Sandy was pottering around behind me, dishing out pearls of wisdom. I was hardly listening but tried to nod and grunt in the right places.

"Ring me if you're worried about anything, promise?"

Uh-huh.

"Don't let him take you anywhere secluded."

Uh-huh.

"I'm just talking to myself, aren't I?"

Uh-uh. Silence, and then I realized what she'd said. "Oh sorry, Sandy. I'm just nervous."

She smiled. "I know. But don't be. You'll be fine. He'll love you — why wouldn't he?"

"Thanks."

The sound of an engine in the lane outside made us both jump, and I felt my face flush. I peered through the window and watched as Ray pulled his helmet from his head and ran his fingers through his hair. He looked so handsome, my heart skipped a beat. It was hard to believe that someone like him — dark, handsome and mysterious — could like someone like me, an ordinary girl who worked in a clothes shop in a small seaside town. I prayed I wasn't about to mess it up, make him realize he'd made a big mistake, taking me out.

"Right, this is it, then. I'll see you later."

I pecked Sandy on the cheek and ran down the stairs, my bag across my chest, and flung open the front door. Ray was sitting astride his bike, his helmet in his hands, another helmet in front of him. He cut the engine so I could hear him speak.

"I brought you a helmet this time — thought we'd better be safe today."

"Thank you."

He looked me up and down, his eyes appraising. "You look great."

My face burned. I'd spent ages deciding what to wear, of course — what girl wouldn't? But I didn't really have a clue what you were supposed to wear for a date on a motorbike. I'd decided on cropped trousers, pumps and a jumper, and hoped I'd be warm enough as we zipped along the country lanes.

"Thank you." I took a moment to look at him properly too. He looked more handsome than I remembered, and his face was clean-shaven as though he'd made an effort for me. His hair was slicked back neatly, although the helmet had ruffled it a bit, and his dark eyes watched me intently. "You too." Not exactly smooth, but I couldn't tell him how I really felt.

He chuckled and I took the helmet from him and placed it on my head. I couldn't seem to get it done up, though, and he reached over to help me with the strap. As his hands brushed my chin I almost gasped at his touch, and I was sure he must have been able to feel the heat of my skin burning him. He clipped it shut and smiled. "There. You're safe now." He nodded to the back of the bike. "Want to climb on board?"

I nodded dumbly, unable to get any words out, and slung my leg over the back of the seat. I was almost shaking at the thought of being so close to him again and I knew I needed to speak to break the tension.

"Where — where are we going?" My voice wobbled and I prayed he didn't notice.

"It's such a beautiful day I thought we'd just drive along the coast, see where it takes us. I don't know it very well round here yet, it'll be nice to explore a bit." I didn't tell him I knew the north Norfolk coast as well as I knew my own flat; I didn't want to dampen his enthusiasm, so I just nodded and smiled. He smiled back. "Then maybe we can stop for lunch somewhere, get to know each other a bit better too." He twisted round to look at me but I couldn't make out the look in his eyes. "Sound OK?"

I shivered at the suggestiveness of his tone, and at the thought of getting to know him better, then felt myself blushing again. "Yes, perfect."

He turned back round and I put my hands on his waist, not sure what to do with myself.

"You'll need to get closer than that," he shouted, as he started the engine. "Wrap your arms right round my waist and squeeze in as tight as you can. I won't bite."

My heart almost thumped out of my chest as I did as I was told. My arms snaked round his waist and found his stomach and I shuffled forward until my chest was pushed hard against his back. I could feel the joints of his spine as he moved, his muscles tense and firm. I'm

114

surprised I didn't faint and fall off before we even started, to be honest, but I managed to keep it together.

Then we were off! We pulled slowly out of the little lane and onto the road towards the sea. For the first few minutes all I could think about was how close Ray's body was to mine. But as we made our way towards the seafront, I noticed people meandering along eating candyfloss on sticks, children carrying buckets and spades, and dads with pasty legs poking out from socks and sandals. Slowly I started to relax. The usually grey North Sea sparkled in the sunshine, the electric blue of the sky reflected back on itself, the sun twinkling off the waves like stars. A tiny red ship sailed lazily across the horizon way in the distance, while close by the beach filled up with bodies desperate for a bit of warmth, layers of reserve being stripped away with every degree the temperature climbed. The breeze was cool through my jumper, but I felt warm behind Ray.

We started to climb the hill out of town, past caravan parks and rows of gorse bushes, up and down and winding round through tiny villages, past stone cottages and oversized churches, until the landscape slowly started to change, flattening out to reveal acres of marshes dotted with reeds, reaching as far as the eye could see all the way down to meet the waves.

We carried on for several more miles and my legs started to go numb. Just as I thought I was going to have to ask Ray to stop, we reached the little resort of Wells Next the Sea, a place I loved where I had spent many a happy weekend. It was busy in the sunshine as we approached the seafront, with people milling all over

115

the road, carrying chips wrapped in newspaper, rolled-up mats, bags of towels. Ray pulled over and squeezed his bike into a small space between two cars on the side of the road. When he cut the engine the silence was surprising, and the sudden change made me feel shy again about being so close to him. I jumped off as though I'd been electrocuted.

"You're in a hurry." He grinned and I watched the dimples form in his cheeks again.

"Sorry." I handed him the helmet, wondering why I always felt the need to apologize for everything.

"I thought we'd take a walk along here and find somewhere for lunch, what do you think?"

"I think that sounds great."

He stashed the helmets under the bike and we set off along the seafront, the waves more gentle than usual but the breeze still stiff. A boat chugged towards the horizon and seagulls flapped high above our heads, answering each other's squawks and calls. I loved being by the sea: the sounds, the smell, the feel of the fresh sea air in my lungs. It was where I grew up and it felt like home, as though it were calling to something in my soul. I couldn't ever imagine living somewhere else, somewhere where you couldn't hear the squawk of the seagulls as you lay in bed, or look out of the window and see the thundery storms whipping the waves into a frenzy, hammering angrily into the cliff edge during the long winter months. Days like this were my favourite, though, with a gentle breeze, sunshine, fluffy clouds scudding across the horizon far out to sea in a rare

116

bright-blue sky. You didn't get much better than this. I wondered whether it had the same effect on Ray.

I was distracted from the sea, though, by Ray taking my hand, which made my whole body shudder. For a minute all I could think about was the warmth of his palm against mine and I walked stiffly behind him. I wasn't used to someone so sure of himself. Dates were usually much more fumbly and awkward than this, hand-holding taking much longer to reach than someone just grabbing it. But I liked it. I moved level with him and gripped his hand firmly back, as though it was a perfectly normal thing to do.

"So, what do you do?" He glanced at me as we walked hand in hand. I was finding it hard to focus on anything other than how close to me Ray was.

"Do?"

"You know, as a job. Work."

"Oh, right. Well, I work in a clothes shop, in town. That's the number I gave you, at the shop."

"And do you like it?"

I nodded. "Mostly. But — well, it's not my dream job."

From the corner of my eye I could see his head turn to look at me but I kept looking ahead. "So what is your dream?"

"My dream?" I was starting to sound like a parrot.

"You know. What would you do if you could do anything at all in the world?"

"Oh. I don't really know."

"Come on, everyone has a dream. You must want to do something?"

I did, as it happened, but I'd never told anyone about it because I knew it sounded too silly, fanciful. I didn't want to let Ray down, though; I wanted to seem interesting, more exciting than just boring old Jan who works in a shop. More like someone he'd be drawn to. So I told him.

"I'd love to design clothes."

"Really? That's cool."

I felt myself flush as his approval. "I've always loved making things, sewing, mending — I made these trousers. But it's not a career, not for someone like me."

"Someone like you? What's that supposed to mean?"

"Well, you know," I shrugged. "Someone normal. I — I don't have any parents, they died when I was little, so — well, it's just me now, and I need to earn money. I can't risk it."

A beat of silence followed my little speech before Ray spoke again. I was too busy wondering where that had all come from to wonder what he thought of me. I never spoke like that to anyone: what was it about Ray that made me open up like this? I hardly even knew him.

"You should never say that. Anyone can do anything if they really want it. You could definitely be a designer. Why not?"

I shrugged again, aware half my conversation was taking place via my shoulders. We walked along the promenade in silence for a few moments; a little girl flew past on her bike, pigtails blowing behind her, dress flapping in the breeze, her feet off the pedals. A small boy ran past chasing a seagull, his parents shouting after him to stop, his sandals slapping on the promenade. Everywhere people were getting on with their lives. But all I could think about was the warmth of Ray's hand against mine.

I cleared my throat, desperate to take the attention away from me. "So, what about you? What do you do?"

"Me? Oh, I — not much, really."

I frowned. He'd been so adamant about me doing something meaningful; why was he being so evasive now?

"You must do something?"

"Well, I play bass guitar in a band, and apart from that I'm just sort of — between jobs. You know. Looking for something. But I'm — I'm in sales. You know, usually."

I felt my heart flutter slightly at the mention of a band. It was such a cliché but it felt so cool, so unlike my life. I couldn't help wondering once again what he saw in me.

I wanted to ask him so many more questions, to know all about him. But it was the first time I'd seen Ray looking flustered and I couldn't help wondering why. Was there something he was trying to hide? I didn't have time to think too hard about it, though, because just then he stopped in his tracks and my arm jerked back hard in its socket. I stopped and turned to look at him. His face was serious and my heart thumped.

"What —" But before I could get any more words out he stepped towards me and planted his lips firmly on mine. They were warm and tasted slightly sweet, and as his tongue gently parted my lips my whole body shivered. His hand was on the small of my back, pulling me closer, and for the first time in my life I didn't care that I was standing in the middle of a busy place, people passing on every side, kissing someone. I couldn't care about anything else but me and Ray.

I have no idea how long the kiss lasted. It could have been seconds, it could have been hours. But when he pulled away he kept his face near mine and lifted my chin with his hand.

"I guess that was OK, then?"

"I —" My voice caught in my throat. "Yes. Yes, it was very much OK."

He looked at me for a few more seconds and I felt as though he could see inside my head, know what I was thinking. Know that I was thinking of nothing but him. My face burned. And then he grabbed my hand again and pulled me along next to him, past a little cafe with a thatched roof, past the kiosks selling ice cream and candyfloss, and across the road to a pub facing the mudflats. It was dark inside and he led me to an even darker corner where we sat staring at each other across the sticky wooden tabletop. "Yesterday Once More" by the Carpenters drifted across from the jukebox.

"Right, I'll order some sandwiches, and what would you like to drink?"

I'd never really drunk during the day and wasn't sure what to say. "Er, half an ale please."

"Coming up, ma'am." He did a little bow then disappeared towards the bar, leaving me alone for a few

120

minutes. My head was all over the place, thoughts racing around it like cars on a track. But each one was of him. I pinned one down; the memory of his lips on mine, the softness with which he kissed me, so at odds with his mysterious, sexy persona. It made me want to know more about the man behind the dark, sultry eyes. I shivered as Ray came back with the drinks and sat down opposite me again, spilling some of his pint onto the table.

"So. Tell me some more, then." I watched his lips as he spoke, those lips that only minutes ago had been on mine, and in my mind I dared myself to lean over and kiss them again, or reach up and stroke my fingers across them. But I wasn't brave enough and instead I sat and told him all about myself.

"Well, my dad died when I was a baby. It was just me and mum, for years. She was my best friend, we did everything together. But then when I was twelve she was diagnosed with cancer." I paused, took a deep breath, remembering. "She died a few months later."

"Oh no." I looked up and saw Ray's eyes boring directly into mine, his gaze intense.

"She — I missed her so much. It felt as though my heart had been torn out of my chest. But I went to live with my grandmother, my mum's mum. We didn't get on. She obviously didn't think it was her job to look after me, and I always felt as though she resented me being there, so the minute I was old enough to leave, at sixteen, I did. I left school, got a job and found a flat, with Sandy. She's my best friend, we met at work."

I stopped, aware I'd been talking for ages and hadn't even paused to ask him a single question. But when I looked at him, he was studying me earnestly, making me feel as though I was the most interesting woman in the world. As though nothing else mattered but me and him, here and now.

"So, that's me, in a nutshell. What about you?"

"Oh, you know. There's not much to tell. I'm not working at the moment. Parents live in London but I never see them."

"Why did you move up here? Seems a weird place to come, out of the blue."

He shrugged, his jacket riding up his neck as he did. "Just — needed a change, I suppose. Get away from London. Start afresh." He tipped his head back and finished off the dregs of his pint then placed it firmly back on the table. I longed to ask him what he needed to get away from but it was clear our conversation was over. Our sandwiches arrived and we ate, then left; he drove me home, back along the coast road, and back to my flat. Having refused my offer of a cup of tea, he arranged to pick me up to go to the cinema on Friday before getting back on his bike and disappearing into the darkening evening, leaving me standing there with a ridiculous smile on my face.

I went back in and told Sandy all about it.

"I really like him, Sandy."

"You don't say," she said, grinning at me. "Just promise me you'll be careful?"

"I will, I swear," I agreed.

It wasn't until later that night, as I was lying in my bed unable to sleep, my mind filled with memories of our date and that amazing kiss, that I realized Ray hadn't told me anything about his life at all. All I knew was that he didn't have a job (at the moment), that he'd needed to get away from London for a reason that he didn't seem to want to tell me, that he played bass guitar in a band, and that he rode a motorbike — which wasn't much more than I'd known before I went out with him.

Before long, though, my eyes were closing and I was drifting off, dreaming about Ray; about the dark eyes that looked as though they hid so much, about the dark hair that blew about in the wind, about the stubble that gave him a dangerous, sexy look. I didn't think I'd ever be able to think about anything else again.

Because I knew, without a doubt, that I was in love. And it felt great.

I also knew, even then, that my life was about to take a very different course. And I couldn't wait.

CHAPTER
SIX

1975–1976

I lay back on the beach, pebbles digging into my back, sand burrowing itself into my hair, and watched the stars above me, the sky stretched out like a dome of twinkly lights to infinity. The moon stared back at me like a belligerent child, challenging.

A hiccup erupted from my throat and it made me giggle. I sat up and the world tipped with me, until the stars and the moon were replaced by a straight line where the sea and the sky met, the rippled surface of the water the only way to tell the two apart. Every now and then the line tipped, before tipping back the other way. I rubbed my eyes.

"Oops, I think I might have had one too many." I put my hand over my mouth as I felt another hiccup emerge, and suddenly I was flat on my back again, Ray on top of me, my ribcage squashed into the firm sand beneath his weight. His face loomed over mine, the stars twinkling on either side of his face, his breath warm on my skin. His hair flopped forward, the gel clearly no match for gravity, which pulled it down towards the earth to tickle my forehead, and it made me giggle again.

"Hey, I can't breathe, you big bully!"

His weight lifted from me slightly and I gasped in some air, but he stayed where he was, his face serious.

"What? Why are you looking at me like that?"

"Just looking at you. I'm allowed, aren't I?"

"I suppose so."

He went silent again and slowly, agonizingly, he moved his head downwards and sank his lips onto mine. They tasted of salt and beer and the outdoors, and they were warm and dry. I responded hungrily, and wriggled underneath him as he pressed his body into me. Then as suddenly as he'd arrived, he rolled off me and hunched forward to light a cigarette in one smooth move, cupping his hand round the flame to stop it going out.

I sat up again and snatched the cigarette from his hand and sucked in a lungful of nicotine. I was still new to this, and my head swam and the stars blurred into one in the black sky. He just grinned, plucked another one from the packet and carried on.

I loved being here on the beach at night, when it was quiet and peaceful and the sky was lit up like a ballroom, like our own private show. I watched as the smoke from my cigarette floated up into the sky, the ash dropping from the end onto the sand and glowing for a few seconds before dying out.

I glanced across at Ray, who was smoking quickly as though his life depended on it, his cheeks sucking in greedily and blowing smoke out in little "o"s. I watched the profile of his face outlined against the lights from the promenade behind us: the straight run of his nose, the full lips, the chiselled cheekbones, accentuated by each in-breath, the sprinkle of stubble that always formed on his chin by the end of the day. It was a face that had become so familiar to me over the last three months I could have drawn it with my eyes closed. Our love affair had spiralled quickly since that very first date on his motorbike, and now my life had become entirely about this man, who, although I was getting to know him better, was still an enigma. But for me, it was a challenge. I liked the idea that there was something to discover; it made life more fun.

We spent most days together when I wasn't at work, and when I was he would wait for me at the end of my shift, leaning on his motorbike across the road, puffing on a cigarette and looking like my very own James Dean. My heart swelled with love and pride every time, and as I climbed on the back of his bike and wrapped my arms round his chest I hoped other women were watching with jealousy. I knew I would be.

Ray still hadn't told me the exact reason he'd come to Norfolk — maybe there wasn't one, not really — but he did admit he didn't have anywhere proper to live, that he'd been bunking down on friends' sofas and floors.

"You can stay with me whenever you like," I said, just a week after we met. I didn't ask Sandy in case she said no, and by the time he turned up, rucksack in hand, that first evening, it was too late. His toothbrush became a permanent fixture in our little flat and his clothes hung from the back of the chair in my bedroom, and, although I knew Sandy wasn't thrilled, she didn't say anything. She'd never tell him to leave. She knew I was happy and that was all that mattered, and I loved her for that. He slept in my single bed with me, our limbs entwined, but fully clothed. I wasn't ready to sleep with him, not yet, however much I longed to.

He didn't have a job but seemed to keep himself busy most days. "I've got meetings with people, you know, who might have some work for me," he explained. But even though the work never seemed to materialize, he always seemed to have just enough money for whatever he happened to need — running his bike, buying food, taking me for dinner.

"But what exactly *do* you do?" I asked one night, as I served up a dinner of pork chops, boiled potatoes and peas. He tucked in, cutting his chop up roughly and shoving it into his mouth. I waited while he chewed and swallowed, then he put his knife and fork down carefully on the edge of the plate and rested his elbows on the table.

"I just buy and sell a few things, that's all. It's nothing major, just enough to keep me going, just until I find a proper job. You know. So I can keep taking you out." He took a swig from his glass of beer and wiped his mouth with his sleeve. "Lovely pork chops, thanks." And that was that, end of conversation. He was good at closing things down when he didn't want to say any more.

I didn't push him for any more details of how he earned his money. To be honest, I wasn't sure I wanted to know. As long as he had some money and wasn't in trouble, it didn't seem to matter.

Most nights we stayed in, snuggled up in bed, the bedroom filled with a fug of smoke that hung like a mist swirling round the lampshade. Other nights we sat in the lounge with Sandy, watching a bit of TV or listening to records: David Cassidy, Rolling Stones, Fleetwood Mac. But some nights we went out, just me and Ray, and they were the nights I liked the most. Like tonight, when we'd been to watch Ray's band play in a pub near Norwich.

"You were brilliant tonight," I said now, the air in front of me filling with smoke from my cigarette as I spoke.

"Thanks. Aren't I brilliant every night?"

"Ha ha. You know what I mean."

"Yeah. Well. Thanks."

"What was that song you played at the end?"

"It's a new one, only just learned it. 'Killing Me Softly', it's called. Did you like it?"

I nodded. "I loved it."

"Good. I hoped you would."

I paused, tracing a love heart in the sand with my finger. "I think those girls at the front liked it too."

There was a beat of silence before he spoke. "Which girls?"

"You know which girls. The ones with the faces full of make-up and the tiny skirts who were standing at the front of the crowd practically salivating over you."

"Huh."

I snapped my head round. "What does huh mean?"

He shrugged. "It just means huh. I hadn't noticed."
"Really."
He nodded. "Really. Well I mean, I saw them, obviously. But I saw a lot of people. There are always girls hanging around. It doesn't matter. Not to me."
"I see." My voice was cold and I turned away and looked back out towards the horizon, my eyes threatening to fill with tears. I sniffed noisily and felt Ray's head turn towards me.
"You don't have anything to worry about, you know."
I kept my gaze trained resolutely out to sea.
"Don't I?"
"No." His voice was softer now and he shuffled across the sand until his hip was touching mine, and held his hand up to my cheek. I turned to face him finally, and saw his eyes were dark, intense. My stomach flipped over. "I'm not interested in anyone else. Only you."
"Only me?" My voice was a whisper in the dark.
He nodded. "Yes." His eyes flicked down to the sand, and then back to meet mine. "I love you, Jan."
I felt a gasp form in my throat and I coughed to cover it up. He loved me! He loved me! I thought I was going to faint.
"Aren't you going to say anything? You just going to leave me hanging like a lemon?"
"Sorry, I —" I cleared my throat and forced the words out. "Oh gosh, Ray, I love you too." Blood rushed to my face and I was glad it was dark so he wouldn't see me blushing as he pushed me back onto

the sand again and kissed me, my world filling with nothing but him.

Like most things, the first few months of excitement soon settled into something more normal. I introduced him to my friends, and they all loved him.

"You want to hold onto that one," Pamela said, grinning.

"Yeah, I'm not sure I'd want him hanging round with other women in pubs all the time if he was my boyfriend," said Shirley, giving me a look that said she thought I was mad.

And I knew what they meant. Most women seemed to love Ray; he was like a magnet, girls swarming round him wherever we went, hanging on his every word. But it didn't matter because, as he'd assured me, he really did seem only to have eyes for me, his gaze meeting mine over the tops of bouffy hairdos, his mouth tipped into a smile.

Besides, most of the time he was with me anyway. When we were together we spent our days zooming along the coast on his motorbike, eating chips on the beach when the sun shone, sheltering in pubs when it was cold and wet outside. Some days we'd just go to the end of Cromer pier and watch the fishermen catching oysters, and I loved sitting there on the old metal bench with the wind blowing my hair, just being with Ray and watching the waves dance and crash over each other way out to sea. It felt like a glimpse into the future, at the long-married old couple we could one day

130

become, even though deep down I doubted Ray was the marrying type.

When it rained we'd go to the pictures, buying tickets for the latest James Bond or whatever was on, and huddle on the back row kissing, only watching half the film as Ray slipped his hand underneath my blouse and cupped my bra, making me gasp.

Some evenings we went out with the girls, tripping down the pier to the arcade, shovelling money into slot machines, the lights whirring round our heads and making us dizzy, the sound of coins tumbling onto metal trays, music pumping, voices shouting.

Other nights I went to watch him playing in pubs. We'd go on his bike, just the two of us, or I'd take the coach with the girls, piling on in our high heels and hot pants at the bus station in town, piling off again excitedly an hour later in Norwich.

I felt so proud as I watched him up on stage playing his guitar, the bright lights highlighting his dark eyes as he lost himself in the music. But the best part was when the band took a break and came to sit with us at the bar. I knew it was pathetic but I loved the envious looks on the other girls' faces as they made their way towards us and Ray planted a kiss on my lips. I'd never been that girl before and it felt great.

There was one girl in particular who caught my eye, though — someone I'd noticed had been at Ray's concerts on more than one occasion. She was always on her own, standing at the front by the stage to the right, the side where Ray usually played. She danced, her hair swishing from side to side, as she sang along to the songs, her arms in the air. And if you hadn't been looking for it you probably wouldn't have noticed, but it was clear to me that she was only there for Ray. She hardly took her eyes off him, and as he walked towards me at the end of the night and wrapped his arms around me she was always standing on the other side of the room, watching, before picking up her coat and walking out of the door.

One night I decided to mention it to Ray as he came off the stage, his face slick with sweat, his hair flopping forward into his eyes.

"She's here again."

"Who's here?" He pushed his hair back with one hand and wiped his other hand on his jeans.

"That girl I always see. Over there." I nodded across to where she was standing, sipping her drink. She averted her gaze when Ray looked round, but he knew who I meant.

"Oh, her. Yeah, she comes to most gigs we do." He took a sip of the beer I'd bought him, tipping his head back quickly and righting it again.

"Don't you think it's weird?"

He shrugged. "Not really. Maybe she just likes our music."

I nearly spat my vodka and orange all over him. "Oh come on, Ray, you know it's more than that. She stands and watches you the whole time you're on stage, then watches us when you're with me. Maybe she thinks she's being subtle but it's creepy."

"Just ignore her. I do."

132

I glanced over to where she was standing, pretending to look for something in her bag. She was tall and slim, and tonight her dark hair was piled on top of her head, her tiny skirt tugging at her slim thighs. I glanced down at the flares I'd thought were so cool when I'd chosen them, their lack of sex appeal obvious to me now, and grimaced.

"I worry, though, Ray."

"What about?"

"Well . . ." I fiddled with the buttons on my blouse. "What about the nights I'm not here? I know you said you're not interested, but she clearly is, and if she persists, then . . ."

Ray took hold of my chin and gently pulled my head round to face him. "Listen to me. I don't know who she is and I don't know why she's here but you have to believe me, I'm not interested in her. Not at all. Not ever. You have to trust me."

His face was close to mine and I could smell his breath, a mix of beer, cigarettes and something else, something musky, and I breathed in deeply. I had to stop this. I had to trust him. I knew he loved me, he'd already told me; what else did I want?

I let out a breath of air. "I'm sorry." My voice was barely more than a whisper. "I know. I do trust you. I just —" I didn't trust her, but I didn't say it. Instead I leaned forward and planted a kiss on his lips, and when I pulled away and looked across the bar, she'd gone.

On a rare night when Ray was out and I hadn't gone with him, I plonked myself down next to Sandy on the sofa where she was watching television, tucked my legs underneath me and said: "Right, who is it you fancy, then?"

She whipped her head round quickly. "What?"

I grinned. "Come on, I know you, you've been mooning round here for weeks now. There's clearly someone."

Sandy's face reddened and she looked away, picking at a non-existent hole in her sock. "I haven't been mooning." Her voice was cross but I knew she didn't mean it.

"Oh, OK. Sorry, my mistake." I stood and smoothed my trousers down and started to walk to the door.

"OK, so there might be someone."

I swivelled round, triumphant. "Ha, I knew it!" I sat down next to her again and pulled my knees up. "Come on, then, tell me."

Sandy's face was even redder and she cleared her throat. I'd never seen her so unsure of herself. But then I'd never seen her interested in a man before either. I was excited.

"Um. Well." She ran her hand across her face and looked at me. "It's Mal, OK?"

I gasped. "Mal? As in Ray's Mal?" Mal was the drummer in their band. I'd had no idea Sandy was interested in him. He was so quiet, thoughtful, hardly spoke to anyone, least of all to Sandy.

She gave a tight nod. "But you have to promise not to tell anyone. Not even Ray. Especially Ray."

"Ha, I knew there was someone. But why can't I tell anyone? Mal's lovely, he's bound to like you too. Ooh, just imagine it, we could go out on double dates, go away together . . ." I trailed off.

"No." Sandy's voice was sharp. "You can't tell him."

"But why?"

"I just —" She pushed a stray hair behind her ear. "If he hates me I'll never be able to come out with you again. It will ruin everything, Jan."

"But he won't hate you, Sandy. How could anyone hate you?"

She shrugged. "I just — it's too embarrassing." She looked at me, her eyes pleading. "Promise me?"

I looked at her for a minute. I was shocked to see Sandy so unsure of herself, so scared. It wasn't like my best friend at all. But I realized as I looked at her that actually, in the four years I'd known her, she'd never been out with anyone, never even shown any interest in anyone. This was clearly a big deal for her.

"OK, I promise."

"Thank you, Jan." She stood then, and walked out of the room and into the kitchen, and moments later I heard her close her bedroom door and go to bed.

I meant to keep my promise to her, I really did. But I thought I was going to burst if I didn't tell Ray, so I did. And a few nights later, when we all got dolled up to go to a dance at the local youth club, I knew straight away that he'd told Mal too.

"How could you?" I hissed. "You promised."

He shrugged. "Yeah, well, you promised Sandy and look where that got us." He grinned. "Anyway, it's fine. He likes her too. And if you're going to drag us all to

135

the sticks to go to a dance then we might as well have some fun."

I punched his arm playfully. "Well, you'd better not have ruined everything or I'll kill you."

He grinned. "We'll see."

I'd been excited about this for weeks. It was just a dance at the youth club, but Ray had promised to come, and it was the first time I'd ever taken a boy to something like this. Usually I spent the night huddled in a corner with the girls, trying to avoid the attention of the local boys on the other side of the room. Now, though, I was arriving with Ray, a man three years older than me, and I felt so proud. Even better, he'd convinced his bandmates to come along as well — Mal, the drummer, Tom, the singer, and Ken, the guitarist. For the first time in my life I felt like one of the cool ones.

As we approached the hall we could hear snippets of Al Green's "So Tired of Being Alone" pouring through the doors every time they opened and I could feel my heart start to race. I was here, holding Ray's hand, and I had never felt happier in my life. And as we walked through the doors I thought I was going to burst with happiness as all eyes were on us, wondering who these strange men were.

We bought drinks and settled at the tables that lined the room. I noticed as we sat that Mal had placed himself next to Sandy and I hoped it was deliberate. I grinned at Ray next to me, who placed his hand on my knee under the table. His hand felt warm on my skin,

136

and I shivered as he moved it slowly towards the hem of my skirt.

He leaned towards me, his breath warm against my ear.

"Is this OK?"

I nodded. I felt faint, as though I was going to fall off the plastic chair, as he slipped his hand under the hem and towards my knickers. I couldn't breathe, and my head whirled as he muzzled my neck with his lips and inched his fingers up so slowly. My heart hammered and for a few moments it was just me and Ray and nobody else in the room, and I was desperate for him.

But then as quickly as he had started he stopped, pulling his hand back down my leg to my knee and moving his lips away from my neck. I felt bereft and I looked over at him questioningly.

"Not here," he mouthed, and despite my crushing disappointment, despite the fact my whole body was singing out for him, I knew he was right. I wanted the first time we got properly intimate to be special, not a quick fumble under the table in the village hall. I shifted my knee away from his hand and stood. "Shall we dance?"

He took my hand and stood and gave a little bow. "Of course."

And as we swayed on the almost-empty dance floor to "My Cherie Amour" by Stevie Wonder, for the first time in my life I didn't feel embarrassed that everyone could see me. As we spun around on the polished wooden floor I watched my friends laughing and joking at the side of the dance floor, the light that spilled from the bar area, and I felt so happy with the weight of Ray's arms wrapped round me. I watched as Sandy and Mal stood and walked onto the dance floor next to us, and I smiled, then rested my head on Ray's shoulder and drifted off to the music.

Hours later, as everyone was sweaty and dancing to the Rolling Stones, Ray grabbed my hand and dragged me out of the front doors. As they swung shut behind us and the cool night air hit us I gasped in shock, and Ray wrapped his leather jacket round my shoulders and planted a kiss on my lips.

"We need to get out of here."

I nodded. I knew what he meant. I'd been desperate for him to touch me all night, and now that Sandy was busy dancing with Mal we knew we had at least a couple of hours before she'd be home.

"Let's go." I grabbed his hand tightly and towed him behind me all the way along the seafront and back to my flat. We stumbled up the stairs and into my bedroom and the second the door closed we were tearing at each other's clothes, pulling off skirts and shirts, tugging on the too-tight jeans that stubbornly refused to slip off. I giggled as Ray sat on the bed fumbling with them in frustration.

"God, sorry, Jan, this wasn't part of the seduction plan." He grinned sheepishly and as he finally wrenched the jeans free from his ankles he stood and pushed me onto the bed, jumping on top of me. I felt as though my body would burst as he planted kisses on my neck, my shoulders, and down across my body. I'd always hoped the first time would be amazing and I knew that, with Ray, it was going to be.

He was the one.

He was mine.

And that night, I gave myself to him completely.

CHAPTER
SEVEN

June–July 1976

Six months passed in a blur of happiness.

I was a regular fixture at his gigs, and we went on double dates with Sandy and Mal who were spending more and more time together. I was glad she seemed to have found love too, and it made me feel less guilty that I was leaving her behind for Ray. We went out on Ray's motorbike; we went to parties, swigging back bottles of beer, eating chips on the beach. I couldn't imagine anything changing. Ever.

But of course it had to. It always does.

Because I had some news for Ray, and I had absolutely no idea how he was going to take it. To be honest, I wasn't quite sure how I felt about it myself, and I didn't know how to break it to him. So in the end I just blurted it out one morning over breakfast.

"Ray, I'm pregnant."

He stared at me across the Formica table in mine and Sandy's kitchen, which was scattered with the crumbs of breakfast, as though trying to find another meaning to what I'd just said. My heart just thumped on and my hands shook uncontrollably, and I didn't dare look him in the eye, scared of what I was going to see there. I was terrified I was going to lose him to these three little words. After all, a baby hardly fitted into his life, did it? Into our lives, I mean. I hadn't even come to terms with it myself. I was only nineteen.

I waited, watching as he blew smoke from his nose and stubbed out the end of his cigarette on the edge of a crumb-covered plate. His face was a mask.

"Are you sure?" His words were slow and measured, his tone unreadable.

I nodded. "Fairly sure."

"How sure?"

I swallowed down the lump in my throat, desperate not to cry in front of him. "Sure."

He nodded and pushed his hand through his hair. Bits stuck out wildly, giving him a crazed look, and his eyes darted round the room, looking at everything apart from me. He didn't speak for so long I was starting to wonder if he was ever going to say anything again, so I spoke first.

"Ray? Is — is this OK?" My voice sounded wobbly and I hoped he didn't notice.

Finally his gaze settled just behind my left shoulder, out of the window towards the sea. He still didn't speak and I wondered whether he'd heard me.

But then his eyes met mine and I gasped. There was a look in his eyes that I'd never seen before. A mixture of hurt and confusion and — rage. I almost didn't recognize him and I had no idea what to say. From the moment we'd met I'd always been scared that he'd realize I was nothing special after all, that I was just boring old Jan from Cromer, and walk out and leave me. But now, for the first time, I was truly terrified that that was about to happen.

My heart almost leapt out of my throat when he pushed the chair back with a loud scrape and stood, his shoulders filling the space in the small room, making the air feel thick and heavy.

"I —" He stopped, looked at his feet. I waited for him to speak again. "I'm sorry, Jan. This is — this has come as a bit of a shock. I —" He stopped, ran his hand through his hair again. It was as though he could hardly bear to look at me.

"It's a shock for me too." My voice was small and I hated myself for sounding so pathetic. I needed him to realize he needed me, not think of me as needy. "Can we — talk about it?"

He took a sharp intake of breath and let it out in a huge puff, then rested his hands on the table. He looked defeated.

"Can we — do you mind if we talk about it later? I just need a bit of time. To think. Alone."

"OK. Yes. Course."

"Thanks, Jan. Right, see you later, then." He looked at me one last time, then turned and walked out of the room. I listened to his heavy footsteps hammering down the stairs, then to the sound of the door opening and shutting. Then I stood and watched out of the window as he jumped onto his bike, revved it up and sped away as fast as he could down the road. He didn't look back at me once and, despite being determined not to cry, I felt tears prick my eyes and start to run down my face.

142

That hadn't gone well.

I sat back down on the chair with a thump and let the tears flow. What if I'd lost him already? What if he left me alone to cope with this? I wasn't sure I could do it. My hand found my tummy, which, if you were looking for it, had a slight swell to it. Otherwise, you would never know there was anything in there.

But I knew. I could feel it.

"It looks as though it's just you and me against the world, then, little one," I whispered through my tears.

I must have fallen asleep because when I woke the sun was high in the sky and I was lying on my bed on top of the sheets. It smelt of Ray, of shampoo and cigarette smoke and something else, something familiar yet indescribable. I took a deep breath and stretched my body along the bed, feeling the tension release.

And then, like a meteor, the memory of what had happened when I'd tried to talk to Ray earlier came crashing down and almost crushed me, taking my breath away.

I sat up and looked round the room for clues that Ray might have come back while I was asleep. But there was nothing, and the flat was completely silent. Sandy was at work and I desperately wanted to go and find her and tell her what had happened. I hadn't even told her I was pregnant yet as I'd been determined to tell Ray first, but I knew she'd know what to do. She always did. But now I'd have to wait until she got home.

I climbed off the bed and walked into the kitchen to make myself a cup of tea, then sat by the window where

I'd watched Ray zoom away from me earlier, and sipped the tea as I stared out towards the sea. It sparkled in the bright sunshine like jewels, and normally the sight of it made my heart swell with happiness. Today, though, it was as if it was taunting me, mocking my misery.

Every now and then I glanced back down at the lane in the hope that I'd see Ray pulling back into it on his motorbike, coming to say he was sorry and that everything was going to be all right. That he'd stick by me, and we'd be happy forever.

But there was no sign of him.

For the rest of the day I didn't know what to do with myself. I didn't want to go out in case Ray came back, and there wasn't much to do indoors. So I sat and listened to the radio, drank tea and chain-smoked until there was a dull fog hanging over the flat, and I stared out of the window feeling utterly miserable as the baking sun poured through the glass, turning the place into a furnace.

And then, as the sun finally started to drop behind the buildings opposite, casting shadows across the lane and into the corners of our kitchen, a miracle happened.

There was a knock at the door, more of a hammering, and with a pounding heart I ran down the stairs to answer it. And there, like the answer to my prayers, was Ray.

I hadn't heard his motorbike approach and when I looked down the road it wasn't there. He must have seen my confusion. "I've had a couple of drinks." His words were slightly slurred and when I looked at him more closely I could see his eyes were glazed over as well. "Left the bike, got a lift."

He stumbled towards me and I took his arm and led him up the stairs to the kitchen. Up close I could smell the alcohol on his breath, and stale smoke mixed with the smells of other people's aftershave and perfume. I tried not to think about where he'd been and with whom. All that mattered was that he was here now, back with me.

We sat down on the chairs we'd left a few hours before when I'd broken the news to him about the baby. For a few moments he didn't speak, just looked at me until I started to feel uncomfortable, a lopsided smile on his face.

I didn't know what to say so I waited for him to speak. It seemed to take forever but finally he made a noise.

"What was that?"

He tried again. "I'm really sorry, Jan. I love you."

It might sound pathetic, but it was all I needed to hear. I sprang up and threw my arms around him, almost tipping him off his chair onto the floor. His arms closed round my back and he sat there, swaying slightly, for a few minutes, until I realized that he was starting to fall asleep. I climbed off him and pulled him from the chair and half dragged him to my bedroom, where I tugged off his leather jacket and T-shirt, yanked his jeans off his legs and pushed him back onto the bed, pulling the sheet up tight round his neck. And then, not wanting to have to face Sandy and tell her what had happened, I climbed into bed next to him even though it was still early, curled my body round the curve of Ray's warm back and fell asleep.

The good weather had broken by the time we woke up the next morning and the open curtains revealed a grey sky, full of anger. It felt like a reflection of Ray's mood too, as he woke like a bear with a sore head.

I brought him a coffee, still managing to avoid Sandy in the kitchen, and put it carefully on the table next to the bed. I sat down next to him and waited for him to sit up. For some reason I felt shy with him this morning. Perhaps it was because I didn't know what he was going to say.

"I feel bloody terrible." He wiped his arm across his mouth and grimaced. "Mouth's dry as a dry thing."

I picked up the coffee cup and handed it to him wordlessly and he took a gulp and plonked it back down on the table.

"Thanks." It was more of a grunt than a word, but I let it slide.

We sat there for a few moments listening to the wind whistling down the lane and making the ancient windows rattle in their frames. Squally rain whipped past horizontally, landing in fine spots on the smeary glass.

Through the door I could hear Sandy up and about, clattering cups and plates in the kitchen, the sound of Brotherhood of Man's "Save Your Kisses For Me" on the radio and Sandy's voice singing along. I tried to

146

block her out and concentrate on what was happening in the room right now. I took a deep breath.

"So."

Ray looked at me, his lips curled in a wonky smile. He shrugged. "So."

I didn't want to push him, so I waited. Eventually he spoke again.

"Look, I'm really sorry, OK. I'm sorry about last night, and I'm sorry for walking off and leaving you. I just —" He paused, and sighed. "I wasn't ready for this. I'm still not. It's a bit of a shock."

"I know. But you're not the only one, Ray. It's not exactly what I was expecting either."

"I know."

He sighed and turned his gaze towards the window. I had to ask him something, even if I didn't really want to know the answer.

"So — is that it, then? You're not leaving me?"

His head snapped round and he leaned towards me, rumpling the covers and gripping my upper arms tightly.

"Of course I'm not going to leave you, Janny. You must never think that. I just —" He stopped, sighed and rubbed his hand across his face. "I'm so sorry if you thought that's what this was all about. It's not. Not at all. It's just — this is such a big deal. It's going to take some getting used to, that's all."

"You're telling me." I gave him a wry smile and he smiled back. "And listen, Ray. I didn't mean for this to happen. Neither of us did. We're having fun, we're still young. But to be honest — well, I'm glad it's happened, in a way."

He frowned. "Glad?"

I nodded. "Yes. It's a baby, Ray. Mine and yours. It can only be a good thing, can't it?"

He shrugged. "Yes, I suppose so."

I stepped towards him so he had to look at me. "It will all be all right, I promise."

He stood still for a moment, not giving anything away. And then he nodded. "You're right. This will be a good thing. For both of us."

His voice sounded uncertain but I was sure that was just the shock. I hoped that once he'd got used to the idea, he'd realize it was meant to be. To bring us closer together. To keep us together forever.

He pushed the covers off and revealed his slim, tanned body in just his pants and I couldn't help it, a shiver went down my spine at the sight of him almost naked.

"What are you grinning at?"

I tore my eyes away and smiled sheepishly. "Oh, nothing." I could feel my face flaming and I hated that I felt so self-conscious round Ray all of a sudden.

"Come here, you." His arms were held wide and I lay down in them and snuggled into his body, breathing in the scent of his skin. I felt so happy, so relieved that he was back here with me again that I didn't care what the future held right then. Because if we were together, then everything was going to be OK. I just knew it.

I was right. For a while, at least. Later that day we got up and went for a walk along the seafront, hoods pulled tight round our faces to keep out the wet wind, and stood at the sea wall watching the murky North Sea swirl and dip, the white tips of the waves gathering in a swell of anger before crashing down wildly onto the beach. It was hard to see where the sea ended and the sky began through the blur of grey, and the clouds moved quickly across the horizon, one indistinguishable from the next. As we stood there, staring out to sea, hands linked, something about the day felt like the beginning of a new chapter.

Soaked to the skin, we ducked into a cafe, where the windows were steamed up so that outside became nothing more than a blur, a backdrop to the life going on inside. We sat at a table and ordered hot chocolate and scones, and while we waited we held hands across the table. I grinned happily and he smiled back. The smile didn't quite reach his eyes.

"What's the matter?"

"Nothing."

He pulled his hands away from mine and laid them on the table in front of him, his fingers linked, then he looked at me with a serious face.

"We should get married."

"What?"

"Me and you. We should get married. Do the right thing."

It wasn't the most romantic proposal in the world but after everything that had happened I wasn't about to turn him down.

"Are you serious?"

He nodded. "I love you, don't get me wrong, but I wouldn't be thinking about getting married if it weren't for — you know." He pointed at my belly and my hand flew to it instinctively. "Not yet, at least. But, well — I want to do the right thing. I have to do the right thing. So — what do you think?"

I wanted to squeal with happiness. OK, so he wasn't down on one knee presenting me with a glittering diamond ring, but he'd said he wanted to marry me and that was enough for me if it meant I was going to keep him.

"Yes." I wiped a tear that had escaped down my cheek, and cleared my throat. "I'd love to marry you, Ray."

"Right then. Good." He fumbled in his pocket and for one ridiculous moment I thought he was going to produce a ring. But then he pulled out a cigarette packet, flipped it open and held it out to me. "Want one?"

I took one with shaking fingers and waited while he lit it. Then we both sat there quietly, inhaling and exhaling until the already overheated room was filled with lingering smoke. I knew it was impossible but I was convinced I could feel the baby inside me already, somersaulting around, letting me know everything was going to be all right. I rested a hand on my almost-flat stomach and sighed. Maybe the baby was right. Maybe everything really was going to work out OK after all.

And so right there, with a cup of hot chocolate in that overheated cafe on a rainy June day, Ray and me toasted our engagement. And despite everything, I felt happier than I'd felt in a long time. This, right here, was my future. I could feel it in my bones.

Days passed and I went back to work, at last, although I wasn't sure how long I was going to keep my job if I kept taking days off the way I had been. I tried to care, but all I could really think about was Ray, and the fact that he loved me. Silly, love-struck girl.

Sandy was glad to have me back, though, at home and at work, and I told her everything over breakfast one morning when Ray had gone to see someone about some work. She raised her eyebrows when I told her about the proposal.

"Shotgun wedding. That's romantic."

"Oh Sandy, don't be like that. I'm really happy."

"I know. I'm sorry, Jan, but I just — I'm worried about you, that's all. Ray's lovely, he really is. But I don't want you to get hurt and this just all seems so fast."

"I know. But I won't get hurt. I know what I'm doing."

"The refrain of girls in love everywhere." She smiled to soften the words but I couldn't help feeling annoyed. Sandy was my best friend, why couldn't she see that this was making me happy?

We sipped our tea in silence, the radio playing Dolly Parton's "Love Is Like a Butterfly" in the background, the air between us humming with unspoken words. Mine, at least. Sandy never held back from what she was thinking.

Her voice broke the silence, shattering the tension into tiny pieces. "It's brilliant about the baby, though. Does this mean I'm going to be Aunty Sandy?"

"Of course! I want this baby to love you almost as much as it loves me. And its daddy, of course."

She fell silent a moment. "I assume this means you'll be moving out? In with Ray?"

"I — I hadn't really thought about it." It seemed strange but it was true. I hadn't. In my mind I suppose I'd assumed we'd stay where we were, living with Sandy in a happy little bubble, going out with her and Mal, just the same as always but with the baby in tow. But the truth was, of course, that it was unlikely to work once the baby arrived.

"Well, you'd better think about it. Ray won't want to be living here with me, you and the baby. And to be honest, Janny, I'm not sure I want that either. It would be — weird."

I nodded. She was right. It would be weird. It was something I needed to talk to Ray about.

In the end, though, I didn't need to bring it up at all, because he did it first.

The sun was dipping below the horizon by the time Ray returned later that day, and his face was alight.

"Ray, what's happened?"

He stumbled through the door and I could smell alcohol on his breath again.

"Oh Ray, are you drunk?"

He smiled at me, his face lopsided.

"I've only had a couple of pints, to toast the baby," he said, and snaked his arms round my waist. He

152

dipped his head level with my belt and whispered, "Daddy's going to look after you, you know. I promise."

I pushed him away, laughing. "Don't be daft, it can't hear you." But I was secretly pleased that he seemed finally to be accepting that this was happening. That he was going to be a daddy.

"She can."

"What makes you so certain it's a she?" I said, smiling.

"Course it's a she, proper daddy's girl. But anyway, even if she can't hear me it's better to be safe than sorry." He pecked me on the nose and walked up the stairs. I shut the front door and followed a few seconds behind. Sandy was in the living room but Ray ignored her and walked straight to my room, and I shrugged an apology as I passed.

I shut the bedroom door and turned to find Ray sitting on the edge of the bed, watching me. His face was serious.

"Ray, what's the matter?"

He watched me a moment longer and then his face broke into a huge grin.

"Nothing's the matter — I've got great news!"

"What?"

"I've got us a house!"

I looked round at my little room, where I'd lived for more than four years.

"But I've got a house."

"Yes, but you can't live here when the baby's born. When *our* baby's born. And when we get married we want to be together, don't we?" He grinned and, even though I'd hoped this would be something we could decide together, not just have him decide for me, I couldn't stop myself grinning back. At least he wanted us to be together, a proper little family.

"Yes, I suppose so."

He nodded. "Good. Great. Well, I've sorted it all out. I've rented us a little house with a garden so the baby can play outside, and it's got two bedrooms. And there's more." He paused and I waited for him to continue. "I've got a job!"

"A job? But — you've got a job. Sort of."

"Yes, yes, I know, but — well, playing in the band isn't exactly reliable, and I can't just keep buying and selling things for the rest of my life. So I've got myself a job in the sweet factory in town."

"A factory?" I couldn't help it. I knew he meant well but this was totally wrong for him. "But — that's not what you want to do. Not at all. What about all your dreams of making your fortune with a band? You're never going to do that, holed up in a factory every day."

He shook his head. "You're missing the point, Jan. I've got to grow up now. It's not just about me any more, and about what I want. It's about me, you and the little one." He reached out and pressed his hand on my tummy and I moved closer. "I've got to look after you both. It's my job."

I shook my head. "Oh Ray, you silly sausage. I love you because of who you are, not despite it. I don't want you to go and get a job you hate just to bring in some money. We can make do with what we both earn, we can get by without you having to give up your dream. It's part of you. It's who you are."

I sat down on the bed next to him and felt the mattress shift beneath my weight.

"But it's not. It's not who I am any more, from this day on. That was me before. Now, I'm going to be a dad. And that means everything has to change."

I loved him for being so enthusiastic, so determined to show he could do this properly. I couldn't help feeling worried about this enormous turnaround, though; it seemed so sudden and unexpected. But when I looked at his face I knew that he wasn't messing around. He really meant this, and I couldn't take it away from him. So I just nodded.

"Well, OK, then. Thank you."

I leaned over and kissed his cheek, his stubble rough against my lips.

"Just promise me one thing."

"What?"

"You won't give up playing in the band? Not completely. You love it too much and I'd hate for it to come between us."

He nodded. "I promise."

"Good. So, where are we moving to, and when?"

"Ah. Well, that's the other thing." He trained his eyes on the swirls of the carpet in front of him, refusing to meet my eye. "The house is in Norwich."

"Norwich? As in the city, Norwich, an hour away from my home?"

He nodded, still refusing to meet my eyes.

"But I live here, in Cromer. I like living here, by the sea. It's my home. I — I'm not sure I want to live in the city. Especially not with a baby."

"I knew you were going to say that."

"Is that why you agreed to rent the house without asking me, then? Because you knew I'd say no?"

"No." He looked up sharply. "No, it's not that at all. I just — I wanted to take responsibility for something, for once. I just wanted to do this right, for you. For the baby. I thought it would be easier to be there, near the hospital. Near to work. I just want us to be together, Jan. Does it really matter where we are?"

I was about to snap, yes, it does matter to me, that this was my home and I didn't like him taking charge of everything, taking over. And that it might be near his work but it wasn't near mine. But something in his eyes made me stop. He'd always been so sure of himself, almost cocky. Yet for the first time I saw something different. For the first time since I'd met him he looked scared, as though he had something to lose. And so I swallowed down the word "yes", and instead I said, "No. No, I suppose it doesn't matter at all. Thank you, Ray."

And that was the day our lives changed again. Forever.

CHAPTER
EIGHT

1977–1979

I walked round the tiny garden — *my* tiny garden — in tight circles, passing the same wall, roses, fence, trellis, honeysuckle, window, wall, roses, fence over and over again until my mind closed down and I couldn't see them any more. In my arms my little baby girl squirmed and wriggled inside her blanket and I held her closely to my chest, trying to calm her down, trying to stop the scream that ripped from deep inside her chest every time I stopped, or every time she detected a change in the rhythm. During each brief respite from the screaming, like right now, I concentrated on keeping my breathing even, on stepping on the same paving stones, the same piece of lawn each time round, to try and prevent her from starting all over again.

The peace, when it came, was such a relief, yet so precarious I could barely enjoy it. My shoulders were hunched and tight. I tried to take deep breaths, in and out, in and out.

This was baby Kate — Kathryn, officially — and although she was only three weeks old, she'd already taken over our lives completely. She'd been born at Norwich maternity hospital on 12 March 1977 and from the moment I saw her scrunched-up eyes and the tiny blonde quiff that stuck up at the front of her little round head, I'd never felt such love. It felt as if a rocket had ripped through me, taking everything else out and leaving behind nothing but this surge of agonizing adoration, so powerful it was almost painful.

And now, while I still loved her fiercely, at times like this when she screamed and screamed as though she was never going to stop, I wasn't sure whether I could cope. I just didn't know if I was cut out to be a mother.

I was heading towards the end of the small patch of lawn for the umpteenth time when I heard a noise behind me. I whipped round to see Ray's head poking round the side of the plastic back door. I made another turn and walked along the back of the garden, then walked slowly towards him, placing my feet carefully on the paving slabs as I reached the patio. "Hi," I whispered, aware of Kate's ear pressed against my sternum. I risked stopping, but kept my body moving gently up and down in the hope that she wouldn't object.

"How long have you been out here?" Ray's voice was low.

"Not sure. It feels like hours. What time is it?"

He glanced at his watch. "Four."

"About twenty minutes." I glanced down at the fluffy little head beneath my chin. "I think she might have finally dropped off."

"Great. Coming inside for a cuppa?"

I nodded and we stepped into the kitchen together. I lowered myself gently into a wooden chair and leaned back, slowly letting out a lungful of air. "So, how was work?"

I studied the back of Ray's head as he spooned tea leaves into the pot and took cups from the mug tree. His hair was longer than I'd ever seen it and it brushed the top of his collar. I longed to run my fingers through it but I knew he'd probably shake me off, irritated. It was the way he always reacted to me touching him these days, as though he wished I wasn't there. It hurt like mad; it was such a change from how he used to be. But all I could do was hope it would pass.

His shoulders rose and dropped again and he put the teaspoon down heavily on the worktop and turned to face me, puffing out his cheeks and letting out a rush of air through his lips. "Oh, it's OK. Same old same old." He rubbed the back of his neck furiously. "Get paid tomorrow, though, at least."

He looked dejected, so unlike the bright, funny Ray I'd met just over a year ago that I felt my heart lurch.

"You know you don't have to do this job, don't you? We don't care."

"I know. But I do have to, that's the point. I've got responsibilities now I've got you two to look after, haven't I?" He sat down heavily on the chair opposite me and leaned forward, his legs parted, elbows on his knees. "It's just — it's so soul-destroying, being in that bloody factory day after day, week after week. Nothing ever changes in that place, they all think it's the centre of the bloody universe. It's depressing."

"So leave."

Ray sighed. "I can't just up and leave. We've got the rent to pay on this place, bills, food. We've got an extra mouth to feed now as well. Not that I'd change her for the world, of course." A smile played at the corner of his mouth when he looked at his daughter, peaceful in my arms now, and for a moment he looked like the old Ray again, the man who'd whisked me off my feet and promised me the world. I wished he had the same look of adoration on his face when he looked at me, the way he used to.

Things had changed a bit since the day we moved in. Ray had been so excited, so full of hope. Sandy had taken a photo of us standing next to Ray's motorbike outside our little flat before we'd left, and it had felt like the end of an era. I would have felt sad but Ray was so excited, like a little puppy, that Sandy and I just hugged and said goodbye, no tears, and then we drove off. His enthusiasm had been infectious, and even when we'd pulled up outside the tiny little bungalow on the outskirts of Norwich later that morning and he'd removed his helmet and turned to me with that grin on his face, I'd swallowed down my disappointment at the tired garden, the scruffy paintwork and the sagging curtains at the windows, and had smiled back just as happily. And before we knew it, it had felt like home. Perhaps it was because it was just me and Ray and it had felt so grown-up, so exciting. I'd bought pictures for the walls from the junk shop down the road and we'd spent our weekends painting the house from top to bottom, even putting up wallpaper in the bedrooms. The baby's room was the most important, of course, and the day Ray came home with a second-hand cot he looked so chuffed I thought he was going to burst.

He'd changed as soon as we moved in, of course. I mean, as he said, he had responsibilities now. Both our lives had changed, only for me the change was mainly about leaving my job in the clothes shop in Cromer that I'd loved, and starting to prepare for the baby, while for him it was deeper than that, more profound. He'd always been free to do whatever he liked and go wherever he liked. He'd played his heart out in tiny pubs and clubs, sometimes to rooms of no more than two or three people, but he'd always given it the same amount of effort, the same passion. He'd always done exactly as he pleased, with no one to answer to. Even when he'd met me, his life barely changed. I just went along for the ride, loving every minute of sharing it with him.

But then he'd become a dad-to-be, and he'd taken it very seriously. Instead of throwing his efforts into playing his bass guitar, he became the epitome of the perfect dad: working long hours to pay the bills, spending weekends decorating the house. He even started wearing his hair neat, taming his wild curls. I didn't like it very much, I missed the old Ray, the Ray I'd fallen in love with, but I didn't dare say anything. He was trying so hard.

We'd had a small wedding ceremony, just me, Ray, Sandy and Ray's friend Pete, at the registry office in town. I'd worn a lovely green dress I'd seen in the shop down the road that I'd had to let out to accommodate my growing bump, and then we'd had a few drinks in the pub afterwards.

So I was no longer Miss Bennett. I was Mrs Wood, and I liked how it sounded, how it felt.

I liked what Ray had become in many ways, too, but I also missed the fun, carefree Ray I'd met. And I couldn't help worrying that this was all a dream — because this behaviour just wasn't Ray, and we both knew that. Oh, I knew he loved me, that was never in any doubt. But I worried that things had changed so much, so quickly, that one day Ray would wake up and realize what had happened to his life, and just walk out and leave us, leave me and Kate behind.

And then what would we do?

Which was why I didn't want him to feel tied to a job he hated. Because if he did, then that day might come sooner than either of us expected.

"Want to hold her?"

Ray nodded and I carefully passed his sleeping daughter into his waiting arms. His arms looked huge wrapped round her delicate little body, and I thought my heart was going to turn into a puddle on the floor just watching them. He gazed down at her, his eyes almost liquid with tears, and gently pressed his lips into her soft, downy hair.

"She's totally worth it, you know. You both are." The words were so quiet I almost wasn't sure I'd heard them right, but when he looked up and smiled at me, I knew I had. I stood and walked across to him and perched myself awkwardly on the end of his knee and leaned into him, feeling his warmth. I wasn't very comfortable and my neck ached but I felt so happy in that small moment, the three of us there together, that I didn't move. At least, not until the pan of water on the stove for the tea threatened to boil over and spill all over the cooker.

I made the tea and placed a cup on the table next to Ray, then we sat and watched the steam rise from both our cups into the silent air. The only sound was the hum of cars outside, and the occasional murmur from Kate, snuggled into her daddy's chest.

I took a sip, the hot liquid scalding my tongue.

"Why don't you go out tonight, have a bit of fun? I can see to Kate." I knew he missed his friends, missed going out with them whenever he liked, and, although he still saw them from time to time, I knew he usually just told them he couldn't go out, that he had to stay at home with us. I hoped spending some time with them might do him good, cheer him up a bit.

"I don't know. I don't know what my mates are up to."

"Go and find them, then." I blew my tea gently, watching the ripples move across the surface. "They can't be that hard to find and it'll do you good to have a night out."

He sighed. "I don't know."

"Go on. We'll be fine. Really." I leaned over and took the sleeping Kate from his arms and kissed the top of his head. "Go. Go on."

He planted his hands on his knees and stood up, brushing his trousers down.

"OK. I'll see if I can find someone, have a couple of pints. But I won't be late back, I promise, OK?"

"OK."

He turned to leave, then stopped. "Jan?" I looked up to see him silhouetted in the doorway. "Thank you. You're the best."

"I know." I smiled and he winked at me, then, ten minutes later, I heard the front door slam, and he was gone in a fog of aftershave.

I must have fallen asleep on the sofa, because I woke up with Kate asleep on my chest and the lamp still glowing. Trying not to wake Kate, I moved my body into a sitting position and laid her gently down on the sofa. She stirred and wriggled her padded bottom in the air, then settled down again with a sigh. I walked into the kitchen and glanced at the clock above the sink. It was 2.30 in the morning. I frowned. Did that mean Ray wasn't back yet? Or had he come in and seen us there and decided to let us sleep? I walked out of the kitchen and down the corridor to the bedroom at the front of the bungalow and opened the door quietly. The light from the streetlamp just outside the window gave the room an orange glow through the thin curtains. I could hear a gentle snoring sound, soft and regular, and when I looked at the bed there was an outline of a body under the covers. Ray's jacket was slung across the chair and his feet stuck out of the bottom of the bed, still in socks. I leaned over him to get a closer look. He was still fully dressed. His breath smelt stale, of beer and whisky and cigarette smoke, and he was snoring gently.

I stepped out of the room and made my way back to the living room, where Kate was still fast asleep. She'd wake for a feed soon, so I made up a bottle then picked her up and carried her through to her little bedroom. It was darker in here and I picked my way carefully to the chair and sat down. As I waited for her to stir I tried not to think about where Ray had been and who he might have been with. I knew he loved me, and to be fair to him he'd never given me any reason to doubt him, to think that he'd cheat on me. And let's face it, it was me who'd told him to go out in the first place, so I couldn't really complain. But there was something about the fact that he hadn't woken me, and had passed out, fully clothed, that bothered me. A lot.

Despite myself I couldn't help images of him with another woman in a smoky club swirl round my mind, eluding attempts to be caught, thrown out. Just the thought of it was too painful even to contemplate.

My thoughts were pulled away by the sudden and loud wailing of Kate waking up, desperate for her bottle, and, grateful for the distraction, I picked it up from the floor and popped it in her mouth, watching her suck greedily.

Ray insisted, the next day, that he hadn't been very late back and that he'd just been for a couple of drinks with the boys.

"You both looked so peaceful I didn't want to wake you," he said.

"OK." I nodded and carried on buttering the toast, my back to him.

His arms wrapped round my waist and he rested his chin on my head. "Come on, Janny, don't be like that. You told me to go out. You have to learn to trust me."

I shrugged. "I do."

But it was hard while I was sitting at home, just me and Kate, to remember his words, and to convince myself that everything was fine. Which was why, for me, that night felt like the beginning of a change for us. It wasn't even that Ray went back to being his old self — at least, not the old self I'd known — because the old Ray wanted to be with me all the time. It was as though, once he'd had a small taste of the freedom he'd been missing, he realized he wanted a huge bite of it.

And so he started going out most nights. He'd come home from the factory, have dinner, and then leave, promising not to be late. And some nights he wasn't. Some nights he'd come home after a couple of hours and we'd sit and chat about our day, about how Kate had been, what we'd done. From time to time he'd even help me put Kate to bed, before dragging me into bed with him — and those days I truly started to believe that everything was going to be OK.

But then other nights he went out and I wouldn't see him until the morning after he stumbled in late, drunk and smelling of smoke. He started playing with the band again as well, and they were nearly always late nights. Sometimes I was sitting up in the dark with Kate when he came back, feeding her or holding her, and he wouldn't even notice us. Those were the times I felt the most bereft. However much I tried to tell myself that Ray's behaviour was perfectly normal, that he was just letting off steam, I felt rejected and lonely. I hated that he chose to be out with God knew who, drinking, over being at home with us: his wife and baby. And his attitude to us made me realize how different we really were.

I filled our days as best I could while he was out at work but the truth was, I was lonely. I hadn't made any friends since we'd moved to Norwich, and some days I literally spoke to nobody all day. I missed the sound of the sea, the call of the seagulls and the bite of salt in the air. I felt smothered by the hot, stuffy city.

But I would never leave Ray.

And so nothing changed.

At least, not for a while.

Then one day, a few months after Kate's second birthday, in June 1979, I had something to tell Ray that I hoped would change everything.

I waited for him to come home from the factory one evening and I'd made his favourite dinner: bacon, eggs and chips, because I hoped it would mean he'd sit down and eat it with me rather than rushing straight out again.

I was in the kitchen taking the chips out of the fryer, waiting for the sound of his key in the lock and wondering what kind of mood he'd be in when he got home. The factory nearly always made him grumpy. Kate was strapped into her bouncy chair on the kitchen floor, laughing happily. As I placed the plates on the table, the front door opened and my heart leapt in my chest. Seconds later he was at the door.

"What's all this?" He indicated the table with a nod of his head.

I shrugged nervously. "I just thought it would be nice to sit down to some tea tonight. You know, have a chat. I hardly see you any more."

He stared at me for a few seconds, then back at the table, and down at Kate, gurgling on the floor. Then he shook his shoulders, swung his jacket over the back of a chair, scooped Kate up from her bouncy seat and plonked himself down. "OK, why not. I'm not going out till later tonight anyway."

I held my tongue, determined not to get him riled. I needed him to listen to me.

I sat opposite him and he kissed Kate on the cheek tenderly before placing her carefully back in her chair. He picked up his knife and fork and dug in. I pushed my food around my plate, occasionally spearing a chip and chewing it slowly.

He shovelled a forkful of egg into his mouth and looked up.

"You not eating?"

"I'm not very hungry."

He shrugged and swallowed his mouthful. "I know I moan about work but I do love you and Kate, you know. It's just — well, you know me. I need my freedom as well. And the factory doesn't exactly give me that." He smiled. "At least you don't mind me having fun in the evenings."

168

I gave him a weak smile back. I didn't dare tell him that I hated him going out all the time and I wanted him back home with me, with us. Away from temptation. It wasn't the right time. Instead I just nodded and took a deep breath.

"The thing is, Ray, something's happened."

His fork stopped midway to his mouth and he lowered it slowly back to his plate. His face was white, his eyes wide. He looked terrified, as though there was a 10-ton truck heading towards him and he knew he didn't have time to move out of the way. I didn't know what he was expecting me to say, but it clearly wasn't good news.

"Something?" His voice was croaky, and he cleared his throat and tried again, his voice harder this time. "What sort of something?"

I waited a beat, then just let it out.

"I'm pregnant."

The silence in the room seemed to grow, making the walls expand and the air feel huge, filling my lungs, my head, my body. I felt light-headed. Why wasn't he saying anything?

I watched him, his face reddening, his shoulders slumped. I didn't know what was going through his mind but I could only remember the last time I told him I was pregnant, when he'd walked out and left me thinking it was over. I wasn't sure I could bear that again.

The silence was broken by the clattering of knife and fork against table and the scrape of a chair being pushed across the lino floor, and I held my breath, wondering what he was going to do. He stood still for a moment, his eyes wandering from me to Kate and back again. Then he spoke.

"Wow. This is —" He stopped, looked down at the lino again, looked up. "This is big, Janny."

I nodded, unsure what to say. Big good or big bad? I waited, as Kate babbled away in the background.

"I don't know what to say. I wasn't expecting this."

"Me neither, Ray. But it's happened."

"But we've hardly —"

"I know. You've hardly been near me." I tried to keep the bitterness out of my voice. "But it only takes once, Ray. Once."

He nodded. "Right. Well. Jesus."

"That's not the reaction I was hoping for."

He looked up at me, his face set. "What *did* you want from me, Janny? Did you want me to dance a little jig in celebration? Did you want me to sweep you off your feet and swing you round the room?"

"I don't know," I snapped. "I just thought — hoped — you might be a bit more — encouraging. Happier." I trailed off.

"Well, I'm sorry. I just think — look, it's fine. It's good. I just need —" He hooked his jacket from the back of his chair and slung it across his arm. "I'm going out for a bit. Sorry. I'll be back later, promise."

He pushed his arms roughly into his jacket, swiped the can of beer I'd placed on the table and shoved it in his pocket. Then he left.

Again.

It shouldn't have been as bad as last time and in some ways it wasn't. He'd said he was coming back, for a start. But I couldn't shake the feeling that this was about more than just the fact we were having another baby. After all, he was hardly ever here anyway, what difference would it make to him? All I could see was the look in his eyes when he'd heard the words. He looked so upset. As though I'd done this to trick him, to set a trap.

Numbly, I picked up the plate of half-eaten food from the table where he'd been sitting and scraped the whole lot into the bin. I dumped my food in there too and then sat down and watched Kate banging her plastic beaker on the side of her chair. She had no idea there was anything wrong, and why should she? I hated the fact that one day she might grow up and realize her daddy was never there.

But I loved him and we needed him. All three of us. And so I'd wait and hope that he would work out whatever was going on in his life, and then I'd take him back and carry on and hope that, this time, things really would change.

They say a leopard can't change his spots, and I know from experience that it's usually true. But this time Ray really did surprise me.

He came home later that evening, slightly tipsy but nothing I hadn't seen before. I was sitting on the sofa, Kate asleep on me for company, the TV flickering noiselessly in the background so as not to disturb her, when he came in and stood in the doorway looking down at us. The light from the TV moved across his face, making his expression hard to read, and I could only make out his outline.

"Jan?"

He stepped into the room and sat down next to me quietly. His face was serious, the frown etched into his brow accentuated by the flickering light.

"I'm so sorry."

"It's OK." My voice came out as a whisper so I didn't wake Kate. "Let me just go and put Kate down."

I stood and walked to her bed and as I laid her down I wiped away a tear. I didn't want Ray to see me cry. He was back now and it looked as though he was sorry for walking out. I had to give him a chance to explain.

I left Kate sleeping and went back to find Ray. He'd taken his jacket off and his head was tipped back on the sofa, his eyes closed. When he heard me come in he lifted his head up slowly. He looked older than usual and I wondered what troubles were hiding behind that handsome face.

"You're back."

He nodded. "I'm sorry, Jan. You didn't deserve that." He paused, his eyes darting round the room, taking in the TV, the electric fire, the freshly painted walls. "I just — I wasn't expecting it."

"Me neither. But it can't be as much of a shock as last time . . ."

He shrugged.

"I dunno. There was just . . . I don't know. It was just the last thing I expected, to be honest."

"So are you back now? Are you staying?" I hated the desperation in my voice but I couldn't hide it. I needed him.

He nodded. "Of course, Jan. I'd never leave you, you must know that." He sat up, slicked his hair off his face again. "I'll be the best dad and husband there's ever been from now on. You won't recognize me. I promise."

He looked so serious I couldn't help letting out a laugh. "You silly sod, I still want to recognize you. It's you I love, not a stranger. But I would like you to be here, with me and Kate and — well, with the baby, when it comes."

"I know. You're right. And I will. I will." He lifted his hand to stroke my cheek and just the gentle touch made me shiver. I knew I could never lose him. I knew I would do anything to keep him.

True to his word, things did seem to change after that night. In fact, so much so that it started to get on my nerves a bit.

"What on earth have you been buying this time?" I watched as a large square frame wrapped in brown paper walked into the room. It stopped and was moved carefully to the floor and from behind it Ray's face popped out, a grin plastered across it.

"It's a picture. For above the fire."

I looked at the blank wall above the ugly electric fire. Bless Ray. He meant well, trying to make the house homely; he came home with something different every day from the thrift shop down the road: cushions, blankets, pictures, toys for Kate and the baby. He made

173

plans, talked about the future, about all the amazing things we could do together when the kids grew up.

"We'll go on holidays to the seaside, maybe we'll even go abroad. You can fly to Spain pretty cheap these days, you know." Or: "We can buy a bigger house with a garden, somewhere the kids can play all day."

I didn't have the heart to point out we'd never be able to afford that on his wages.

He came home after work every night, no longer going out drinking or whatever else he'd been doing.

"You can go out for a drink sometimes, you know," I'd tell him. "You don't have to stop completely."

"I know. But I want to. I want to be here, with you."

I couldn't help feeling thrilled that, when push came to shove, he'd chosen us over his friends, over his life of freedom. And I loved this Ray, the caring, thoughtful Ray, the Ray who wanted to spend time with us, be a happy family. But really, I spent most of the time worrying that, before I knew it, the day would come when it wouldn't be enough for him any more and he'd be off again. I always half expected him to leave at any minute.

I tried to swallow the worry down, and I didn't let Ray know how I was feeling. Instead I tried to embrace the happiness, and let myself believe this was how life was going to be from now on.

And to make things easier I even arranged a babysitter from time to time and went along to watch Ray playing with the band again, to make an effort. And it felt pretty good to have a taste of our old lives. It made me feel young again.

174

In fact, the future seemed pretty good, from where I was sitting. At least, that's what I told myself, until I even started to believe it.

My tummy grew bigger and Ray wouldn't let me do anything, treated me like a delicate flower. He went crazy if I even tried to get plates from the cupboard over the sink in kitchen, or carried a load of washing from the bathroom to the sink.

"Let me do that," he said, taking over and making sure I sat down instead. "You need to look after yourself."

It got pretty tiresome, but I didn't have the heart to argue. Besides, what could he do when he was at work and not there to stop me? Those hours in the middle of the day when Ray was at the factory were the only time I could really be myself.

I waved goodbye to him one morning in early September 1979. I say one morning as though I can't remember it clearly, but of course I can. It was 10 September. It was 8.35 in the morning and Kate and I stood at the door of the bungalow and I held her hand and made it wave goodbye to Daddy as he made his way down the road and out of sight. And then we went back inside the house and shut the door.

The morning had been cloudy and clammy, the sort of weather that feels as though the air is sticking to your skin, clinging to it, suffocating it. We spent the morning indoors, playing with toys on the new rug that Ray had brought home a couple of days before. My tummy was clearly round now, although I was still less than four months pregnant. Kate loved to touch it and say "baby", and it made my heart swell with happiness. We had lunch, fish paste sandwiches, at the kitchen table, and then I looked out of the window and saw that the sun had started to streak across the back garden.

"Let's go outside and play, shall we?"

Kate grinned her almost-toothless grin and I stuck a hat on her head and carried her down the back step onto the grass. We found some shade by the fence where it wasn't too hot, and I went and fetched her push-along trike so she could trundle round the lawn with it. I sat down as she toddled about, stretched my legs out into the sunshine and tipped my head back. This was lovely. Maybe, just maybe, things were going to work out perfectly after all.

We hadn't been out there long, though, when I thought I heard a banging noise. I strained to listen and realized it was someone knocking on the front door.

"Ooh, that must be Aunty Sandy," I said, scooping Kate up and walking quickly inside to answer the door. It didn't occur to me that it could be anyone else because, although she normally told me when she was coming, she did turn up unannounced from time to time, when the buses were running at the right times for her to get here. I left the kitchen, Kate balanced high on my hip, and walked down the short hallway towards the front door where we'd waved Ray off a few hours before. I could see a figure through the mottled glass on either side of the door and I frowned. The figure was much taller than Sandy, and wider. In fact, it looked like a man. I stopped, suddenly, and Kate turned her little face to me quizzically. For a split second I wasn't sure what to do. I didn't know who this was, and nobody apart from Sandy ever came round to see me. But now they must have spotted me through the glass, walking towards the door, so there was no pretending I wasn't in. I stood frozen for a few seconds, my heart thudding against my ribcage, my mouth dry, unsure what to do next.

Then I shook my head. "Oh, snap out of it, Jan, it'll just be the postman or something, or a neighbour. Stop being such a drama queen." I resumed the short walk to the door and opened it wide.

The man that stood there was, as expected, tall and broad, his shoulders filling his white shirt, the buttons straining to keep his chest covered. His face was serious. I stared at him for a second, waiting for him to speak, before I noticed a woman, standing slightly to his left, out of view of the door. She was smaller, her blonde hair pulled back neatly in a bun at the nape of her neck, her eyes wide. She looked quickly down at the ground as I met her gaze, as though she'd rather be anywhere but here. I looked from one to the other and back again, trying not to panic, but holding Kate closer to me, just in case. I glanced over the man's shoulder, to see whether anyone was watching us. The street was empty.

"Can I help you?" My voice wobbled a little and I cursed it. I wanted to sound strong, in control, not scared.

"Are you Mrs Wood?" His voice was deep.

I nodded. "Why?"

He glanced at his partner, and my heart thumped. "Is it Ray? Has something happened?" The words were pure panic, any control lost now at the silent front they were presenting at my door.

"I'm so sorry, Mrs Wood. I'm PC McDonald. This is WPC Greene. I'm afraid we have bad news. Your husband — Mr Wood — has had an accident."

My body started to shake and I had to cling to Kate to stop her falling from my arms. "What kind of accident?" I didn't care about my wobbly voice now.

"Can we come in?"

I wanted to scream, *No, just tell me now, right here, don't make me wait!* But instead I stepped aside and let them come in and led them blindly into the kitchen where the remains of our lunch still sat on the table, crumbs scattered across the floor. We sat down at the table, Kate on my knee. WPC Greene was the first to speak this time.

"I'm so sorry, but he was knocked off his motorbike. In town. I'm afraid he had no chance . . ."

No chance.

No chance to live.

No chance to be here, to watch his children grow up.

No chance.

I wanted to scream, to let my lungs fill with air and let it out into the heavy summer day, a high, intense, deafening sound. But nothing would come, and instead the sound became lodged in my throat, suffocating me. Besides, I had to stay calm for Kate. For my baby.

"No." It was all I could get out, the only sound my mouth would form, and it scratched my throat, my dry mouth, my parched lips, as it left.

But I knew it was true.

178

And then, as if it also knew something terrible had happened, as though it wanted to let me know it was there, and that, actually, everything was going to be all right, there was a soft thump against my pelvis.

It was my baby's first proper kick.

CHAPTER
NINE

September 1979

I had to leave the house, the city, everything. I had to get away. It was the memory of Ray in everything, of the hope he'd had for the future in the little bed, the excitement he'd felt when he'd brought home that ridiculous painting above the fire. Everything reminded me of what I'd lost.

I got through the funeral, although I don't really remember it much. I can see snatches of it in my mind: sympathetic looks from Ray's colleagues, a hug from Sandy, the pain in my chest that made me feel as though I'd never breathe properly again.

But then I had to leave.

I packed a couple of bags with clothes for Kate and me, bottles, milk, a few bits and pieces of food, toiletries and nappies. I didn't really have an idea of where I wanted to go, so I more or less picked somewhere out of thin air. It was a little village just south of Norwich, where some new houses were being built. It was only a bus ride from the centre of the city but I knew nobody there, and it was far enough away to leave the bad memories behind me. I hoped.

I'd seen a little house advertised for rent in the local paper and Sandy had helped me sort it out, even driving over in her brand-new Morris Marina to pick up the keys for me. So when we arrived on a hot, sticky September afternoon, it felt as though, for the first time since Ray had died, I might just be able to do this.

Maybe.

It was a little terraced house with two bedrooms, one for me and one for Kate and the baby.

"It's lovely," Sandy said, running her hand over the flowered wallpaper in the cool hallway as we stepped inside for the first time. But all I could see was a house without Ray.

"Thank you, Sandy." I turned to her, gripped her arm for support to stop myself collapsing there and then in the entrance of the house. "For everything."

Her arms wrapped around me. "Don't be daft, Jan. I'm always here." She pulled away and caught my eye. "Always. Do you hear?"

I nodded numbly and walked along the soft-carpeted hallway to the kitchen. I had to make the best of this. I had to get on with things, for Kate and my unborn baby, even if I didn't feel as though I'd ever breathe normally, live normally again.

And to start with, the four walls of that house were my world. I didn't see anyone, apart from the occasional visit from Sandy, and I didn't want to see anyone. I didn't make friends, I didn't talk to anyone apart from the woman behind the counter in the corner shop when I had to. I knew they all wondered who I was and why I was here, pregnant, on my own with a small child. But I couldn't tell them. I couldn't tell them about Ray, about him being knocked off his motorbike in the centre of Norwich, about him being killed almost instantly, his skull smashed into the tarmac. I couldn't tell them about everything I'd lost, about the hopes for the future that had disappeared the moment I'd opened the door to those two police officers that sunny summer morning. I couldn't tell them because I couldn't form the words. I couldn't even bring myself to think about it, so how could I explain it to anyone else?

So it was easier to lock myself away and try to grieve, try to get through the pain that filled my heart, my belly, my head, without letting Kate down.

"Please tell me if you need anything. Anything at all," Sandy said on one of her regular visits. She always came with a bag of food from the grocer's and made me something to eat, something I had to force myself to swallow for the baby's sake if not for my own. It always felt as though it was going to get stuck in my throat, choke me.

"I will, I promise. Thank you, Sandy."

She was my rock, those first few weeks. The only person I saw. But it was hard for her to get there too often, from Cromer, and so I was almost always alone, just me and Kate.

The days passed in a blur that September, and soon it was October and my belly was getting bigger. I'd been surprised to learn that Ray had left some money in a bank account — not much, but more than I ever knew about — but even that was running out now and

182

I was vaguely aware that I needed to find some work once the baby was born. Maybe mending clothes, or ironing or something.

"I'll help you all I can," Sandy said.

But it wasn't fair to rely on her, no matter what she said. And maybe it would be a distraction from everything to spend time looking for work, would help me claw my way through the fog of grief that hovered over me, waiting to crush me at any moment.

Days were spent playing with Kate, scrubbing the house, trying to stay busy. I just wanted the baby to arrive now, but it wasn't due until well into the new year.

Then one day in early November, everything changed.

I woke up feeling a little under the weather, but nothing I could put my finger on. A low-lying tummy ache, a little shivery. Kate didn't care, though, and she was yelling her head off from early in the morning. I dragged myself out of bed and padded through to her room, holding my tummy. The air was chilly and I shivered as I opened the door to her bedroom to find her sitting up in her bed.

"Morning, sweetheart." I walked across to her and planted a kiss on her head.

"Hewo mumma." Her smile could melt a thousand icebergs, and I scooped her up and held her on my hip as we opened the curtains. It was a grey day, almost weatherless, the air still, the sky grey and unmoving. The street was empty apart from a small black cat darting across the road, and we stood there for a moment, looking out.

"Right, let's get you downstairs for breakfast, shall we?"

"Brekkie!"

I carried her to the top of the stairs, but the pain in my stomach was insistent so I put her down and held her hand as she cautiously took one step at a time. We counted the flowers on the carpet as we went down.

In the kitchen I lifted her carefully onto a chair and walked round getting out plates and plastic cups and spoons, putting water on to boil. I poured cereal into Kate's bowl and mashed it up with some milk. My stomach was aching and I felt a little dizzy, so I plonked myself down on the chair opposite Kate with a heavy sigh to wait for the water to heat.

"Want Mummy to feed you?"

Kate waved her spoon in the air and squealed with delight, so I leaned forward and plucked it from her hand. I gasped as a pain shot across the front of my stomach and round my back, then disappeared as quickly as it had come. I frowned. I was sure it was nothing to worry about, just a cramp or a trapped nerve.

I spooned cereal into Kate's mouth and she giggled wildly as I pretended the spoon was a bee buzzing round her head.

"More!" she yelled, and I floated the spoon towards her open mouth. When we were done I chopped a banana for Kate and made myself a cup of tea, then sat and sipped the steaming cuppa while she smeared

184

banana all round her face. I was cold but I didn't have the energy to walk up the stairs to get a cardigan, so I wrapped my hands round the mug and blew the steam into my face.

Breakfast done, I lifted Kate from her chair. And then I nearly dropped her as the pain shot across my abdomen again; only this time it didn't disappear, but deepened, intensifying like a tight band from my belly button round my side. I put Kate quickly on the floor and sat back down heavily, leaning right forward to try and catch my breath. The tightening was getting worse by the second and I could feel my heart knocking on my chest like a hammer. The walls of the kitchen bulged out and in again, and I sucked air in and out as slowly as I could while my head spun. I couldn't get comfortable; there didn't seem to be a position that helped ease the pain, so I stayed still and concentrated on breathing. I knew Kate was watching me but I didn't know what to do.

"Mummy's OK, go and find some toys, sweetheart."

But she shook her head and came closer, fear etched on her face. I wrapped my arm around her and kissed her cheek and tried not to panic.

Slowly the pain subsided and I stood, my legs wobbly beneath me. I held Kate's tiny warm hand in one hand and clutched the back of the wooden chair with the other, then shuffled slowly through to the living room. I flipped open the top of the little toy box in the corner and we pulled out some teddies, a couple of cars and a plastic record player that Sandy had given her and I sat her down on the carpet to play. I stayed right next to her so she didn't worry, and lay back on the sofa, my legs out in front of me. My eyes followed the Artexed pattern of the ceiling and I tried not to think about what this pain might mean. It was too early for the baby to be born, I was only just over six months pregnant. It couldn't come yet. I had to relax.

I lay there for some time listening to Kate's chattering and the odd car driving along the road. The net curtains hid the street from view and the dim, neutral daylight was failing to squeeze much light into the room, leaving it empty and colourless. I carried on tracing the Artex with my eyes, and breathed steadily in and out, in and out, my chest rising and falling, my heartbeat gradually slowing.

The pain was still there, but it had subsided to a dull ache, as if I'd been wearing too-tight jeans for too long. I wished Ray was with me, and then I wouldn't feel so scared. But, like everything else from now on, I had to do this alone.

"Mumma." Kate was standing next to me, holding her little hand on my tummy.

"Hi, sweetheart. Mummy's OK." I kissed her little nose and she watched me for a few more seconds, then, as though she was finally convinced, she turned and sat back down again, pushing cars round the flowery carpet.

I couldn't just lie there all day. If I got up and the pain got worse, I'd take myself to the doctor's and get it checked out. Everything would be fine. Carefully, I swung my legs over the side of the sofa and planted my feet on the floor, pushing my body into a sitting position. So far, so good. I pushed myself up and straightened my legs slowly. But as I stood the pain came back, worse than before, and I gasped, bent double, and fell back onto the sofa, clutching my stomach.

Kate whipped her head round, her eyes wide.

I tried to smile at her but nothing would come and she watched me with serious eyes. It felt as though a knife had been plunged through my side and into my belly . . . I was on fire; the pain ripped through me, tearing my stomach, my womb, my baby from me. I needed to get to the bathroom, this couldn't happen here. With a superhuman effort I launched myself from the sofa to the door and, each step utter agony, climbed the stairs to the bathroom. I stumbled through the door, and as I did a final roaring pain ripped through me. I heard screaming and remembered Kate, then realized the noise was coming from me. I fell to my hands and knees and watched as blood spread on the floor, around and out towards the sink, the door. With each convulsion I felt myself doubling up, wanting to scream but not wanting to scare Kate any more. I needed to get to her but I couldn't move from where I was and all I could do was hope that she was OK, and still playing with her toys, blissfully unaware.

I have no idea how long I was on that bathroom floor, but what could have been seconds, minutes or hours later I was shivering on the cold tiles, covered in blood, and there was a tiny, still mass beside me. I couldn't bear to look at what should have been my baby, cold and lifeless on the bathroom floor, a symbol of everything that I'd lost. Instead, numb, I grabbed a towel from the rail and wrapped it round the baby and picked it up and pushed it unceremoniously to the side of the room. I needed to get down to Kate, but first I had to clean myself up. I stripped everything off, the pain in my stomach and groin almost tearing me apart, and jumped into the freezing ceramic bath and ran the taps. The water was lukewarm but I splashed it all over myself hurriedly, watching the pink water running down the bath and into the plughole. Shivering, I grabbed a clean towel from the floor and wrapped it around me, pulled on some clean knickers and a sanitary pad and walked as quickly as I could down the stairs, holding onto the rail as I did. I went straight into the living room and my heart almost stopped; there were toys abandoned in the middle of the carpet, but no sign of Kate. My head felt as though all the blood from my body had filled it and I grabbed hold of the door frame for support. Oh God, not Kate as well now. Where was she?

My eyes whipped backwards and forwards, scanning the small living room for clues. And then I spotted her, just a few tufts of hair sticking up above the arm of the chair. I walked over and found her crouched behind it, her legs drawn up to her chin, her arms wrapped round them, pulling them closer. There were tears and snot all over her face and she was looking at me with utter terror in her eyes.

I put my arms out and she reached hers towards me and I scooped her up and held her close to me. I was shivering in just a towel but I didn't care, I had my Kate and she was safe and she was all I had left in the world now. We sat carefully on the chair, and I wrapped my arms tightly round her and felt her hot little cheek press against the cool skin of my shoulder. She was shaking, but I was too and we sat there together, huddled in a ball, for ages. I buried my nose in her fluff of hair and slowly, slowly, she stopped shaking and looked up at me, her eyes dry now.

"Mumma cry?"

I kissed her eyes, her nose and her little rosebud lips. "Yes, Mumma was crying, but it's all OK now. I'm here, I'm never leaving you again. Not ever."

She smiled, a weak little smile, and we sat a while longer, listening to the clock ticking and the odd shout from the street. It felt wrong, disjointed, to hear life going on as normal, given that so much had changed in the last few minutes in this house.

I got up and carried Kate upstairs with me while I got dressed. I wasn't really thinking as I pulled on my trousers, my jumper and tied my hair back into a ponytail. My stomach was still convulsing, but the ripples of pain were getting more manageable as the minutes passed, until they weren't taking my breath away every time one came. I wasn't really thinking as I strapped Kate into her pushchair and headed out for a walk, my head down so I didn't have to look at anyone. I wasn't thinking as I pushed her on the swings and made her laugh, or as she hauled herself up the steps of the slide and made me watch her stutter her way slowly down. And I definitely wasn't really thinking later, after I put Kate to bed and pulled on my tatty old nightdress and realized I finally had to do something about what had happened earlier.

I pushed open the bathroom door, praying that somehow it would all have been cleaned up and the room would look spotless, as though nothing had happened there at all. But of course it was exactly as I'd left it earlier. I stared straight ahead into the mirror above the sink and saw my face, pale and grey, my hair scraped back and my eyes bruised and swollen. I lifted my nightie up from the bottom and looked at my belly, still slightly swollen but already the evidence that there had ever been a baby in there disappearing before my eyes, leaving just some bleeding and waves of pain in its place. And then I knew I had to look down, at the floor by the radiator. I took a deep breath and turned my head and lowered my eyes. There it was. A perfectly ordinary-looking bundle of towelling, containing all my hopes and dreams for the future, shattered into pieces.

I didn't know how I was going to do this. There was a huge lump in my gut, and I really felt as though I was going to throw up if I had to pick up that little bundle.

I tore my eyes away and looked back at the mirror. The me I saw before me was an empty shell of the me who'd been reflected back just a couple of months before. I was hollow.

I had nothing more to lose.

Without thinking about it any further, I turned and scooped the bundle off the floor with both hands, and held my arms out in front of me, slightly away from my body. The only way I could do it was by telling myself there was nothing inside, it was just a towel. Nothing more.

I walked carefully down the stairs, turned sharply at the bottom and went into the kitchen. Shifting the bundle into one hand, I reached up for the key above the door frame and unlocked the back door before stepping out into the chilly early evening. It had been dark for a while and I was glad of the blanket of privacy. I didn't really want to do this here, but I couldn't leave Kate alone and I had to do something, so I walked to the end of the garden and placed the bundle carefully on the cold ground. I didn't have anything to dig with so I grabbed a stick and bashed it into the soft, damp earth in the corner of the garden, frantically pulling at the soil and moving it to the side. It was taking ages, so I knelt down and scooped up handfuls of soil with my hands, and didn't stop until the hole was a good few feet deep. I stopped and wiped my hands on my trousers, my breath coming in short, ragged bursts, and wondered what the hell I was doing. Could I really just do this, and carry on as if nothing had happened? Was I actually losing my mind?

I sat, hunched over for a few minutes, until the cold crept in. Then I took a deep, ragged breath, and picked the bundle up from under the hedge. I held it in my arms for just a moment longer and brought it up to my face.

"Bye-bye, little one. I'm sorry we didn't get to meet, but I'll never forget you. Be free." Then, with tears pouring down my face and falling in the hole, I tipped my baby's remains into the ground. And as I covered it up with layers of soil, I knew I would never be the same person again.

CHAPTER
TEN

24 November 1979

The next day dawned bright and as the light pushed its way round the edges of the curtains I closed my eyes and prayed that what had happened yesterday had been nothing but a terrible dream. But the pain in my heart and my belly told me what I already knew.

It was all too true.

I rolled over onto my side and laid my arm gently across Kate's body. I hadn't slept a wink all night and at around three in the morning I'd brought her in with me, desperate to have someone close. I watched as her chest went up and down, up and down with each breath, and I could hardly believe she was right here next to me, that I hadn't lost her as well.

My face was damp and I lifted it from the pillow, which was soaked with tears I hadn't even known I'd been crying. I wiped my cheeks with the back of my hand and sat up. My stomach ached, a dull, throbbing reminder of everything I'd lost. I knew I ought to go and see someone, to tell them what had happened.

And as I'd lain awake in bed that night I'd worked out a plan. I'd go to the hospital, tell them what had happened, get myself checked over and then arrange for someone to come to the house and sort everything out. I couldn't leave my baby buried out there in the garden; I needed some sort of closure, some formal goodbye. I knew it would be hard admitting what I'd done, but I hoped people would understand my grief, after losing Ray.

I hoped.

I went downstairs and into the kitchen, leaving Kate sleeping on my bed. It was still early and the air was so cold I could almost see my breath. I stood by the window overlooking the back garden and I stared at the spot where I'd been digging last night. There was just a small patch of earth overturned at the edge of the lawn near the flower bed. It hardly looked like anything at all; you wouldn't notice it if you didn't know it was there. It didn't seem real. But then I glanced down at my hands resting on the edge of the sink and I could see that it was; my nails were torn and there was mud packed underneath them, despite my best efforts to scrub myself clean again last night. I turned the tap on and held my hands under the water until it warmed up, and scrubbed them again, over and over, until they were red and sore. The mud still hadn't shifted.

I turned away from the garden, unable to look any more. I felt odd; my body didn't feel like my own, my limbs heavy and aching. I filled a glass with water and drank it down in one. It felt like ice sliding down my throat and I was glad of the uncomfortable feeling, as though it was all I deserved. Then I put the glass down and walked back upstairs to Kate. When I walked into the bedroom she was stirring and I sat down on the

193

edge of the bed and watched as she rubbed her eyes and slowly opened them. She blinked and looked round the room in confusion, then saw me watching her and her little face broke into a smile.

"Mumma!"

"Morning, sweetheart. Did you sleep well?"

She nodded and looked round the room. "Mumma room?"

"Yes, it is Mummy's room. Mummy needed cuddles, is that all right?"

Her serious eyes watched me as she nodded her head slowly. She might have only been two and a half but sometimes she seemed wise beyond her years.

She sat up and I lifted her and took her downstairs for breakfast. As she spooned cereal into her mouth I couldn't help remembering the same moment yesterday and I shuddered. I hadn't had a clue about the horror that was to come.

It was still early, and I wondered whether we should wait before we made our way into town to the hospital. It wasn't something I was looking forward to and I knew I should just get it out of the way. I wished, not for the first time, that Ray was there. Or Sandy. She'd know what to do for the best. But I couldn't face dragging her into this, it wasn't fair. Which meant I was alone, and that was the way it was. That was the way it was going to be, from now on.

In the end I decided to wait until after lunch to make my way to the hospital, in the hope that Kate might sleep in her pushchair.

194

And so, after lunch of spaghetti hoops on toast, I wrapped Kate up in her coat, gloves and hat. "We're going for a little day out, OK, sweetheart?" I said.

She nodded. As I took Kate to the bus stop in her pushchair my belly still ached; I'd used several sanitary towels to stem the flow of blood. I felt uncomfortable, worried everyone would know what had happened, that they'd see the guilt in my eyes, the grimace on my face at every twinge. But nobody even looked in our direction. We were invisible, and I liked it that way.

While we waited at the bus stop it started to rain, a light drizzle that hung in the air and clung to our faces, our hair, our clothes, rather than reaching the ground. I shivered in the cold November air.

Finally the bus arrived and we climbed on. I sat Kate on my knee, the pushchair folded on the floor in front of me, and we watched out of the window as the world went by, Kate pointing at doggies, babies, cars. I wanted to concentrate on what she was saying, but my mind kept drifting to what was going to happen when I got to the hospital. I tried to imagine telling someone what had happened last night and what I'd done afterwards. I tried to imagine their faces: the disapproval, the contempt, the disgust. I didn't know how I was going to do this. But I knew I had to.

Worse, though, I was dreading going back to this hospital. Since Ray's death I hadn't seen my midwife, and when we moved I hadn't told anyone where we'd gone. I hadn't seen a doctor or a nurse since, and I was terrified of seeing the midwife now and having to face her questions, her sympathy.

Finally, the bus let out a huge gush of air and shuddered to a stop, and when I looked up we were there, in the city centre. We climbed off the bus and I strapped Kate back into her pushchair and started walking down the busy street towards the hospital. I passed people laden down with shopping bags, all going about their day as though nothing had happened, while all the time the pain in my gut and in my heart reminded me that everything *had* happened.

I listened to the wheels of the pushchair bump, bump, bump over every space between the paving slabs, and instinctively held my breath and gripped the handles tightly as we went down through the underpass, past buskers and beggars. When we came out the other side we were only a short walk from the hospital and the sound of my heartbeat was so loud it was thumping in my head, my ears, my brain. I held onto a low wall and took a deep breath. Everything would be OK. I just had to get through this.

I walked slowly the rest of the way, Kate laughing and pointing at the buses as they whooshed past. And then there it was. The black railings were the first thing I saw, separating the red-brick building from the rest of the street. It was set way back and I walked through the gate, my heart heavy. I cut across the forecourt and slipped down the side of the building towards the tall concrete block behind, and tried to look confident as I approached the doors of the maternity hospital. I tried not to look at heavily pregnant women going in and out, their swollen bellies ready to give them the most precious gift in the world. Instead I kept my eyes focused straight ahead, and walked through the sliding doors and towards the reception desk.

But before I got there I stopped dead. What the hell was I doing? I couldn't just march up to the poor woman at the reception desk and tell her I'd miscarried and buried my baby and could she help. I needed to find the right people, the right place. I needed to think.

I swerved past the reception and made my way to the lift. There was a list of the floors and my eyes passed over them blindly as I waited for the lift to arrive. Finally the doors slid open and I pushed the chair inside.

"Me buttons!" Kate said, reaching over to try and press something. She pushed on "five". I glanced at the list. "Five: Postnatal". Mums with their babies. There would be someone there I could talk to, I was sure of it. I shrugged. "OK, five it is."

The doors slid shut and slowly we started to move upwards. We stopped a couple of times to let people in, and finally the doors opened at floor five. We stepped outside and as the doors closed behind me again I looked up and down the corridor. It was surprisingly quiet, just the odd wail of a newborn baby which made my sore tummy clench and my heart squeeze. I gripped the handles of the pushchair tightly and walked slowly up the corridor towards the sounds of babies, of chatter, and soft, squeaky footsteps on the linoleum floor. I felt as though I were in a dream, that any minute now I'd wake up and be back at home in my bed, still pregnant. The pale-green walls didn't feel solid as we made our way along the shiny floor, and I shook my head to try and clear the feeling. I just needed to find one person to talk to, to tell them what had happened, and then everything would be out of my hands. I wouldn't have to worry any more. Suddenly it felt as though the world was tipping away from me, as though the floor had disappeared beneath my feet, and I stopped dead and laid my hand heavily on the green wall to help me stay upright. I lowered myself carefully into a chair and put my head between my knees while I waited for the wave of dizziness to pass.

"Are you OK, love?"

I snapped my head up, too quickly. A woman stood in front of me, in a blue uniform. A nurse. I needed to tell her. But the words wouldn't come and I just nodded.

"Mmm-hmm."

She stood there a moment longer as though deciding whether to believe me, then, clearly in a hurry to get somewhere, she left, her shoes going "eeee, eeee, eeee" along the corridor towards the lift. I stood carefully and started walking towards the swing doors, shoving them open with the pushchair. I thought all eyes would swivel towards me as I entered, wondering what on earth I was doing there among all these brand-new mums. But nobody even noticed me, and bodies just flew round me, carrying swaddled babies, bottles of milk, clean towels. Bewildered dads stood there, holding flowers and looking lost, wandering like zombies round the wards. I'd come at visiting time, which made me invisible.

I stood for a minute, hoping someone would notice me, ask me again if I was OK. But nobody did. I probably just looked as though I was visiting someone, rather than being a bereaved mother, yet still I couldn't bring myself to stop someone, ask them for help. Instead I started walking again.

Lots of the doors were shut, and I caught occasional glimpses of visitors round beds, happy smiles plastered on faces, tears of happiness running down cheeks. A knife pain twisted in my heart and I tried not to think about my poor baby, in the back garden, in the cold, all alone. I thought I was going to be sick.

I sat, pulling the pushchair out of the way, on a hard plastic chair outside one of the rooms. I needed to get some air in, calm down. It was a mistake, coming here, to this floor. I should have stayed downstairs, as distant from the newborn babies as possible. I should have gone to the phone box outside my house and rung to speak to the midwife; I should have asked Sandy to help me. I couldn't do this alone.

But it was too late now, and I was here. All I knew was that I had to get out, to get home, and get this over and done with.

I looked up, rubbing my hand down my cheek. The door opposite me was propped open and I had a clear view of the room behind it as a young woman stepped out. She was wearing a hospital gown and was clearly exhausted after giving birth. Part of me felt for her and part of me hated her. Her baby was alive. Mine was dead.

I shook the thought away. This wasn't her fault.

I watched as she walked away from the room and made her way slowly down the corridor. A tug of recognition pulled at my mind: the dark hair piled scruffily on top of her head, the slim legs poking out from the bottom of her hospital gown. I knew I'd seen her before but I couldn't quite place her. And then it hit me.

She was that girl from the pub. Pubs. The one who was always there, watching Ray, watching me. I was sure it was her. What on earth was she doing here? She was so young, surely she was too young to be having a baby? I glanced into her room, and then back at her. And then I saw what she had in her hand. A packet of cigarettes. She was going outside to smoke.

I looked back again at the room she'd just left and saw, at the end of her bed, two tiny cribs. Two. She had two babies. I had none. Rage bubbled inside me.

As she walked through the doors at the end of the corridor without a backward glance I found myself staring, then standing and walking slowly towards the open door of her room. I just wanted to see the babies. Before I knew it I was standing in the doorway. There was nobody else in there. I could see the two tiny bundles wrapped in swaddled blankets. They both had their eyes shut, and were sleeping peacefully.

My heart swelled with love, and my arms ached for the baby they should have been holding. I didn't think about what I was doing as I reached out and gently picked up one of the babies. I just needed to hold it, just for a moment. I pulled it into my chest and lowered my face to the top of its head and breathed in. The smell of newborn baby was overwhelming and my belly ached, my breasts ached, heavy with milk. My whole body hurt with the pain of what I had lost.

I turned and walked out of the room, back towards Kate, where I had left her in the corridor in her pushchair. She looked up at me, confused, and I smiled, then slowly started pushing her back out of the ward and towards the swing doors with one hand. I was still holding the baby with the other hand, clutched to my chest. The doors looked as though they were a million miles away and I knew I was never going to make it without getting stopped. But then, unexpectedly, we were through them and out the other side, walking down the pale-green corridor towards the lifts.

I expected, at any minute, a hand to land heavily on my shoulder and tug me back, to rip the baby from my arms, to scream at me to give her back. And I would have done, I know I would have done. I expected it, and I knew it was coming, yet still I kept going, moving forward, out of the hospital. I would explain myself then, but for now, I needed to hold this baby in my arms as long as I possibly could. I needed this. I needed it.

I deserved it.

We were at the lifts.

"Press the button for Mummy, sweetie."

Kate leaned over and pushed the button and miraculously the doors slid open straight away to reveal an empty lift. We stepped inside and glided slowly down to the ground floor. The doors opened again and still I had the warm body pressed against mine, sound asleep.

My arms ached from holding the baby with one arm and pushing the pushchair with the other, and I risked stopping to swap arms. Still nobody came. Nobody even gave me a second glance and before I knew it I was through the sliding doors and out into the chilly November evening. The rain had stopped by now but the air was still grey, and I pulled my coat round the baby to keep it warm. It. I still didn't even know if it was a boy or a girl. I wasn't going to stop to look now.

A few people were milling around but there was no sign of the baby's mother, of that woman who'd haunted my dreams for so long. I never knew whether she'd tried to seduce Ray — he'd always insisted she hadn't — but it hadn't stopped me thinking about the possibility. I wondered where she'd gone to smoke her cigarette, and whether she was back yet and raising the alarm.

I quickened my pace and headed round the red-brick building of the main hospital and back towards the black iron railings, retracing my steps from what felt like a lifetime ago but was really only about twenty minutes. I listened for footsteps behind me and the sound of people shouting "Stop!" But none came. And then I was out of the gates and on the street, just an ordinary mum leaving hospital with her newborn child.

A voice in the back of my mind was nagging, telling me to turn round, go straight back up to the fifth floor and take the baby back to where it belonged: with its mother, with its twin. But the other voice was saying I deserved this, that I deserved this baby, and that I should keep going and not look back. And although I knew it wouldn't last, that I'd get caught and the baby would be taken away from me, whether that was in five minutes or five hours or five days, I just couldn't bring myself to do it.

I wanted as long as I could get.

And so I kept going forward, through the underpass and out the other side, up the busy street past the people with shopping bags, and back to the bus stop. As we waited for the bus I realized I had nothing to feed the baby if it woke up. There was a Mothercare across the road. Should I risk going in and buying some supplies, or was it better to get on the bus and get out of here? Without thinking too hard I dashed across the road, pushchair in one hand, baby in the other, and bought formula milk, bottles and nappies. I felt as though what I'd done would be obvious, that someone was bound to sound the alarm at any moment. But nobody batted an eyelid at this new mother with her toddler and baby, buying nappies.

Moments later we were on the bus, moving slowly through the traffic and away from the hospital, away from the terrible thing I'd just done.

We were going home.

CHAPTER
ELEVEN

November 1979–1980

I don't think I ever truly believed I was taking that baby to keep. In my grief-stricken state, I believed that I was taking it to hold for a few minutes, or hours, or however long I got, before I had to hand her back to her real parents. I was borrowing her from that woman, and I had every intention of giving her back, sooner or later. It's just it started to become later rather than sooner.

Not once during the rest of that day did I think about the poor mother, back at the hospital, when she realized her baby was gone. Not once did I think about the frantic search, the minutes ticking by, the police coming, the family arriving, the pain the mother would go through as the hours passed and her baby was still missing.

And neither did I think about the consequences for me, once I was discovered, for snatching a baby from a hospital.

But I had plenty of time to think about it all afterwards, in the lonely, sleep-deprived days to come.

In fact, as the hours turned to days, I started to realize that this wasn't just a game. This wasn't just a grieving mother needing to hold a baby.

I'd snatched someone else's child.

And, even though I'd told myself I deserved this baby, and that she — the real mother — didn't, I knew deep down I was wrong, and that I had to take her back.

But how?

How could I take the baby back without anyone knowing it was me who took her? I couldn't just walk into the hospital and hand her over, no questions asked, and I certainly wasn't going to dump her out in the cold and hope someone found her.

But the main problem was bigger than all of those practicalities. The main problem was that, simply, I didn't want to take her back.

How could I? Not only because she was keeping the grief at bay that I felt at losing my husband and my baby. But also I knew it would be worse than losing my baby the first time round, because this time I'd have lost a real-life baby, one that I had held in my arms and kissed with my lips and hugged to my chest.

A baby I already loved like my own.

She *was* my own.

I just couldn't do it.

And so I didn't.

And then I didn't do it some more, until it all became too late.

Despite all this, we quickly slipped into a routine, me, Kate, and the baby. Even though her name tag had said "Louisa Foster", I was calling her Georgie. Georgina Rae Wood. It suited her, and I was sure she smiled when I said it.

It was lucky for me that I hadn't made any friends here because I had no one to explain myself to, to explain why Georgie had a mop of dark hair when me and Kate were so fair — although you only had to look at a photo of Ray to draw your own conclusions as to where that had come from, so I doubted anyone would question it. But it was just easier on my own, at first.

And so it was just the three of us, cocooned in our little house, in a little bubble.

I expected a knock on the door any minute, for someone to come and drag my baby from my arms, to take Georgie away from me. But with each day that passed without anyone coming, the knot of anxiety in my stomach loosened just a little.

But I still couldn't relax completely. So much so that when Sandy came round out of the blue I couldn't even let her in. I opened the door cautiously, and there she was, smiling at me as though everything was normal. Which, to her, I suppose it was. But I couldn't let her see that I wasn't pregnant any more; I couldn't have that conversation, or let her see that the baby was here already. I wasn't ready to try and work out what to tell her, what story to come up with, although I knew I'd have to sooner or later. Instead I stood, my lower half covered by the door, peering round it suspiciously.

"Aren't you going to let me in, then?" Her face furrowed into a frown.

"No, I er . . ." I stopped, glancing behind me and praying that Georgie wouldn't start crying.

"Jan, are you OK?"

I nodded frantically. "Yep. Yes, I'm fine, Sandy. I'm just a bit tired, that's all. Do you mind if you don't come in, today?"

I could see the hurt on her face, but what choice did I have?

"Oh. OK. It's just I've driven all the way here, to make sure you're all right." She stepped forward and I closed the door a fraction of an inch more. She noticed, and stepped back again, peering at my face in the shadow of the porch.

"Jan, are you sure you're OK? You look very pale. And — not right. Please, let me in."

"I'm fine, really. Sorry, Sandy, I really need to go now." And before she could reply I closed the door in her face and walked back down the hallway to the lounge where Kate was playing and Georgie was sleeping in a basket on the floor. My heart was going wild, my breath coming in frantic bursts, and I sank onto the sofa, blinking back the tears. Sandy was my oldest friend; what was I doing? Surely I needed her now more than ever? Part of me wanted to run to the front door, yank it open and run after her, beg her to come back to look after me, and tell her everything. But the other part of me, the part that didn't want to lose my little girl, knew I couldn't do that. Don't get me wrong, I knew Sandy would want to help me keep my secret. But it was such a big, bad, dark and terrible secret, I wasn't sure even she could keep it for me. So instead, all I could do was sit and let her walk away, wondering what on earth she'd done wrong. I could only pray she'd come back again one day soon, when I was ready.

After that the days passed slowly. One day, when Georgie was just a few days old, we decided to venture outside for the first time. It was more by necessity than by choice as we'd almost run out of formula and I needed to buy some food for me and Kate. It had rained almost constantly since we'd been home, and this was the first day it was dry. So shortly after we got up that morning I got me and Kate dressed, as usual, and I changed Georgie's nappy, as usual, and we had breakfast, as usual, just a couple of stale slices of toast and a scraping of butter we had left in the fridge.

"Me hungry, mumma." Kate pointed at her mouth and banged her hands on the table.

"Yes, I know. We need to go shopping."

I lifted her down and she toddled over to the pushchair. I shook my head. "Not today, sweetheart. You need to walk while Mummy pushes Georgie in the pram." I pointed to the corner of the kitchen where the second-hand pram I'd bought in preparation for the baby sat, taking up most of the small room.

"But me pram!"

"No, you'll have to be a good girl and walk with Mummy. Georgie needs the pram."

"Nooooo!" The scream was so loud it made me jump backwards and I bashed my head on the door frame. At the same time Georgie woke up, and within seconds the air in the room was replaced with noise, and my head was throbbing. I sank into a chair and put my head in my hands, trying to block out the tantruming toddler

208

and the crying baby. I wanted to scream myself, but I didn't have the energy.

With no signs of the racket from either of them abating, I picked Georgie up and placed her in the pram, her face bright red. I covered her with a blanket and stuck her hat on her head, shoved my bag in the basket underneath, and grabbed Kate's hand and pulled her, still screaming, towards the front door.

As though she realized I wasn't taking any notice, her screaming stopped almost as soon as we stepped out into the cold air, and she walked beside me, slowly, holding my hand in her gloved one, in silence all the way to the shop at the other end of the village. We passed the odd person and they nodded at me and I nodded back, my heart hammering, wondering if they'd guess who I was and what I'd done.

But of course they didn't and we got to the shop without incident. I manoeuvred my way through the door, struggling to get the pram up the step and into the shop.

"You can leave it outside, it'll be perfectly safe," shouted the woman from behind the counter at the other end of the shop.

I looked at the pram and back at the step. I glanced up and down the street and back down at the pram again. I couldn't do it. I couldn't leave my baby out here in the cold, where anyone could take her. She was coming with me, everywhere, forever.

I'd never let either of my girls out of my sight again. I knew better than anyone what could happen if you did.

I struggled some more, and finally the wheels made it over the lip of the step and the door shut behind me with a jangle as I let it go, almost tripping over as I did. The aisles were narrow and I carefully navigated the pram through the shop to the other end.

I smiled at the woman behind the counter. I'd seen her a few times when I'd been pregnant, but I'd avoided talking to her for long, anxious to avoid the subject of why I was a mum on my own, without a husband. But now, with a new baby in tow, I knew I probably didn't have much choice.

"Ooh, you've had the baby, then? You didn't look that pregnant, you must have carried it well. Well done, love." She came to the front of the counter and peered into the pram, and I smiled weakly.

"Hello, sweetie, aren't you gorgeous," she cooed, stroking her finger gently down Georgie's face. It was all I could do not to shout "Get off her!" but I bit my tongue and waited for her to stop.

Finally she turned to me. "Well done, it must be hard, on your own."

I knew she wanted me to elaborate, tell her the story of how I came to be living here, in this little village, pregnant and alone. But I wasn't ready to talk about it, not yet. It was still too raw. I was still too raw. So instead I nodded and forced my lips into a smile.

"Yes, it has been hard but I'm OK. We're doing well." I pulled Kate towards me and squeezed her hand.

"Big sister." Kate smiled proudly and pointed at Georgie.

"Oh bless her, isn't she sweet as well?"

Kate beamed as the woman stepped back behind the counter, clearly disappointed that I wasn't going to tell her anything more.

"So, what can I get you?"

"I just need some more formula milk, please. And some bread, cheese and juice and a few other things."

"Well, the formula's here —" she indicated behind her — "and the cheese and anything cold. But you can help yourself to everything else; it's all down there, at the front."

I walked to the front of the shop and grabbed bread, apples and oranges and a few tins, then plopped them on the counter where there was already some formula milk, cheese, milk and butter. I was grateful for the thoughtfulness. I picked a newspaper from the pile as well and folded it into the bottom of my bag.

I paid and bundled the bags of shopping into the bottom of the pram, and slowly manoeuvred my way back to the front of the shop.

"Here, let me get the door for you."

The woman — I really should have remembered her name — held it open for me while I wiggled the pram out and down the step, trying not to let it tip over and spill its precious cargo. Finally I made it and turned to thank her.

"You must let us know if you need anything. Anything at all. We're all pretty nice really, I think you'll find." Her eyes wrinkled at the corners as she smiled and I couldn't help smiling back, properly this time.

"Thank you." It came out as a whisper, but I knew she'd heard and she turned and walked back into the shop.

I wobbled my way back down the road towards home. That hadn't been as bad as I'd thought. Maybe, eventually, I'd get to make some friends round here after all.

All in good time.

It wasn't until later that evening, when Kate was eating her tea of cheese sandwiches on the floor by the fire, and Georgie was lying next to her, contented after a long feed, that I remembered the paper I'd picked up at the shop earlier. I stood and pulled my bag out, unfolded it, and smoothed it across my knees. It was the local paper, the *Eastern Daily Press*, and across the front page was a story about a raid on some embassy in London. I glanced at the date. It was a few days old. That was odd. But it didn't matter, I hadn't read or seen the news for weeks.

My eyes glanced across the details to the smaller stories down the side. I licked my finger and flicked to the next page, and it was the words I saw there that made my heart stop.

BABY SNATCHED FROM LOCAL HOSPITAL

I gasped out loud and almost dropped the paper on the floor. My hands were shaking, making the paper shudder as well, the words swimming in front of my eyes. I tried to hold it still, to focus on the story. How much did they know? I stared at the page and forced the words to fall into line.

A newborn baby girl was snatched from Norwich maternity hospital last night.

The baby, who had only that morning been named Louisa by her distraught mother, Kimberley Foster, was taken from her crib at the end of her mother's bed in the Norfolk and Norwich maternity hospital between the hours of 1630 and 1700 hrs yesterday afternoon. Her other child, twin Samuel, was left alone in his crib.

Ms Foster, 17, of Colindale Avenue, Sprowston, was too distraught to tell us any more, and is being consoled at home by her mother, Margaret. But Pamela Newsome, another new mother on the same ward, said: "This is every mother's worst nightmare. I can't believe this has been allowed to happen, and I can't believe that nobody saw anything. Kim has to get her baby back."

Police are calling for any witnesses, or anyone who has any suspicions of who the perpetrator may be, to call the number below or call into Norwich police station.

My heart thumped so hard I thought it was going to fall out of my chest and the room started to spin away from me as the words sank in. Of course I'd known that a baby being snatched would be big news and that it was bound to be in the newspaper. But knowing it and seeing it for real were two entirely different things. I'd been so locked away in my own little bubble that the outside world had seemed like a different place entirely, somewhere that didn't affect me.

But now this was here, in black and white, for everyone to see. Worse, there was the baby's mother — her name was Kimberley, it said — staring out accusingly at me from the page. Her eyes were empty, full of pain, pleading with me to bring her baby back. She was so young, but lines etched her forehead. I'd done that. I'd brought her that pain.

And yet I knew I couldn't do anything to stop it. It was too late now.

I tore my eyes away from the page, away from the sadness in hers. I thought I was going to throw up. I sat perfectly still for a few seconds, the newspaper still spread across my lap, waiting for the wave of nausea to subside. I couldn't lose my babies, I just couldn't. I'd lost everything else.

What had I done?

"Mumma, all gone."

Kate's voice broke into my thoughts and I looked at her blankly. She pointed to her plate where a few bits of half-eaten crust lay strewn. I was glad of the distraction. I folded the paper so I couldn't see Kimberley's face any more and laid it down carefully on the sofa, then stood and took Kate's plate from the floor. Crumbs dropped onto the carpet and I crouched down to brush them onto the plate, trying to ignore the aching cramp in my belly. Kate's arms snaked round my neck and she buried her little face into my shoulder.

"Love oo mumma."

I dropped the plate, the crumbs scattering everywhere again, and wrapped my arms right round her, pulling her as close as I could. She smelt of shampoo and sandwiches and grass and I breathed in her scent. She looked up at me.

"Mumma sad?"

"What? No, Mummy's not sad."

She pointed at my face and I realized it was soaked with tears.

I wiped them away and gave her a weak smile. "They're happy tears. Mummy's happy, because she has you, that's all." I kissed her head.

"Ge-ge kiss too." She pointed at her little sister and we both leaned down to kiss her soft, warm head. I watched them both, in the glowing heat of the fire, and my heart swelled with love. These two girls were the only reason my heart hadn't broken in two when I lost Ray and then my baby. They were the only thing helping to mend it, slowly. I couldn't lose them too. The pain would be too much to bear.

I stood and brushed the crumbs from the floor again and headed into the kitchen. I ran water into the sink and plunged my hands into the soapy suds and stared out of the window at the garden beyond. I couldn't bring myself to look at the pile of soil that had been disturbed at the end, by the shed, where my baby was buried. I had to concentrate on the two girls I had and try to forget about it.

So instead I stared blankly out of the window as I thought about everything that had happened in the days since, and I thought about that newspaper cutting, the sad, desperate eyes of the baby's mother. I knew what I'd done was wrong. I knew I should come forward and give Georgie back to her rightful parents.

But I couldn't. I just couldn't.

I'd lose everything.

Instead I had to hope that nobody would realize it was me, and I had to keep my girls safe.

I vowed to never let them leave me. Ever.

Over the next few weeks I tortured myself; I bought the local paper every day and scoured it for updates, trying to work out if the police were any closer to discovering who had taken baby Louisa. Trying to work out whether I was one step closer to losing my children, or one step closer to being able to keep them with me forever.

It had become part of the daily routine for us. We'd get up and dressed and walk to the shop, buy milk, bread and the paper, then go home and read it. It was like an obsession, but in a strange way I was glad of the routine. It brought some structure to the day.

Sandy still hadn't come back to see me. I knew she was probably hurt and confused about why I'd treated her like that, shutting her out. But I didn't have a phone, and I wasn't sure what her new number was, so I couldn't even ring her from a phone box. I just had to wait and hope she came round again. I was sure she would.

I didn't have any visitors most of the time. Mrs Doyle from next door had popped round once, though. I'd been feeding Georgie; she was sucking greedily on her bottle and I answered the door awkwardly, still holding her in my arms.

"Hello, dear. I'm sorry to bother you but I thought you might like these." She held out a small wicker basket covered with a white tea towel. "It's just some scones I made yesterday and there are far too many for me. I thought you and your little one —" she nodded at Kate who'd popped her head round the living-room door — "could enjoy some."

"Thank you, that's very kind."

Realizing I couldn't take them from her, and that I wasn't going to invite her in, she hovered for a moment longer then bent down and placed them just inside the door.

"I'll just — I'll leave them there for you, then."

"Thank you."

She hesitated, looking at me and Georgie for a moment longer. "Let me know if you need any help with, you know, anything. I'm always here."

I was so overwhelmed at her kindness but didn't dare let myself cry in case I never stopped, so I took a breath and whispered "Thank you" one more time and then closed the door. I knew I seemed rude but I wasn't ready to talk to anyone, to try and explain anything, not yet.

And so I carried on, following the story, watching for new developments, waking up each day wondering whether today was the day.

I was constantly on edge. I felt as though my chest was full, my breathing shallow, my shoulders hunched and tight. Staying inside our four walls as much as possible, just me and the girls, felt like the only way to survive.

And then one day the news changed slightly. The stories in the paper had been getting smaller every day, becoming lost amongst the adverts for washing powder and department store openings, and I'd started to believe that, with the press forgetting the story bit by bit, perhaps the police were too.

But this day, 5 December 1979, eleven days after I'd taken Georgie, there was a new development. The police had a suspect.

The headline outside the shop made me stop dead, of course, and I almost threw up on the pavement. I even looked round, half expecting there to be a police officer behind me, waiting to arrest me there and then. I picked the paper up and read it at once, trying to keep my hands steady. The relief, when it came, was so great, I felt as though my legs might fail beneath me, collapsing like jelly onto the concrete.

The suspect wasn't me.

In fact, it was even better news than that. The police were now focusing their attention on the father's sister. From what I could piece together, Kimberley and the twins' father weren't together, and he had more or less disappeared. Samuel — the other twin — and Kimberley were living with her mother, Margaret. And it was the missing father's sister, Sheila, that the police were looking for now. They didn't say why.

I read it three times to make sure I hadn't misunderstood, but it seemed I hadn't. I wasn't naive enough to think that it was all over for me, that I needn't worry again. But it did mean that, while they were looking for someone else, they weren't looking for me. And the longer it went on, the less likely they were ever going to look for me.

With Kate toddling along beside me I pushed the pram inside the shop again, and went to the counter to pay. I had got to know the lady behind the counter quite well by now, as I saw her every day, and I now knew her name was Joyce. She smiled as we approached, and I placed the paper on the counter and smiled back. I was still shaking.

She nodded at it. "Terrible business, this, isn't it?"

I didn't dare look down at the paper again so I tried to keep my face blank. "Yes, awful."

She looked down at Georgie asleep in the pram and a roaring started in my ears. Had she . . . Would she . . .?

"I mean, just imagine if it was your little one. It would be — it would be like torture, wouldn't it, not knowing where she was? That poor mother." She looked at me and I realized she was waiting for an answer.

"Yes. It's the worst possible thing imaginable."

We both stood for a moment, looking at Georgie. The roaring in my ears got louder. Then Joyce sighed heavily and said, "It doesn't bear thinking about."

"No. No, it doesn't."

A beat of silence, then we moved on. "Anyway, anything else I can get you today?"

I shook my head. "No, just the paper, thanks."

"Ten pence, please."

I handed her the coins and started to back out of the door.

"You know, I do mean it, about helping out," she said. "It must be tough for you, with the two littl'uns. If you ever need a break, or anything at all, you will ask, won't you?"

"Yes, I will. Thank you." I carried on backing out, desperate to get some air, and then I stopped.

"Actually, there is something."

I saw her face light up. "Oh, what?"

"I need to earn some money but I can't leave the girls. I was thinking about starting to do some ironing, or clothes repairing, something I can do from home. Do you think it would work, that people would, you know, want that sort of thing?"

She nodded. "Ooh, yes, I'm sure they would. Especially if I put in a good word for you." She reached under the counter and brought up a pile of postcards. "Tell you what, why don't you put an ad in the window? And I'll tell people about you too."

I didn't like the idea of my address being up for all to see, or the thought of people I didn't know knocking on my door. But, despite everything that was going on, I knew I had to earn some money. I was almost out of it and we had rent and food to pay for. We couldn't live on fresh air.

"Yes, OK. Thank you."

I scribbled my details down and she took the card from me, resting her hand on mine on the counter. "I'll find you some work, don't you worry." It was the first human contact I'd had other than with the girls for weeks, and it felt surprisingly good. I smiled and then turned and left. I could see her Blu-tacking the ad to the window before I was even out of sight.

It wasn't until I was back at home and had Kate safely installed in her highchair with a drink and a snack that I had time to really think about what this new development meant for me. I smoothed the paper down and read it again, devouring the details. I hadn't misunderstood. It looked as though I was safe, for now at least. As I read it for the umpteenth time the doorbell ding-donged round the little house and I nearly fell over. Surely my advert hadn't worked that quickly? Perhaps it was Mrs Doyle again.

Leaving Kate in her highchair and Georgie sleeping peacefully in her pram, I walked towards the front door. It wasn't until I was almost halfway there that it occurred to me it could be the police. The story this morning could have been a red herring. Perhaps they'd tracked me down and didn't want me to do a runner.

My heart hammered as I walked slowly towards the door. I wasn't sure I could take all this stress; I was going to end up having a heart attack. I reached out and pushed the handle down, then pulled the door towards me, peering round it.

"Sandy!"

The relief was so great I threw the door open, rushed towards her and wrapped her in a tight hug. She pulled away and looked at me quizzically.

"You OK, Jan?"

I nodded, unable to speak in case the tears started. I'd been desperate to see her, but terrified she'd never come again. Now she was here, I wanted her to stay forever.

"Can I come in?"

"What? Oh yes, sorry, course." I stepped back and she walked in, shaking her jacket off and hanging it on the peg to the side of the door. The sight of her, the smell, the sheer presence of her, was so familiar, I felt a lump form in my throat. I'd been so lonely, and now she was here. My best friend.

We went through to the kitchen and Sandy walked straight up to Kate and scooped her out of her highchair. "Hello, little one, I've missed you." Kate giggled wildly as Sandy lifted her high into the air above her head. She brought her down and shifted her to one side, balancing her on her hip. Her eyes flicked down to my belly and my heart stopped again as her face was pulled into a question mark.

"I know I haven't seen you for a while, but — you've had the baby and you haven't even told me?"

My face flamed and I couldn't answer. Sandy looked round the room and saw the pram in the corner. She walked over and peered inside, and my heart hammered so hard I thought I was going to fall over. Sandy knew me so well, would she notice anything was wrong? She stayed like that for a few moments, just watching Georgie sleep. I'd had a story planned, that the baby had come early and it had been such a shock I wasn't ready, and I wasn't ready to see anyone either, but the words wouldn't come. Instead I just stood there, desperate for her to say something, anything, even if it was bad. I just couldn't stand the silence.

222

"She looks like her dad, don't you think?"

The words were out before I could even think about them, edit them, as though they'd been lurking, waiting to be tried out.

Sandy turned her head towards me, then looked back at Georgie, and back at me again. "Yes. Yes, I suppose that must be where she gets her dark hair from." She watched me thoughtfully for a few more seconds and her gaze was so intense I felt as though she could see right inside my head, to my deepest, darkest thoughts. But then her face broke into a smile.

"She's beautiful, darling. I just can't believe you didn't tell me, especially as she must have come so early."

"Yes, sorry. I — it turns out I got the dates wrong. You know, it's not that accurate. I must have fallen pregnant before I thought, and — well, it was a shock and I just didn't get the chance to tell you, but — I kept thinking about walking up to the phone box to ring you at work, but I just — well, it's tough, that's all." I knew I was jabbering but I needed to fill the silence.

"I know. That's why I thought I'd come over and try to see you again. Because I thought it must just be your hormones, giving you such a tough time. Plus, I missed you."

"I missed you too. So much. I wish you lived nearer."

"I know. Me too. Maybe I'll move here. You know, soon." She shrugged awkwardly.

"You'd be nearer to Mal as well, I suppose, then, wouldn't you?"

She shook her head. "No. Me and Mal are no more, I'm afraid."

"Oh no, what happened?"

She shrugged again. "We just weren't suited. Plus he was sick of me talking about you all the time. Said it was as though you meant more to me than he did. Thought I should forget about you, leave you be. Well, I wasn't having any of that. Stupid bugger." She smiled sadly and my heart nearly broke for her.

"Oh Sandy, I'm so sorry."

She nodded. "It's OK. And he was right, really. You *are* more important to me than him. Which says a lot." She smiled sadly again. "Anyway, let's sit down, shall we, this one's getting heavy."

"Yes. Do you want tea first?"

"In a minute. Sit first." I sat and she took the chair opposite me, placing Kate carefully on the kitchen floor. She toddled off to find some toys.

"So. How are you? I mean, obviously you've got — oh my goodness, I haven't even asked what her name is."

"Georgie. It's Georgina Rae Wood."

She snapped her head round to look at me. "You're giving her Ray's surname, then?"

I frowned. "Of course. Why wouldn't I?"

"I don't know. Sorry. Of course you would, of course she'd have the same surname as you and Kate. I just thought — well, I don't know what I was thinking, truth be told. Ignore me."

Her face was red and she looked flustered. I wondered what she'd been about to say but I didn't dare ask. I wasn't sure I'd really want to hear the answer.

"I've been OK, thanks. Coping."

"Bet it's been hard, on your own?"

I nodded. "Yes. I miss Ray, all the time." I couldn't tell her about the baby I'd lost too. That would have to stay my secret, locked up inside my heart forever.

"I know."

There was a moment of silence. "Do you want tea now?" I jumped up, desperate for something to do. It felt weird, being this anxious around Sandy. But I was terrified she'd see straight through me and see what I'd done, if I let her.

"Yes, tea would be lovely, thanks."

I put a pan of water on the hob and leaned against the counter. "Do you want to hold her when she wakes up?" I glanced at the clock. "In fact, she's due for a feed soon, you can give her her bottle if you like?"

"I'd love that, thank you." Her words sounded stilted, but I put it down to the fact I'd shut the door in her face last time she'd tried to help me. Anyone would be cautious after that.

As if on cue, a loud cry pierced the air. I lifted Georgie from her cot and placed her gently in Sandy's arms. Sandy gazed down at her. Would she notice she looked nothing like me or Ray? Would she ever suspect?

Sandy turned her face to me, tears shining in her eyes. "She really is beautiful, Jan."

"Thank you." The words were a whisper, barely audible above the noise coming from Georgie's lungs, and as Sandy watched me intently for a few seconds I felt as though I must be giving myself away, somehow. But then the moment passed.

"Right, where's that bottle, then? There's a little girl who's desperate for some milk here."

I handed her the bottle and she stuck it in Georgie's mouth and the silence was instant. I let out a breath I hadn't realized I'd been holding and Sandy laughed. "Noisy little bugger, isn't she?"

"She certainly is."

I made tea and we sat for a while, Sandy feeding Georgie and Kate, having returned, sitting on my knee, and I realized I hadn't felt this relaxed for a long time. Maybe it was because, for the first time, I had someone to help me out. Or maybe it was because I felt as though I'd passed the first, most difficult test. If Sandy believed Georgie was mine, why should anyone else suspect she wasn't?

And as the days turned to weeks and the weeks turned to months, I slowly started to relax and think that maybe, just maybe, I had got away with it. That I was going to be able to keep my little family together after all.

I still read the newspaper voraciously, looking for any changes in the story, any indication that the police had a new suspect, someone else to investigate. It was almost like a comfort blanket, something to reassure me when I started to doubt myself.

And then, almost as quickly as it had started, the story stopped appearing in the paper.

Everyone had forgotten about it. At least, nearly everyone.

The girls started to get bigger. Georgie looked nothing like me, but everyone just nodded and smiled when I said she looked like her dad. I started to meet people, although I kept them at arm's length so I never felt I had to tell them anything. It would have been too risky. And I took on some work: bits and bobs of ironing, sewing, mending. It wasn't much to start with but it soon grew until I seemed to spend most of my days either with the hiss of an iron or the hum of a sewing machine.

It became a way of life in our house and, whether they liked it or not, it was the girls' world.

Because I knew I was always going to keep my promise to keep them safe. To protect them from harm. I vowed I would never let them go. Never.

And even though I've thought about Kimberley from time to time, about what I put her through, I have to be honest and say that when it came down to it, I didn't really care. I didn't know her, so I didn't care. Not really.

And so I can't honestly say I've ever truly regretted what I did. How could I? I have Georgie to show for it. And even if she finds out the truth and never forgives me for what I've done, I know she'll always love me, deep down. And I'll love her too. Forever.

And love is all that matters.

Part Three

Georgie

CHAPTER
TWELVE

28–30 October 2016

The house is quiet; Matt's at work, Clem's at school, and Georgie's called in sick to work again, something she hates doing. But she can't wait any longer. She needs to get started, to be doing something.

She perches at the dining table and opens up the laptop, then stops for a moment, staring at the blank screen. Next to her sits the pile of cuttings she's read through so many times. The black-and-white photo of the poor bereaved woman staring out from the top one has jagged white lines all across it where it's been folded, screwed up and flattened out again, making her gaze seem less penetrating than it had before. But she can still see the sadness in the eyes, even through all of that.

She smooths the paper down and reads it again, even though she knows it almost off by heart.

A newborn baby girl was snatched from Norwich maternity hospital last night.

The baby, who had only that morning been named Louisa by her distraught mother, Kimberley Foster, was taken from her crib at the end of her mother's bed in the Norfolk and Norwich maternity hospital between the hours of 1630 and 1700 hrs yesterday afternoon. Her other child, twin Samuel, was left alone in his crib.

Her other child, twin Samuel.
She has a twin.
In all the horror of her discovery, this was the one thing that hadn't really sunk in, until now, despite her words to Aunty Sandy yesterday.
She's a twin.
She stands and walks across to the fireplace and gazes at her reflection in the mirror above it. She studies her dark hair, so unlike her mother's; the wide green eyes, the narrow snub nose, the high cheekbones. The little dimple in her cheeks when she smiles. Her mother has none of these and, in the one photo of her father she's familiar with, neither does he, apart from the dark hair. But, with no reason to question any of it, she never has.
Until now.
She traces the outline of her lips, and tries to imagine someone else out there who — not looks like her, because he's a boy: a man — but just someone who *fits* better. Someone she's just more like. The idea makes her head spin.
She sits back down at the table and takes a deep breath. She's going in.
She opens up Google, the most obvious starting point. She could go to the library and see what else she can find in the newspaper archives. But she'd need to

travel into Norwich so this is the easier, more obvious place to start, with just a name and a forty-year-old address.

Her hands shaking, she types in "Kimberley Foster" and "Colindale Avenue, Sprowston".

Less than a second later there are hundreds of thousands of results in front of her, and she swallows. She's not expecting to have any luck — who knows what Kimberley's name is now, or even whether she's still alive? But she has to start somewhere.

She begins at the top of the list, her eyes skimming the results quickly, dismissing most of them. One catches her eye, a Kimberley Foster who works at the local college, teaching English to adults. But when she clicks on her photo she can see she's far too young, even younger than herself.

She scrolls down, her eyes searching for clues, scanning pictures for the same sad, empty eyes from the hazy picture in front of her, even though she's not sure she'd recognize her now anyway. But there's nothing.

After half an hour or so of scrolling through the results she stops and rubs her face. Her eyes ache and she's no further forward in her search. There's no Kimberley Foster anywhere near or around Norwich: at least not one who's done anything to turn up on Google. She's not sure if that's a good thing or a bad thing. She's tried Facebook, but nothing there either.

She sighs. Google was worth a shot, but she's afraid she's going to end up going in ever-decreasing circles. She's going to have to try something else. Maybe if she had some more information about the family that would help? Maybe she could look for her father instead, try and find him?

She riffles through her papers until she comes to the one where her father was mentioned. She reads it again. Her parents had had a fling, nothing more. It doesn't seem likely that he'd still be involved in the family's lives, but it has to be worth a shot. She digs out the newspaper story: *Barry Thomson, the twins' estranged father*, and carefully types in "Barry Thomson, Norwich". Once again thousands of entries fill the screen, but a cursory glance reveals none is the Barry Thomson she's looking for. Or at least, if they are, there's no way of telling.

She sighs heavily and sits back in her chair, the light from the laptop giving the room an eerie glow. It had been worth a shot, but it was what she'd expected. Now, she needs to do more.

It's time for action.

It's time to go and knock on some doors.

It's still early but it's already starting to get dark by the time she pulls into Colindale Avenue, and she can hardly make anything out in the semi-darkness through the wildly whipping windscreen wipers. She pulls into a tiny space and cuts the engine, peering out through the rain-streaked windows at the street beyond. It's narrow, cars parked along both sides, the houses small but mostly neat, lined up like soldiers into the distance. She squints to read the number of the house next to her but it's impossible. She pulls her hood tightly round her ears, opens the door and steps into the pouring rain.

234

She's not sure what she's going to achieve, but she's here now. She peers more closely at the house number next to her and, just as she makes out the number 38, she notices a movement at the window and someone glares at her before angrily pulling the curtains shut. She takes a step back and looks up and down the street. It's longer than she'd hoped and she's not sure where to start. Can she really go and knock on doors at random and ask if they know a woman who lived here almost forty years ago? And what will she do if they say yes? She can hardly introduce herself to Kimberley as her daughter, not after all this time.

And yet.

She has to do something, now she's here.

Before she can think about it any more she's marching up a short path and ringing the doorbell. Water drips down her forehead and into her eyes and she brushes it away impatiently. Moments later a light flicks on behind the glass panels and a short older man opens the door, pushing his glasses up on his nose. "Hello?"

"Oh, um, hello. I — I'm looking for someone who used to live here and wondered if you might know them."

"Here? I doubt it, I've been here for thirty years." He pushes his glasses up on his nose again and peers at her over the top of them.

"Well, actually, it was longer ago than that. It was —" She stops, unsure what to say. "It was almost forty years ago."

"Hmm." He clicks his teeth together and waits.

"Her name was Kimberley Foster. She would have been about seventeen, back then. So late fifties now."

He shakes his head briefly. "No, I've never heard of her. I'm sorry."

He goes to close the door but Georgie's not done yet. "I don't suppose you know anyone who might know her?"

He pulls the door open again and sighs. "No, I don't. I'm very sorry, young lady, but I don't think I can help you."

The door closes firmly in her face and she steps back out from under the porch into the rain. She's soaked within seconds as it pours from her hair down her neck and drips off the end of her nose. She stands at the end of the path and looks up and down the street again, hoping for inspiration. Knocking on every door will take her all night and most of tomorrow. Maybe she'll try ten more, then give up, for today.

She knocks on the next door along, and then the next, and the next. There's a real mix of people and some just slam the door in her face straight away. Some are renting, some are young, some are out, leaving her standing hammering on an unopened door, while others are interested but just can't help. And before she knows it she's knocked on ten doors and has absolutely no more information than she had before she started. She glances at her watch. She's only been going half an hour. She's soaked through and is aware she must look a bit mad standing out in the rain.

It's only 4.30 but it's almost dark. People will be getting home from work soon. Maybe she should try for a bit longer.

And so she carries on knocking on doors, getting nowhere but unable to give up until she feels she's given it her best shot. After all, what's she going to do once she's driven away from this road? This is her best chance of finding her mother, and even if it's not the right way to go about it, she can't give it up, not yet.

She's almost at the end of the street, at number 182. Her feet ache and she's ignored her phone several times, cutting off calls from Clem and Matt. She doesn't want to tell them where she is, not until she's home and in the dry and not feeling quite so desperate. She lifts the door knocker and lets it fall against the peeling paint of the wooden door a couple of times then stands back slightly to wait, listening to the rain hammering on the porch roof above her head. A moment or two passes and all's quiet inside. She's about to give up and walk back down the short path and on to the next house when there's a jingling sound from the other side of the door, of chains being undone and keys being turned. She stops and waits and a few seconds later a small white face appears in the narrow black crack of the open door. The face is chiselled with deep valleys of wrinkles and surrounded by a frizz of grey hair, the eyes buried deep, peering at Georgie standing in the semi-darkness. She doesn't speak, just keeps her gaze trained on her. It's disconcerting.

"Hello, I, er, I was wondering if you could help me. I'm — um, looking for someone." She clears her throat.

"A woman who lived on this road about forty years ago. Kimberley Foster."

Georgie lets the question hang in the air. She's not sure whether the woman has even heard her and the silence stretches out, broken only by the sound of cars creeping slowly along the road, their tyres swooshing through puddles. Georgie's about to repeat the name, when the woman speaks.

"Yes. Yes, I knew her." She keeps the door open only a crack and says no more. Georgie has to grab hold of the door frame to stop herself falling over as the whole world tips on its axis.

"Did you?" Her voice is a squeak and she clears her throat again. "Wh-when? Do you know her now?"

The old woman shakes her head and Georgie feels her heart crash to the floor. "No, not any more. She moved a long time ago. But she lived just there —" Her arm comes out from behind the door and flaps vaguely across the street. "Number 181. Lovely girl. Terrible what happened to her, though."

Georgie looks across the street to the house opposite, which looks almost the same as this one but smarter, well looked after. Lights shine brightly in the window and she tries to make out the people inside as though it will give her a clue to the hidden secrets of the house's past.

She turns back and tries to keep her voice steady while her head spins. "So, do you know any more about her? Where she went? Where she is now?"

The old woman shakes her head. "No, not really. I just knew her and her mother and her little one. Lovely little boy, Sam, his name was, always used to come round for biscuits when his mum was having one of her *episodes* —" she made the speech mark sign in the air with her fingers as she said the word — "but they moved away when he was about ten. Shame, really, I used to like having him round to play; he livened the place up a bit, you know." She sighs. "But after what happened, her little girl being taken and all, she was never the same, really." She looks up at Georgie, the lines between her eyes even deeper than before. "Why do you want to know about them, anyway? Who are you?"

Georgie swallows, her throat scratchy. "I'm, er, just an old friend. Well, my mum was, you know, a friend of Kimberley's. I just — I thought it would be nice to find her, as a surprise . . ." She trails off, unable to lie any more, unwilling to think about the consequences of what her mother has done, and of what she herself is doing now. Is she about to tear someone's life apart?

"Oh, right." The old woman's eyes narrow even further. "Well, I'm afraid I can't tell you much more than that."

Georgie swallows down the disappointment. Her hopes had soared as, just for a moment, she'd thought this little old lady was going to be the key to unlocking her past. But now those hopes are shattered again, scattered like confetti across the doorstep. She gives it one last shot. "I don't suppose you know where they moved to, do you?"

The old woman closes her eyes and Georgie wonders if she's forgotten she's there. But then she snaps them open again, and a smile spreads across her face. "Round Mile End way, I think. Or at least that's where they went for a bit. Woodcock Street. They went together, all three of them, Samuel, Kim and Margaret, her mum's name was. Never really liked her, abrupt woman, never gave you the time of day. But she looked after them all right, the two of them, so I suppose she can't have been all bad." She shrugs and looks at Georgie. "Sorry I can't help you any more than that."

Once again, Georgie lets her hopes lift just a little. It might be an old lead, but at least it's a lead, somewhere to start. "That's OK. You've been really helpful, thank you so much."

"Give my love to them, won't you, if you do find them? Mrs Moore. Hazel. They'll remember me, I'm sure."

"I will, thank you."

The door closes with a soft clunk and Georgie stands there a moment staring at it as though it's going to offer up more clues. Then she turns and walks back to the car and drives home, her mind racing with the information she's just gained. She's desperate to go and find this street, to knock on the doors and continue her search, see where it takes her. But it's dark now, and she needs to get home to her family. Her search for her other family is going to have to wait until tomorrow.

"Earth to Mum?"

Clem's voice breaks into her reverie and Georgie stares at her daughter as though she's surprised to see her there.

"Oh, sorry. I was miles away."

Clementine pouts and flops her lanky body into a dining-room chair, splashing tea on the tabletop which she wipes away with her sleeve. Georgie watches without comment. She has too much on her mind to worry about tea stains.

She feels annoyed and impatient. She had such a successful day yesterday in her search, but she was frustrated that time had run out. When she got home all she'd wanted to do was go straight back out and knock on doors. But she'd been so tired that she'd just had a bath then sat down to eat dinner with Matt and Clem. She hardly spoke a word, the exhaustion washing over her in waves as she twirled her spaghetti mindlessly round her fork.

It wasn't until later, when Clem had taken herself off to her room to do her homework, that she'd had a chance to tell Matt everything she'd discovered.

"So what are you going to do now?" Matt had asked.

"I'm going to try and find them tomorrow, in that road."

"But you don't know if that's where they still are." Matt's voice was gentle but firm. "It's a long time since they moved there, you know. A lot can change in that time."

"I know, but at the moment it's all I've got."

"I'm just worried, George. I don't want you to get your hopes up too much. But also —" He stopped, concern etched into his face. He sighed, rubbed his hand across his forehead. "I mean, what if you *do* find your birth mother? What's going to happen then? What

241

— what if she doesn't want to be found now? Or what if she does, but she can't cope with you just walking into her life? You could end up causing more problems than you solve."

She sighed heavily.

"I know. I've thought about that, I have. And I am worried. But I can't see any other way of doing it." She took a gulp of her wine. "I keep thinking about how I'd react if it was me, if someone just walked into my life after almost forty years, and I just can't picture it, Matt. But I have to find her. Don't I?"

Matt nodded. "I guess you do." He took hold of her hand and squeezed it urgently. "Promise me something, then."

"What?"

"Don't take any risks. I know these people are your family, but — well, you don't know a single thing about them. They might be lovely but they might be — well, just be careful. This is a massive thing for them and they're not expecting it. Kimberley might have moved on with her life, and not want to know you. You need to be prepared for that."

"I know." Her voice was small.

"So promise me you'll be careful?"

Georgie nodded. "I promise."

Later, as they'd sat down to watch TV, the pictures flicking over Georgie without her seeing them, her phone had beeped. It was a message from Kate. Georgie frowned. They hadn't spoken since she'd told Kate she was looking for her family, and she hadn't expected to hear from her yet. She clicked the message open.

I'm really worried about Mum. Things not good. Doctor is coming to see her tomorrow at 12pm. Would appreciate you being there too. Kate

There was no kiss, no "Love Kate", and the uncharacteristic abruptness of the message made Georgie's eyes prick with tears. She knew whatever she found was going to hurt her sister, and she wished she didn't have to choose between the two. But she didn't have any choice. She couldn't live the rest of her life not knowing who her real family were.

She reread the message and clicked it off. The last thing she wanted to do tomorrow was see her mother again. Memories of two days ago were still fresh in her mind and she hadn't even started to work out how she felt about everything she'd learnt. And besides, she had plans.

She showed Matt the message.

"You are going to go, right?"

Georgie shook her head. "I can't, Matt."

"What, because you don't want to see them or because you want to go and find your real mum?"

Georgie shrugged. "Both, I think."

He said nothing for a moment, just studied her in the half-light.

"You know you have to go, don't you? You can't leave Kate to deal with this on her own, whatever's happened between the two of you."

"But —"

"George. She's your mother. And before you say it, yes, I know she might not be. But she has been for your whole life, and Kate's still Kate, and she needs you. It sounds like it's important. You'll never forgive yourself if you don't go."

Georgie didn't know what to say. She knew he was right but a huge part of her still wasn't sure if she could face either of them. Plus, of course, she was desperate to carry on with her search and the thought of delaying it by another day seemed almost unbearable.

"I'll come with you if you like."

Georgie shook her head. "No, it's fine, Matt. You're right. I'll go. I have to."

Matt nodded. "You can carry on your search the next day. It's only one day."

Georgie had nodded miserably.

And now here she is, desperate to go and knock on doors in Woodcock Street, but stuck here instead, waiting to go and see Kate and her mother. To see Jan.

She glances at the clock on the wall. It's still early, only just after eight in the morning. She grabs her laptop and opens it up, typing in the road name she's been given. She also types in Margaret Foster — assuming that is Kimberley's mother's surname as well — and anything else she can think of. She taps Kimberley's name into Facebook again too, just in case, but it doesn't look like there are any Kimberley Fosters living nearby.

She sighs and closes her computer. Clem is still sitting opposite staring at her phone, the glow from the

244

screen lighting up her face. She's only eleven but she's already so grown-up, so different from the eleven-year-old Georgie had been. So worldly-wise. Georgie can remember clearly the day Clementine was born, the moment she saw her daughter's perfect face staring back at her from a bundle of blankets, her dark hair so like hers, her blue eyes wide and searching like Matt's. She'd never loved anyone so much and she knew she'd never love anyone the same way again. She can't even begin to imagine the pain of losing someone that precious before you've even been given the chance to get to know them.

She stands and plants a kiss on her daughter's head, the smell of her lemon shampoo calming Georgie's nerves. Clem lifts her head to peer at her mum hovering above her.

"What was that for?"

"Nothing. I just love you, that's all."

"Oh right. Love you too, Mum." And then she turns back to her phone, not a care in the world.

"Right, I'm going to Grandma's now." Georgie glances at the clock. It's still only 8.30. "Shouldn't you be leaving for school?"

"Yeah, yeah. It's only French this morning."

"Clementine George."

"OK, I'm going." She stands; she's almost as tall as Georgie now, it won't be long before she's towering over her. "Bye, Mum. Say hi to Grandma and Aunty Kate for me."

"I will." Georgie's voice is weak, lost in the noise and shuffle of boots being zipped up, bags being picked up and the door slamming. And then the house is silent. Her eyes wander over the wooden dining table, littered with cereal bowls, crumb-filled plates and half-empty coffee cups. There's a pile of papers on the end of the table that's grown so high it's threatening to topple off and scatter across the floor. She really must sort it out. She knows she won't.

She runs upstairs and showers and carefully applies her make-up. She wants to appear in control today when she sees her sister and mother. She needs to *feel* in control.

Finally, just after ten, she's ready. She's too early, but she's going now, to get this over with.

She picks up her coat and bag and leaves the house. Outside it's turned suddenly cold and the winter air bites through her too-thin coat, making her shiver. The sun is low in the sky, its warmth failing to reach the ground. She gets in the car quickly and turns the heater up high and rubs her hands together, thinking about the day ahead. She knows she should be worried about Mum — about Jan — about what's happening to her, but she's finding it hard to find space for sympathy in her heart, now that she knows what she did.

She drives slowly to Jan's, making the twenty-minute drive last almost forty with a stop for coffee. When she pulls up outside her mother's house, the house she grew up in, she's hit by a pang of nostalgia so powerful it threatens to overwhelm her. She can clearly picture

246

herself and Kate sitting on the front doorstep as young children, having a teddy bears' picnic in the sunshine.

"Come in, you two, you're not supposed to be out the front, you never know what might happen," their mother had said, and they'd dutifully gone inside, never wondering what their mother was so afraid of. But it was always the same with anything they did. Most things were deemed unsafe by Jan, and so they were stopped.

In her mind she walks through the house, seeing it as it was then, with the old-fashioned flowery carpet in the hall and living room, the clock ticking monotonously on the mantelpiece; she can picture the bedroom she shared with Kate, divided down the middle, a single bed on each side. But that was where the similarities ended. Kate's side had always been immaculate, the walls painted a deep shade of pink, with a pink flowery duvet, neatly framed pictures of dogs, Coke cans and arty black-and-white photos of men holding babies. Her books were stacked tidily on the small desk in the corner and her clothes were always hung in the wardrobe. Georgie's side, on the other hand, had been a riot of colour; the walls might have been pink but you could hardly see them for the photos, pictures torn from magazines, snaps of friends, of places, of things that she just liked the look of, taped haphazardly to the walls. Her desk was covered in papers and books, clothes slung over the back of the chair and draped across the floor like stepping stones. It drove her sister mad but she didn't care. It was how she liked it. In her mind Georgie walked down the stairs to the kitchen, where they spent so much of their time. When it was quiet she liked to stand there, with her back to the worktop, and just listen to the comforting sounds of the house, the sounds that made her feel safe: the clicks of the radiators as they warmed up; the creak of the floorboards long after someone had trodden on them, like a memory; the sound of birds and the gentle hum of a lawnmower from Mr Pritchard two doors down, giving his already-neat grass a short back and sides. The kitchen lino had seen better days until Mum replaced it a few years ago; it was always slightly curled up by the back door, and the black tiles there were a shade lighter than the rest, worn by the traffic of so many feet over the years. Crumbs gathered in the corners where the broom struggled to reach, the small kitchen table was stained by cup rings from years of spilt tea and coffee, and there was a larger brown ring on the worktop by the kettle where the teapot had sat for years before it got replaced. The back of one of the wooden chairs had a broken slat, and the iron sat almost constantly on the tabletop, the cable snaking out across the surface instead of being wrapped neatly round the iron. The ironing board was shoved against the wall, standing to attention, and Mum's sewing machine and box were on the floor waiting to trip someone up.

It was chaotic but it had been home. It had been the place she'd felt safe and loved, if a little smothered.

And now that was all about to be ripped away from her.

She takes a deep breath and gets out of the car, hooks her handbag onto her shoulder and walks up to

248

knock on the door. Last time she was here — was it really just a few short days ago? — was when she came to confront Mum, to try and find out the truth about the snatching. She'd come away disappointed, but also shocked by the drastic change in her mother's behaviour in just a few weeks. She'd gone from being a bit confused, a bit scatty and forgetful, to being empty, angry and scared. It was as though she'd literally lost some of her mind in just a matter of weeks and, despite herself, Georgie's worried about what she's going to find here today.

The door swings open and Kate is standing there, her face betraying nothing.

"Come in."

There's no move to hug her; in fact Kate stands so far back to let Georgie pass it's almost as though she can't bear to be anywhere near her. Georgie pretends she hasn't noticed and steps inside, slips her shoes off and lines them up neatly by the radiator the way she always has. The tiles feel cool even through her thick socks and she shivers, trying to ignore the chilly atmosphere between her and her sister.

"Mum's having a nap."

Georgie nods and walks through to the kitchen, Kate following closely behind her. As she reaches the kitchen she stops, surprised. Sandy is standing at the sink, her back to them, scraping plates.

"Oh, Aunty Sandy. I didn't know you were going to be here."

Sandy turns and smiles. "Hello, love." She leans forward and plants a kiss on Georgie's cheek, water and bubbles dripping from her hands onto the floor. Her eyes flick to Kate. "Your sister asked me to come today, she — she thought it might be useful. As I see your mum a lot, you know ..." She trails off, clearly uncomfortable, and Georgie feels a stab of guilt. She's done this. The decision she's made to look for her birth family has already caused a huge rift between her and the people she loves, and they already feel more like strangers. How much further apart can they get before the ties snap? She doesn't know, but she can't stop now anyway, even if she wanted to. She's gone too far.

"I'm glad you're here." She glances at the clock. There's still an hour to go until the doctor arrives and Georgie's surprised by how worried she is about filling that hour. She's never felt this uncomfortable with either Kate or Aunty Sandy, but there are so many unspoken words humming in the air between them they can almost see them. They're impossible to ignore.

"Would you like some tea?"

"Please."

Kate bangs around taking mugs from the mug tree, milk from the under-counter fridge, teabags from the cupboard above the kettle, as Georgie looks round the room. It's neater now, the cupboards updated, but it's still so familiar it takes her breath away. How can this place, where she lived all her life, where she was a child, a teenager, and became an adult, be full of false, damaged memories?

Kate hands her a cup of tea and Georgie takes it and turns towards the window, looking out into the neglected garden. Weeds grow where flowers used to, and the hedge that runs between their garden and next door has grown wild, tendrils waving in the cold winter air. Pots stand empty on the crazy paving Mum never got round to replacing, and a couple of plastic chairs sit forlornly in the corner, turning green.

"We used to love playing out there." Kate takes a sip of her tea — Georgie can smell the scent of peppermint wafting across from her cup — with a sad expression. Georgie feels the need to say something, anything.

"We did. Remember the climbing frame we used to love?"

"Yes. I think it had been there for years even when we moved in, it was probably a deathtrap. But it was fun, wasn't it?"

"It was."

There's a silence again, and both sisters stare out of the window, lost in their own memories. Sandy clatters about in the background, wiping surfaces, putting away pots and pans. Georgie wonders how long she'll have to wait until Kate asks her how it went with their mother, although she assumes Aunty Sandy's filled her in. It's Kate who speaks first.

"I hate this, you know."

Georgie glances at her sister, who's keeping her gaze trained on the garden outside.

"Me too."

Kate turns her head and meets Georgie's gaze. "It doesn't matter how angry I am. I'll always love you, you know that, don't you?"

Tears sting Georgie's eyes and she nods, hiding her face behind her mug. She coughs. "So, what's happening with Mum?" The word jars as it leaves her mouth but she doesn't let Kate see.

"She's just — worse." Kate shrugs, and places her mug on the worktop, running her finger slowly round the rim.

Behind them, Sandy speaks, and they turn. "She's just so angry all the time, at everyone. But we rang the doctor because we realized — me and Kate — that your mum hasn't been eating. We're not sure whether it's because she's forgotten how to cook, or she's just forgotten whether she's eaten or not."

"We found loads of food in the fridge that hadn't been touched for weeks. Even meals I'd made and left there for her, festering at the back, uneaten. I hadn't noticed before, but they'd started to smell and — well, I rang Aunty Sandy and she said she was really worried about her too."

Georgie tries to ignore the pang of pain she feels at hearing that Kate had rung Sandy first and not her. It's not important. At least, not right now. "So what happened?"

"I rang the doctor and he's coming to see her today because she refuses to go there. Says there's nothing wrong with her. But we think she's going to need some care. More care. Help with everyday tasks, that sort of thing. And I just can't do it on my own." Kate sniffs and rubs her eye, looking away back out of the window.

Georgie knows it's terrible news. She's known for ages that her mother has been getting worse, but she's finding it hard to care as much as she should. She glances at the clock again, desperate to get out of here.

252

"It's 11.30, should we wake her up?"

Kate shakes her head.

"Let's give her another ten minutes."

"OK."

The three women sit down at the table, Georgie perched on the edge of her wooden seat, sipping her tea, watching the seconds tick by. The silence in the room is oppressive, each woman lost in her own thoughts; where there's usually warmth, today there's only emptiness; where's there's usually laughter and chatter, today there's only silence.

A bang from the hallway slices through the air and the three of them stand and push their chairs back quickly, rushing into the hallway just in time to see an ornament flying through the air and down the stairs, to land with a crash, tiny pieces skittering across the tiles in all directions. They look up the stairs to see Jan at the top, her face pulled into a mask of rage.

"Mum!" Kate steps over the shards of ceramic and climbs the stairs quickly. By the time she gets there Jan has stepped back into the doorway, a look of terror on her face.

"You didn't come and get me."

"I thought you were asleep, Mum." Kate's voice is soft, pleading.

"You were meant to come and wake me up, I'm going to be late." Jan's voice is louder now, laced with tears. "You promised and now I'm going to miss it."

Georgie looks at this woman she's called her mother her whole life and feels a ball of anger and shame well up inside her. She watches as Jan stands at the top of

253

the stairs, scared and alone. She's lost weight but she looks bigger than usual, bulked out by the countless cardigans she's layered over and over each other until her arms can barely bend, and Georgie can feel something else, a sense of pity washing across her face and down into the pit of her belly.

Kate moves towards her mother, walking slowly up the stairs, her arms held out in front of her, as though in surrender. "Come on, Mum, let's take some of these cardigans off and get your hair looking nice, shall we, then we can come back downstairs. How does that sound?" Kate's voice is soft and pacifying and Georgie wonders how she can do it, how she can be so patient faced with such a nightmare. But she knows, deep down, that she'd be exactly the same, under normal circumstances. It's just a shame that these aren't normal circumstances.

"No, I don't want to. I want to come down now."

"But Mum —"

But Jan pushes her to one side and walks down the stairs, holding onto the banister for support. At the bottom she looks at Georgie, as though trying to work out who she is, shakes her head then turns and walks into the kitchen. She's muttering something under her breath but Georgie can't make out what it is. She hears Kate's footsteps running down the stairs again as she follows her mother into the kitchen and then watches as she opens the back door and marches out into the garden. Jan's walking purposefully now, a changed woman from the scared one who stood at the top of the stairs just a few moments before, and Georgie and Kate

254

watch in horrified fascination as their mother reaches the end of the garden, by the shed, and bends down and starts to scrabble at the earth with her bare hands.

"Jan, what are you doing? Stop it!" Sandy rushes towards her as lumps of wet soil and stones come flying from the patch of ground, Jan fixed on the task. All they can see is the back of her head, her back hunched over under all her cardigans, and the soles of her slippers pointing up to the sky as she kneels. But then Sandy reaches her and grabs her arm, and Jan turns, and they see tears running down her face.

"But I have to get her, she's here, she's here." She struggles to catch her breath and Sandy slowly pulls her to her feet, Jan brushing mud from her hands, her nails black. "Why are you stopping me? You can't stop me, it's nothing to do with you."

Jan tries to pull her wrists away from Sandy's grip but she can't and the two women stand there, locked together in silent battle for a moment.

"Jan, come on, let's stop this. Let's get you inside." Sandy's voice is calm but there's a tremble in it, and she makes to pull Jan gently towards the house. But Jan rips her hand away and screams.

"Get off me! I need to go to her. What's it got to do with you? Why are you always interfering? Why do you always think you know best? Maybe you should just mind your own bloody business, you bitch, and stop telling me what to do." Jan's face is screwed up in a rage that Georgie's never seen before and she doesn't know what to do, how to stop these terrible words firing like bullets from her mother's mouth.

"Is it because nobody else loves you? Is that why you always wanted me to love you? You just have to interfere because you're a lonely old spinster that nobody else wants."

Sandy gasps and drops Jan's arms, and they fall roughly to her sides, almost tipping her off balance.

"How could you?" Sandy's voice is lowered to a hiss and Georgie can hardly make out what she's saying. She glances at Kate, but her sister also seems to be stuck, staring in horror at the scene unfolding. "You evil cow. After everything I've done for you."

Jan's body has sagged now, as though all the vehemence has been exhausted, leaving her weak. She sways on the spot slightly, and suddenly Kate is galvanized into action, walking forward to take hold of her mother's arm and guide her gently towards the house.

"I'm sorry. She doesn't know what she's saying," Kate whispers to Sandy as she passes her. But Georgie can see from the look in Sandy's eyes that it's too late. That her mother has gone too far, even for Sandy's seemingly endless patience.

Sandy wheels around and follows them into the house. As they reach the door she strides in front of them and stops, blocking the doorway. She seems to fill it, such is her rage, and for the first time ever Georgie feels scared of this kind, gentle woman she's known her whole life. She can feel the blood rush to her face as Sandy walks slowly towards them.

"That's it. I'm sorry, Kate. Georgie. I can't do this any more. More than forty years I've been there for

256

your mother, helped her with everything, been there whenever she needed me. I've kept her dirty little secrets — and believe me, she hasn't even got any idea how much I've kept quiet. But I can't do it any more. Not with this . . . this . . . anger. I just can't. I'm done."

"But —" Jan's voice is small, weak, her eyes filled with tears, suddenly remorseful. "I'm sorry."

Sandy looks at her oldest friend for a moment, and Georgie thinks maybe she's going to forgive her, and that everything is going to be all right after all. But then Sandy gives a tiny shake of her head, turns and walks away, out through the kitchen, down the hall and out of the front door, closing it firmly behind her.

Georgie feels rooted to the spot, unable to believe what's just happened. She looks back at the patch of earth where her mother was digging and wonders momentarily what on earth she was doing. She shivers, as a feeling of déjà vu ripples through her, as though she's seen this patch of earth before, dug up and patted down, but she can't for the life of her pin it down, work out its significance.

Kate's voice breaks into her thoughts. "Help me get Mum back inside, will you, Georgie?" Obediently, Georgie grabs hold of her mother's arm and steers her into the living room, where the sound of the clock seems louder than ever, marking time.

Kate fusses around, trying to get her mother comfortable, plumping pillows, removing her cardigans, but Georgie can hardly bear to touch her. Instead, she walks numbly to the kitchen to grab the dustpan and brush. She heads back to the bottom of the stairs and bends to sweep up the mess from the thrown ornament. As she pushes the pieces into the dustpan she can't get out of her mind the look on Jan's face as she screamed at Aunty Sandy. She's never seen her like that before, and she's certainly never heard her speak to anyone like that, least of all her best — and only — friend.

As she clears up the last of the broken ceramic, she can hear Jan and Kate's voices in the other room: Kate's soft, soothing, trying to calm her mother down.

Kate's so patient with her and she knows it's not Jan's fault, it's what she needs. But Georgie can hardly bear to look at her mother at the moment. How on earth is she going to stay calm with her, to help her?

Slowly she stands and walks back to the kitchen, opens the bin and throws the pieces of ornament in roughly, letting the lid slam back down with a bang.

She can't do this. She can't be here pretending to care about Jan and her deteriorating mind when she's got so many other things she needs to do.

She can't help.

She needs to go.

And so, without thinking about it too much, she picks up her bag and walks towards the front door. She feels guilty for Kate's sake, leaving her sister to cope all by herself. But she doesn't feel guilty for Jan's sake. She pulls the door open and shuts it quietly behind her without looking back to see if Kate has heard her leave. She couldn't bear the look on her face if she had.

She walks back to her car and climbs in, pulling away quickly before she can change her mind, peering through the frosted-over windscreen as the ineffectual heater slowly clears it. She needs to get away, to put as much distance between herself and her mother as she can, even if that means stretching the bond between her and Kate so tightly it's in danger of breaking forever.

All she can do is hope that, one day, her sister will forgive her.

The sky's a heavy grey when Georgie gets up the next morning and she hopes it's not an indication of how the day is going to be. She had a tough enough time yesterday.

She's been awake most of the night, going over all the possibilities, all the different outcomes, and yet she still feels woefully unprepared. And what if she comes home tonight and the trail has gone cold? What if she discovers absolutely nothing? What will she do then?

She pulls a jumper over her head, runs her fingers through her hair and peers at her reflection in the mirror. Will she meet someone today who looks just the same as her? She shivers at the thought.

Downstairs, Clem is sitting at the table shovelling down a bowl of cereal. She barely glances up as Georgie walks into the room. Georgie watches her for a minute, feeling a surge of love for her daughter. She can't even begin to imagine how it would feel to lose her, not to know where she was, what she was doing; to wonder whether she was happy or safe or even alive. She shakes the thought from her mind and walks over, wrapping her arms around Clem's neck, pulling her into a hug. "Love you, sweetheart."

"Love you too, Mum." She carries on eating, barely stopping for breath and Georgie breathes in the scent of her daughter, a mix of lemon shampoo and washing powder. She hopes Clementine's world isn't going to be completely thrown if she finds anything out today. Clem doesn't have a clue what's happened so far, but Georgie can't bear to tell her, not yet. Not until she knows exactly what she's facing.

"I made you a coffee, if you have time?" Matt points to the worktop where there's a steaming cup waiting for her.

"Thanks." She takes a gulp and slams it down, spilling some over the side. "Sorry."

Matt lowers his voice. "Nervous?"

Georgie nods.

"Are you sure you don't want me to come with you?"

"No. I need to do this alone."

He accepts this. "OK. But ring me if you need me, OK?"

She nods again.

"And don't do anything silly."

"I won't." She glances at Clem. She's reading the gossip pages of a magazine, not listening to a word they're saying. "Love you." She gives him a quick kiss then turns to leave, aware that when she gets home her life could be turned upside down. It makes her feel dizzy if she thinks about it too much.

Her legs shake as she makes her way to the car and she takes a couple of deep breaths before pulling into the road. She drives on autopilot, hardly thinking about where she's going or what she's going to say when she gets there. The area isn't a part of Norwich she knows at all so as she gets nearer she follows her satnav, turning down streets she's never seen before. She feels lost.

Finally, she's there. Woodcock Street. Her stomach is in knots and her head is throbbing and she sits for a minute, trying to gather the courage to get out and knock on the door.

She'd spent some time online last night, during the early hours when sleep was eluding her, trying to discover whether Kimberley still lived in this street, the street that Hazel Moore had said she'd moved to all those years ago. But she hadn't managed to find anything, and so she was back to banging on doors, hoping someone would be able to help her. The Internet doesn't have all the answers, after all.

She steps out of the car and stands for a minute, looking at the innocuous houses either side of her. It's quite a long street, curving away into the distance so she can't see where it ends, but it's not as nice as the street in Sprowston where she was yesterday. It's scruffier, the houses council-built and less well maintained, paint peeling from windowsills, graffiti on crumbling garden walls and an underlying air of menace that makes her shoulders hunch. She pulls her bag further up on her shoulder and takes a step onto the pavement and up the first garden path.

Her heart thunders as she waits for the first door to open but, as it becomes clear there's no one in, she starts to breathe more easily. She wishes she'd taken Matt up on his offer to come with her, but she can't have them both taking so many days off work. She's already worried the library will think she's pulling sickies.

She moves on to the next house, but the old man who lives there can hardly hear her, let alone help her with her search. At the next couple of houses is a harassed mum with a screaming toddler at her ankles, and a youngish man in tracksuit bottoms who looks as though the doorbell has woken him up, his hair standing on end, the circles dark under his eyes.

She knocks on the glass pane of the next door, ignoring the taped-up doorbell. It takes several seconds for someone to appear, and Georgie's about to give up hope and head to the next house. Then the door swings open and there's a man standing there, about her age. In fact, exactly her age, and she gasps as her legs start to shake.

It's him.

It's Samuel.

It has to be.

Her voice seems to have stuck in her throat and she swallows, trying to unblock it. Samuel — she's utterly certain it's him; he has her green eyes, her cheek dimples, her slightly arched eyebrow — stands patiently and waits for her to speak.

"Are you OK? You've gone really white." His voice is gentle, warm and she feels it seep into her skin.

"Yes —" She clears her throat and tries again. "Yes, I'm fine. I — I was just looking for someone but I think I must have the wrong house, I'm sorry." She can't look at him, can't meet his eye. She's made a terrible mistake, coming here. She can't spring this on him, on his doorstep on a chilly November day. It's not fair. She should have thought this through better but now it's too late and she's here and she needs to get away. "Sorry to bother you." She starts to turn but his voice stops her in her tracks.

"Who are you looking for? I know a few people in this street, I've lived here most of my life."

Reluctantly she turns back around and trains her gaze on the door frame just to the side of him. She holds her hand up to her cheek, hoping he doesn't spot any resemblance. But why would he? He's not expecting his long-lost sister to come knocking on his door. She's being ridiculous.

"I — I'm looking for Kimberley Foster." Her voice wobbles and she's sure she's given herself away, but his face lights up at the mention of the name.

"That's my mum!"

She doesn't say that she knows that. She doesn't say it's her mum too. But all these words are clogging up the air between them, making it hard for her to breathe. Instead, she says, "Oh right. Well. Excellent. Can you — can you tell me where she lives?"

He cocks his thumb behind his shoulder. "Right here." He shrugs and gives a wry smile, the dimples appearing in his cheeks again. "I know, bit sad eh, still living with my mum at my age?" He's so open, so warm, there's no hint of suspicion or defensiveness and she feels guilty for even being there. She shouldn't have come, not like this.

"Who's looking for her?"

"Er . . ."

"Well, who are you?" He smiles warmly again and it's so familiar she feels as though she's going to pass out. She rubs her hand over her face. "It's — er — my mum was an old friend of hers and — I just wanted to say hello. But I'll come back another time."

She takes a step back and the world tips away from her and she loses her footing, almost falling backwards onto the crazy-paved pathway. Samuel reaches out and grabs her elbow, steadying her. "God, are you OK? Do you want to come in, have a glass of water? You look terrible."

She shakes her head. "No, I'm fine. Sorry. I just — I should go."

"I'll tell Mum you were looking for her, shall I? She's just gone out with Gran, she should be back in —" he glances at his watch — "about an hour?"

"Thanks." She turns and hurries back to the car and sits for a minute, feeling as though the sky is pressing down on her. The door to the house is shut now, and it's hard to believe, looking at it, what's just happened. What was she thinking, just turning up like this? What did she imagine was going to happen?

She closes her eyes and tries to picture the warm, kind face of the man who'd just opened the door — her brother — but she struggles to form any features in her mind. She's desperate to go back and have another look, to spend hours drinking in the familiar lines and contours of his skin, the dimple in his cheeks, the dark hair, gelled into short spikes at the front. She pulls the sun visor down and peers at her reflection again. Her

264

eyes are framed by the edges of the mirror and she stares at them; despite the dark rings around them she can see they're just like Samuel's, the shape, the colour, everything. She pulls back and looks at the shape of her face and smiles at herself, wondering whether her smile is as warm and welcoming as his. Probably not.

She leans her head back against the headrest and breathes deeply. She knows without a shadow of a doubt that she's going to go back and knock on that door later and, hopefully, meet her real mother. She has no idea what she's going to say, or how she's going to say it, but she knows that whatever happens, several lives are about to be torn apart — including her own.

She doesn't know how much time has passed when she hears a shout outside the passenger window and her eyes fly open. It takes a moment to remember where she is and she peers out of the window to see where the noise is coming from. There's a little boy running past; she can just make out the top of his head above the edge of the door, and behind him a woman's running, pushing a pushchair. "Stop, Tyler, now!" Her voice is almost a scream as she chases after her son. Georgie watches as the woman reaches him and scoops him up and straps him angrily into his pushchair. Then her attention is drawn to the sound of footsteps approaching behind her and she cranes her neck round to see who's there. Two women are walking up the road towards her, laden down with carrier bags, one older than the other, with a slight limp. When they get close enough for her to make out their faces Georgie stops breathing.

It's Kimberley, and her mother.

It's *her* mother.

She grips the steering wheel, holding her breath as they pass her car as though the sound of her breathing might draw their attention. They walk past, not noticing her, as her eyes follow them from the safety of the car. She watches as they stop outside their house, readjust their bags and walk up the short path. Kimberley kicks the door with her foot, gently, unable to find a free hand to knock with, then Georgie sees her brother again as he opens the door and lets them in. He glances up and looks at her car and she prays he can't see her. As he turns away, taking the bags from his grandmother, she lets out a huge puff of air and waits until her heartbeat slows and she can breathe properly once more.

Part of her wants to go and knock on the door again, introduce herself, watch their reactions as they realize who she is. The other part of her wants to run away and pretend she'd never even started this search, pretend she knows nothing, just carry on with her perfectly happy life as it was.

But she knows she can't do that. She's come too far already. Too much has already changed, or been destroyed. She needs to fix things again.

Slowly she climbs back out of the car, clutching her handbag to her stomach. Her legs feel heavy and it's an effort to make them move, one in front of the other, up the path to the door. It's an effort to lift her hand and knock, and she holds it there, suspended in mid-air, for a few seconds. It seems amazing that what she does

266

next will change her life forever: one knock at a tatty old plastic door will change everything.

And then she knocks on the door, quickly, and steps back, and waits.

CHAPTER
THIRTEEN

30 October 2016

It seems like forever and also no time at all before the door is opened and Samuel is standing there again, and it takes all Georgie's effort not to gasp. His face breaks into his already-familiar smile and he takes a step back into the house.

"Hello," he says. "Mum's just back. I've told her someone was looking for her but she seemed confused. Come in, I'm sure she'll be pleased to see you." Samuel's standing with his back pressed against the peeling paint of the hallway wall, watching her expectantly.

Georgie looks down at the threshold of the door and tries to imagine stepping over it. She tries to imagine lifting her foot up and over the door frame and placing it down again on the thin grey carpet on the other side. It's such a simple movement, hardly anything at all. And yet it's everything.

She glances behind her briefly. It's not too late to turn around and run, far, far down the street away from here, and never come back. She could just run and run until she got home, and then carry on with her life as though nothing had ever happened, and pretend that she'd never even knocked on this door, and seen this man. And maybe that would be for the best, for everyone. Maybe she should never have come here, to destroy these people's lives. Maybe she should just go, right now. She pauses a second longer.

But then, before she can think about it any more, it's as though her body has taken over from her mind and her foot is through the doorway, into the narrow hall; the other one follows closely after and then the door is being closed behind her, and she's there. She's inside the house and there's no going back. The walls seem to bulge towards her, and she presses her hand against the nearest one. She breathes deeply.

Suddenly she's aware that Samuel's looking at her quizzically, waiting for her to follow him. She lets her hair fall across her face and follows him down the hallway, one heavy, dread-laden step at a time. Her hand trails along the wall as she walks, the solidity of it giving her a false sense of security. She deliberately places one foot in front of the other, each step an effort, as though she's walking to her own execution. And then, before she's ready, she's there, at the doorway to the small, slightly scruffy kitchen, and she's looking at the back of her mother's head, her hair grey now, no longer dark, and her heart hammers against her ribcage as she waits for her to turn around, to see her. She thinks she might fall over.

"Mum, that lady's back again. She's come to see you." Sam's words are slow and measured, as though he's talking to a young child.

Kimberley doesn't turn round straight away, but instead spends a few more agonizing seconds placing the tins she's bought carefully in the cupboard, all neatly facing the front like soldiers. Each movement seems to take forever and Georgie wants to shout, "Oh, just hurry up and look at me!" But she doesn't; she stands quietly on the spot, waiting for her mother to turn round.

And then, finally, she does. It takes a few seconds for her to focus properly on Georgie, her eyes wandering quickly across her face, her hair, down across her coat, her shoes and back up to her face again, taking in the details. It's clear she hasn't recognized her straight away — why would she? — and so Georgie waits patiently to see how long it will take for realization to dawn. And then, at last, it does; it's easy to see the moment as Kimberley's face turns ashen and a small gasp emerges from her throat. She takes a couple of steps towards her as though to see her more closely, and Georgie steps back reflexively. She thinks she might throw up.

"Louisa . . ." Kimberley's voice cracks and she takes a rasping breath, her hand fluttering to her chest. She sits down heavily on the chair next to her.

"Mum?" Sam's voice is confused, concerned.

Kimberley doesn't speak, but just stares at Georgie. Georgie can only stare back at the face of this woman, almost forty years older than she was in the newspaper report, but so familiar all the same. Her face looks older than its fifty-four years, but it's something about her eyes that breaks Georgie's heart. They're so full of pain, of suffering and desperation, that she just wants to

270

reach out and hold her and tell her everything is going to be OK. Instead, though, she just stands there waiting for this poor, broken woman to take in the terrifying significance of the woman standing in front of her in her kitchen.

"Mum. Mum, what the hell's going on here?" Samuel is looking from one woman to the other, a deep crevice carved between his eyes.

Kimberley looks at her son, and then back at Georgie. Her voice comes out as a hoarse whisper. "It's her. It's Louisa."

Samuel looks at Georgie again, studying her more closely this time, and her face flames under his gaze. It doesn't take him long.

"Fuck. It can't be."

He stands still, his body rigid, his face as white as his mother's.

For a minute or so there's nothing but the odd bang from the central heating and the sound of the recently boiled kettle clicking as it cools. Nobody knows what to say. Georgie feels as though she ought to speak, to say something, anything, to break the tension in the room, to explain why and how she's there, but the words won't form so she continues to stand there, too warm in her heavy coat, clutching her bag tightly against her body. Her knuckles have turned white.

The silence is broken suddenly and loudly.

"Why does everyone look like they've seen a ghost?" An older woman — who must be Margaret — has walked past Georgie and shuffles slowly towards the table, where she sits down carefully, huffing and puffing as she does so. Her voice is raspy and hard, and if she weren't so frail-looking Georgie would have felt afraid of this woman. Instead, she just watches her watching her, and waits for the penny to drop.

Just as with the others, it doesn't take long. It's as though this was what they'd all been waiting for, for the last thirty-seven years, as though it isn't a huge surprise to them that their missing baby has just walked through the door all these years later, a grown woman — because they'd been expecting it all the time.

"Oh my giddy aunt." An understatement if ever there was one, Georgie thinks. Margaret looks at her daughter, who's still staring at Georgie. "You bloody well *have* seen a ghost."

Samuel steps forward first, and pulls out a seat for Georgie. "Do you want to sit down? You look like you're going to fall over."

Georgie takes the four or five steps towards the table with shaking legs and sits down gratefully on the edge of the seat. Kimberley has torn her gaze away now and is staring at Samuel instead. Her whole body is shaking.

"What . . . How —?" She stops, swallows, starts again, looking at Georgie this time. "Is it — is it really you?"

Her eyes are wide, full of disbelief and hope, and Georgie gives a small nod. "Yes. I think so."

"Course it's her. She looks just like Sam, look at her." Margaret's leaning forward, her breath slightly wheezy as she lights a cigarette with shaking hands, her voice raspy.

272

Kimberley lowers her head into her hands and takes a couple of breaths. When she looks up again there are tears running down her face, pulling her black mascara down with them, giving her the look of a clown. She wipes her hand across her cheek and rubs it on her jeans.

"I thought you were dead." She nods, as if having a conversation with herself, and stares at the trainers poking out from the bottom of her jeans. "I mean, not at first. I thought they'd find you and you'd come home and everything would be all right again, in the end. But after a while, when they found nothing, then — well, I thought you must be dead. Otherwise, how could they not have found you? How could I, your own mother, not have known where you'd gone?"

She stops and slumps back, as though the effort of getting all those words out has exhausted her. Her voice is flat, detached.

"So, how are you here?" It's Samuel's voice this time and for the first time Georgie looks him in the eye. He meets her gaze like a challenge. "I mean, what's happened, right now, to make you be here, right now, in our house?"

Georgie clears her throat, her tongue parched. "I — I just found out about this. It's only been, what, three days, since I found out that my mum wasn't my mum. Since I found out — what she did. I needed to find you and — well. It seems I have, already." Her heart thumps so loudly she's sure they can all hear it and she looks round at Kimberley, at Margaret, whose face, beneath all the wrinkles and lines, is pulled into an expression of pure anger.

"Your *mum?*" Margaret spits the words out, and they land on the table with a thud. "Your mum? You mean the woman who stole you from us? The woman who destroyed our lives, you mean? *That* 'mum'?"

There's so much venom in the older woman's words that Georgie almost wants to push her chair back to get away from them.

"Mum!" Kimberley's voice is more forceful than Georgie's heard it before.

"What? You think we should just nod and hug her and ignore the truth here?"

"I think you should stop talking for a minute and let me think." Her words are a hiss and she stops to gather her thoughts. "I think that we should take this one step at a time. None of this is our fault, but it's not Louisa's either —" Georgie flinches at the name, a reminder of how little she knows this woman who gave her life — "so let's just stop for a minute, shall we? You're not helping."

Margaret pulls her mouth into a thin line and folds her arms across her chest as though she's not used to being told what to do, but she doesn't say another word and Georgie's relieved and grateful.

"I'm so sorry. I shouldn't have come here out of the blue like this. I just — I needed to find you. I needed to do something, when I found out."

"But how —" Kimberley stops, unable to carry on. "How did you find out? Who you are, I mean?"

274

"I found this." Georgie remembers the newspaper cutting she found in the library, that she's been carrying round like a stone in her handbag ever since; the cutting that she's used to break the news to so many people. She pulls it out from the folder at the bottom of her bag and unfolds it, smoothing down the creases as she passes it to Kimberley. Kimberley's eyes move across the page, across the blurred image of her own much younger face, and she turns white again. She passes it back with shaking hands and Georgie feels the need to explain more.

"I was looking for something, my birth certificate, actually, up in Mum's loft. I'd never really been up there before but — well, Mum's not very well, and I didn't want to ask her where it was so I went up when she was out. I didn't find it, in the end, but — well, I did find my sister's birth certificate and her baby wristband, from the hospital. But there was no sign of mine and I thought it was odd." She stops, clears her throat. "I suppose deep down I'd always been expecting something like this. Not — *this* exactly, but . . . Well, some sort of sordid secret to be let out of the bag. So anyway I — I went to the library. And I found this, and loads more —" She stops, clenching her hands together tightly. "And there was no birth certificate for me anywhere there either. I didn't exist, according to the records. I did find a record of Samuel's birth, though, and — well, Louisa's. Or mine, as it turns out. To be honest, it didn't take me long to work it out, after that."

"Oh my God, how horrendous."

"For me?"

Kimberley nods.

"Yes, it was, it is. But it must have been so much worse for you. I haven't been able to stop thinking about you since I found out, about what you must have gone through when you realized I was gone." She looks up at the woman who gave birth to her and meets her eye. "I've got a daughter of my own and I don't think I could have carried on, if I'd lost her. I couldn't bear it."

"I had no choice." Her voice is soft and Georgie has to strain to hear her words. "I had Sam to think about too, I had to carry on." She glances at Samuel and gives him a weak smile. "I just got through each day one at a time."

"Hardly." Margaret's face is like thunder. "You didn't *get through each day*. You struggled through every day, you wanted to kill yourself several times — sorry, Sam, but you know what it's been like, growing up in this house." Her voice is dripping with long-pent-up fury.

"Mum, stop it."

"No, I won't stop it. I won't sit here and listen to you pretending that you muddled along OK, that you coped. The girl needs to know the truth, to know the damage her so-called mother — that *woman* — caused." She stops, struggling to catch her breath. The air pulses with anger.

Kimberley turns back to Georgie. "I'm sorry, Loui —" She stops and gasps. "Oh my God, I . . . I don't even know whether you're still called Louisa. Are you?"

276

Georgie shakes her head and hates herself as the woman's shoulders slump. "No. I'm Georgina. Georgie."

"Georgie." Kimberley tries it out on her tongue and shakes her head. "No, it's all wrong. All wrong." She seems agitated and Georgie reaches out her hand to hold Kimberley's, but she snatches it away as though she's been burnt and hugs her hand to her chest.

"Sorry. It's just — this has been a bit of a shock."

"Understatement of the century." Samuel's voice comes out as a laugh without any mirth in it.

Georgie doesn't speak for a moment, she doesn't dare. The air has changed; it's charged with tension and she doesn't want to say the wrong thing.

Samuel stands, eventually. "I think we should stop now. This has been a massive shock for all of us, and I think Mum — we all — need time to think about it. To get our heads round it, what this means."

Georgie nods and stands too, almost matching his height. "You're right. I'm sorry to have come here, like this, out of the blue. I just didn't know what else to do. I — I hope you'll let me see you all again?"

She looks at the closed faces round the table and gets nothing. Samuel places his hand on her shoulder and starts to guide her towards the door. When they get to the front door he turns to face her.

"I don't know how Mum's going to cope with this. She's not the most stable of people, even at the best of times. And this definitely isn't the best of times. I don't know how any of us are going to cope, to be honest.

You're going to have to give us some time to get used to the idea that you're still alive. That you're here."

Georgie nods. "When can I come back?"

"Give me your number. I'll ring you." He pulls out his phone and types Georgie's number in, checking it carefully. "I'm not just trying to get rid of you, I promise. I just think — well, give us a bit of time and maybe we can talk some more. I'd like to get to know you." He stops and shakes his head. "My mysterious, missing sister." He reaches out his hand to touch her cheek and his hand feels warm to the touch. "So many times I wished you'd never been taken, that our lives had gone just like they were meant to. But then there were other times, when things were really bad, that I just wished more than anything else that you'd never been born. Because then I would have mattered so much more." He pulls his hand away and opens the door for Georgie to leave. "I'm sorry," she whispers, then she turns and walks away, her back burning under his gaze, unsure whether she'll ever see this man, her brother, again.

She climbs into the car and sits for a moment, head tilted back, eyes closed, not daring to look back at the house in case she sees someone watching her. Instead she starts the engine and drives, through the lighter midday traffic, towards home. The house is empty when she gets there and she's grateful to have peace and quiet for once.

It's not until she sits down to process what's just happened that she remembers what happened yesterday with Kate. There hasn't been any word from her sister since she walked out of their mother's house the day before, and the lack of communication speaks volumes. She feels an overwhelming urge to ring Kate, to pick over the details of her day one by one, to tell her what the people she's just met were like, about the strange connection she feels with her brother.

Picking up her phone, she starts to type out a message, an apology for her behaviour. But then she stops. Kate's made it clear she wants nothing to do with this search, and after yesterday she doubts her sister will be very open to hearing from her. So instead she switches her phone off and lies down flat on the sofa. Only then do the tears come: tears for herself, for the family she missed, for her childhood that feels like a lie, and for Kimberley, the sad, broken woman who gave her life.

CHAPTER
FOURTEEN

Early November 2016

It's almost a week before Georgie gets the phone call she's been waiting for, and by then she's starting to believe it's never going to come; that she's lost Kate, her mother, everyone, for nothing. She hasn't been able to think about anything else since the moment she walked into that house and saw her mother and her brother for the first time. She hasn't got the space in her head.

The shrill tone slices through the air as she's sitting in a cafe round the corner from the library in her lunch break, and she snatches her phone up and presses it to her ear. It's a number she doesn't recognize and her heart hammers wildly, her breath coming in short bursts.

"Hello?"

There's a moment of silence on the other end, a beat of time when Georgie thinks she might have got it wrong, that this is nothing more than a wrong number. But then she hears an intake of breath and an already-familiar voice fills the silence.

"Georgie? It's me. Sam."

"Sam." She breathes out heavily, letting the name slip down the phone line. "Thank you for ringing me."

"I'm sorry it's taken so long. It's been a tough few days."

"I can imagine. I'm sorry." She takes a sip of water, then presses her free hand to her ear to try and block out the hum of the cafe around her. She doesn't want to miss a word. "So. Um. How are you?" It's a ridiculous question but she doesn't have anything else right now.

"OK." Samuel sniffs and swallows loudly. "I wondered — we wondered — if you wanted to come round again? Or we could meet somewhere else, if you feel more comfortable."

Georgie shakes her head. "No, no, I'd love to come round again. When?"

"Can you make tonight?"

"Yes, tonight's good."

"OK. So, we'll see you about seven, then, shall we? After tea?"

"Great. Thank you, Sam."

"See you later, then. And Georgie?"

"Yes?"

"Don't worry about Gran. Her bark is worse than her bite. She doesn't mean any harm."

And then the line goes dead. Georgie puts the phone down on the plastic table. She hadn't realized how much her hands were shaking until now. She stares at the half-eaten sandwich in front of her. She doesn't want it now. She stands and puts her phone back in her bag, throws the sandwich in the bin and makes her way out of the cafe into the cold, bright day. The sky is a bright, explosive blue but the sun is giving off little heat and she shivers as she walks briskly back to the library. She has no idea how she's going to concentrate for the rest of the day, but perhaps work will be a welcome distraction until the clock crawls round to seven o'clock.

She hopes so.

It's been a long, torturous day but it's finally time to leave. Matt has already offered to come with her, but Georgie knows she has to do this on her own. She hopes he understands, that he doesn't think she's pushing him away. Although she is, in a way, she supposes.

As she drives up along the dark, unlit roads towards the city her mind does somersaults. There are so many questions, so much she wants to know about these people who are part of her. It's clear from their first meeting that Kimberley is fragile, treading a delicate balance between getting on with her life and tipping over the precipice into depression. Georgie wonders how many times in her life she's plunged over the edge, only to be dragged back again, kicking and screaming. She wonders how much of it has to do with what happened to Kimberley, and how much was in her anyway. Then she thinks about Margaret, so angry, all her rage balled up into one tiny frame and hardened over the years. And she thinks about Sam, her twin brother, with whom she feels this inexplicable connection that she's never felt with anyone else before, not even with Kate. Just being in his company feels so right and she's desperate to get to know him better, to discover what he likes and dislikes, what his hopes and dreams are. And to find out more about how his life has been, living in the shadow of a lost sister for all these years.

Shivering despite the warmth from the car heater, she realizes that they're going to want to know more about her as well. What if she's a let-down to them, after all this time?

She pulls up on the street just down from the house and sits for a moment, taking a few deep breaths. She can do this. There isn't any choice.

Georgie steps out of the car, walks unsteadily to the front door and knocks gently, feeling strangely detached as she waits for someone to open it, as though she's not really there, but merely watching from a distance. A shadowy shape appears behind the mottled glass and as it approaches she squints, trying to make out who it is. And then the door swings open and it's like looking at a male version of herself as she sees her brother in front of her, his face creased into a smile. He looks even more like her than she remembers and she can't believe he didn't know who she was straight away. But then, he wasn't looking for her, was he? They stand for a moment, staring at each other, then, out of the blue, Sam steps forward and puts his arms round Georgie's shoulders and gives her an awkward hug. It's unexpected but it feels so right that she squeezes him back. When he pulls away his face flames and he looks at the floor. "Come in."

She steps in, then follows him through into the cramped kitchen at the back of the house.

"Sit down, I'll just go and tell Mum and Gran you're here."

She sits at the table nervously and looks round, taking in details of the room she hadn't noticed last time. The walls are shabby, with paint peeling off in the corners and a few cracked tiles, but it's cleaner than before, as though someone has made a real effort for her arrival, and she feels touched. There's a plate of biscuits on the side, arranged in a neat circle, and she smiles. You don't buy biscuits for unwanted guests.

There's a movement behind her and she turns to see Sam and Kimberley entering the room. Kimberley's hair is pulled back into a tight ponytail, making her narrow face look even smaller and accentuating the deep lines that run across her forehead and the wrinkles that pucker her lips. But it's clear she's made an effort, with a pair of faded black jeans and grey jumper that cling to her slender figure and make her look younger than her fifty-four years — younger than she did the last time Georgie saw her. She's wearing a smile that wavers at the edges.

Georgie stands and holds out her hand. It's over-formal but she is a stranger still, and doesn't know what else to do. Kimberley takes it and clutches it in both hands. Her hands are freezing cold and dry as paper to the touch. They're shaking slightly.

"Thank you for coming back. It's good to see you."

She walks to the worktop and flicks the kettle on, then turns and places the biscuits on the table. "Please, have a biscuit. Would you like tea?" Her words are slow

284

and measured and Georgie wonders whether she's taken something before her arrival to calm her nerves.

"Tea would be lovely, thank you."

"Or coffee? I've got coffee as well." She turns and holds out a jar of cheap instant coffee.

Georgie shakes her head. "Tea is fine, thank you." She hates how stilted she sounds but it's going to take time to relax.

She sits, jiggling her leg up and down under the table, as Kimberley flits around making tea. Strangely, Kimberley reminds her of her mother — of Jan — the nervous manner she has, the way she's unable to sit still when she's anxious. Georgie wants to tell her to relax, that she's not going to make this difficult for her, that she's not going to ask her any questions she doesn't want to answer, she just wants to get to know her. But the words won't come so she sits and waits patiently, watching as Sam sits down opposite her and pops a whole custard cream into his mouth in one go. Crumbs spill out and he brushes them away, raising his eyebrows apologetically.

Finally Kimberley sits down, spilling tea as she puts the mugs down on the table. They sit in silence for a while as they sip their scalding drinks, and Georgie holds hers to her face, letting the steam rise and warm her cheeks, covering her face like a flimsy mask.

It's Sam who speaks first.

"So, we haven't stopped talking about you since you came last time. Can we — do you mind if we ask you some questions?" His voice is shaky and he glances at Kimberley who gives a faint nod.

"Yes, of course you can. But I don't know very much, not about — what happened. I've only just found out about it myself."

Sam shakes his head. "No, we know. But we just — we want to know more about you. You know. What your life's been like. What you're like. I want to know if we've got anything in common. I mean — I've never had a sister before, let alone a twin . . ." He stops, his voice catching in his throat, the torrent of words suddenly stuck. "Sorry. I didn't mean to go on."

"It's OK. You didn't. There — there's not really much to say, to be honest. I grew up with Mum and my sister, Kate." Her heart tightens at the mention of her sister. Despite everything, she misses her. "She's two and a half years older than me, and she was my only friend for a long time, growing up. I've got an Aunty Sandy too, but she's not really my aunty, she's just my mum's best friend who's always been there for me. For us. Mum —" She glances at Kimberley to see her reaction to her using this word, but her face is blank, her gaze fixed on a point just behind Georgie's head. She wonders whether she's even listening or whether she's drifted off to some other world, a world where she doesn't have to deal with meeting the daughter she thought she'd lost all those years ago. A world where she doesn't have to deal with anything. Georgie carries on anyway, aware of Sam's eyes on her. "Mum hated us going anywhere so it was mostly just me and Kate, growing up. We never really went anywhere or did anything. I still never have — it's why I was looking for my birth certificate in the first place, to get a passport.

286

I never met my dad, he died before I was born and I've only ever seen a few pictures of him. But I've got Matt now — we're not married but I met him at school and we've been together ever since, and we have Clementine. My daughter. She's eleven." She stops, aware that she hasn't talked for all that long, and yet she's covered most of her life already. It can't really have been that boring, can it?

She looks up at Sam to see him watching her, studying her face. They don't look alike, exactly, and yet there's something familiar about the angle of his head, the crook of his eyebrow, the slant of his mouth when he smiles. She wonders what he sees when he looks at her. She runs her hand through her hair self-consciously.

"So I have a niece as well?" A smile plays at the corners of Sam's mouth. Georgie nods. "Yes. Yes, you do. She's — well, she's lovely. But she doesn't know about any of this, not yet. I haven't been ready to tell her yet, but I want to, now I've found you."

Sam nods but says nothing.

"So, what about you? Do you have anyone? Do you work?" The questions sound stilted but she wants him to tell her all about himself.

Sam shakes his head. "No. It's just me. And Mum and Gran, of course." He smiles weakly. "I've never moved out and — well, girlfriends don't tend to like it when you live with your mum." His smile is sad now and he presses his hands together, his knuckles white. "I work at the petrol station down the road. Keeps me out of trouble." He takes a deep breath.

"It's been tough, though, to be honest. Mum — well, Mum never got over losing her baby. Losing you." He glances at Kimberley. Her lips are pulled into a tight line as though she's trying to hold in all her emotions, to stop them spilling out all over the table. But the pain is visible in her eyes and Georgie feels her heart contract. She can't believe her mum — Jan — inflicted so much damage on someone and yet seems to have shown so little remorse. She can hardly get her head round it.

"Mum won't mind me saying this but she's been depressed a lot. She — it's been just me and Gran, a lot of the time." He reaches out his hand and wraps it round Kimberley's small fist. "I know Mum loves me, but it's been like a little piece of her heart went missing that day, and she never found it again. Life has always had a shadow over it. And this —" he gestures at Georgie — "you coming here and, well, just *being*, has kind of thrown us." He rubs his hand over his face and breathes out heavily. "Who am I kidding? It's blown our family apart a little bit, to be honest."

"God, I'm so sorry. I never wanted —"

"It's not your fault. None of this is your fault. But it's not ours either, and our family has been the one that's suffered." He stops, glances at the wall. "I never knew my dad either — he buggered off before I was born — but, well, half the time I didn't have my mum either, because of everything. Because of what your mum did. And that's hard to get over. I don't think we ever will."

Georgie nods slowly. "I'm trying to understand what you've been through. I've felt lost, broken, really, since I found this out. It's only been just over a week and yet I feel as though I've lived a lifetime since then. I've tried to talk to Mum about it, but — well, I haven't got much from her yet."

Kimberley's head snaps up. "Why not? I think she's got quite a lot she needs to explain." Her voice is harder than Georgie's heard it until now and she wonders what lies beneath the quiet, expressionless exterior. Anger, heartache and — what else? Mental illness, she suspects. Georgie takes a deep breath. "It's complicated. Mum — she's not well. Over the last few weeks, no, months, really, she's been getting confused a lot, forgetting things, getting angry over nothing. We're waiting for an official diagnosis but it's very clearly Alzheimer's and we're really worried about her, so I just can't talk to her about it at the moment. At least, not if I want to get any answers. And apart from any of that, I can't face her. I don't know what to say to her. I feel as though my childhood has been stolen from me, and it's all because of what she did. And worse than any of this, I think I've lost my sister too. I think I've lost Kate." Her voice breaks on these last words and she stops, looks down at the tabletop.

"But I've found mine." Sam's voice is gentle and when she looks at him she sees a sad smile. "I can't help being pleased that your mother's suffering now. We've suffered for so long — my childhood was stolen from me before it even began because of what happened." He shrugs. "Sorry if that sounds harsh."

"No. I understand. I do." She fiddles with the strap of her bag and for a few moments it's the only sound that fills the silence. There's a clattering upstairs and floorboards creaking, and it's only then that Georgie realizes Margaret's not there.

Sam must see the question in her eyes before she says anything, because he looks at the door. "Gran wasn't sure if she could see you. But — well, she'll be OK. I think she'll come round. She's just — angry, and she couldn't trust herself to contain it. Not yet."

The clock on the cooker glows. It's not even 7.30, and yet Georgie feels as though she's been in this kitchen for a lifetime. She's not sure she can stay much longer, she's starting to feel a little ill. The walls feel as though they're closing in, the ceiling is coming down and Georgie's lungs are shrinking, until there's no air left in them and she tries to gulp down lungful after lungful but nothing happens. She plants her feet firmly on the floor but it's no good, the world is tilting and she grips the table and then slips forward and then she's falling, falling, falling . . .

Georgie opens her eyes and blinks quickly to block out the harsh strip light immediately above her. She's lying on her back on some cold tiles, and for a few seconds she has no idea where she is. Then a familiar face drifts into her vision and it all comes rushing back. She feels terror wash over her and she struggles to sit up.

"What happened?"

"Don't try and sit up too quickly." Sam is crouched next to her and has his hand on her arm. "You passed out. You're all right now."

290

Georgie puts her hand on her forehead. It feels clammy despite the chill in the air. "God, that's never happened before. I — I couldn't breathe."

"You had a panic attack. I have them all the time." Kimberley's on the other side of the room, standing with her back to the worktop. Her voice is blank, robotic, as though she's reciting the words. Once again Georgie wonders what she's taken, and how much.

She pulls herself up to her feet and stands awkwardly in the middle of the kitchen.

"I'm really sorry. I think I just — I think this is all a bit overwhelming." She pushes her bag back onto her shoulder and sniffs.

"Maybe we should call it a day, for now," Sam shrugs. "Maybe we could meet somewhere else next time, somewhere more — neutral. Sorry, I don't mean to make it sound like a battleground, but you know what I mean."

Georgie nods. "Yes, I think I should be going. Shall we — are you free tomorrow?" She looks from Sam to Kimberley expectantly, but Kimberley's staring out of the window into the featureless black night.

"Sorry about Mum, she's — well, she took something to steady her nerves, but it always makes her seem a bit vacant. Let's meet tomorrow." He glances at his mother again but she doesn't respond. "I'm sure she'll come too."

"OK. Do you — do you want to come to my house?"

Sam shakes his head. "No, I don't think I'm ready for that yet. Maybe somewhere away from everyone. There's a restaurant, a little Italian, Mario's, a mile or so that way." He points vaguely out of the window. "It's nothing special, but how about we meet there for lunch? It might be easier to have something to do while we talk." He smiles wanly and she smiles back. She loves the way he says what he means. She prefers to know where she stands.

"You're on." She holds her hand out and he takes it awkwardly then turns towards his mother. "Mum, Georgie's going now, do you want to say goodbye?"

Kimberley turns her head slowly to look at them, and frowns. "You're off already, are you?"

"Yes, sorry. I don't feel very well. I — I might see you tomorrow?"

She tilts her head and lifts her shoulders slightly. "Yes, maybe. Thanks for coming." Her eyes are blank, staring right through Georgie, her words stiff, detached, as though she's trying to keep a distance to protect herself.

Georgie's glad to find herself, a few minutes later, walking down the path and letting herself back into her car. She'd been looking forward to meeting them all properly, to finding out more about her mother, her brother and her grandmother. But she realizes now that it's not going to be as easy as she'd hoped. She's walked into a broken family — Sam seems OK, at least on the surface, but Kimberley is a woman on the edge, and Margaret is too angry even to look at her. She wonders whether she's made a mistake after all. Perhaps Kate was right. Perhaps she should have stayed well away.

But she couldn't have done. She couldn't have spent the rest of her life knowing there was a family out there that she belonged to and not even have tried to find them. It would have been like living a lie, a half-life, always wondering, always searching the faces of the people she passes and thinking *is that you?*

Before she pulls into the flow of traffic she glances back at the house one more time. Upstairs a curtain is pulled back, and standing there, watching her from one of the bedrooms, is Margaret. She doesn't flinch when she sees Georgie watching her back and they are still for a moment, frozen, looking at each other like a challenge. Then Georgie tears her eyes away and starts the car and drives off, feeling the older woman's gaze almost burning a hole in the back of her head.

She has a feeling Margaret is going to be a tough woman to get to know.

Georgie arrives at the restaurant early the following day and sits at a table for four, unsure who will be joining her, sipping a cool glass of water. Her eyes are trained on the door and every time it opens she jumps, her heart pounding, until she realizes it's not them. She's anxious and on edge and just wants someone to arrive, to get it over with.

She's thought a lot about how yesterday went, and she's determined that today will go better. She wants to find out more about this family, about the kind of people they are, what lies behind the tragedy that hit them all those years ago. And, she's not ashamed to admit, she wants them to like her too. Especially Sam.

She almost jumps out of her chair as the bell over the door jangles again and she looks up to see Sam walking towards her, his shoulders hunched. He's alone, she notes with disappointment. The waiter points him over to her and as he approaches she takes a moment to study him. He's wearing a beanie and a thick Puffa jacket, and his face is half buried inside the collar of his coat so that she can't really see his features. But she does see his eyes, and today he looks wary, unsure of himself. He sits down opposite her.

"Hi."

"Hello." She looks towards the door. "Is it just you, then?"

He pulls his hat off and tucks it into the pocket of his coat as he shrugs out of it. "No, Gran's coming in a bit." Georgie feels a shiver of apprehension at seeing the ferocious old woman again. "I talked to her last night, told her you just want to get to know us and she seems to have come round a bit. You'll have to excuse her, though, because she's spent the last thirty-seven years feeling angry. She's not going to be able to shake that off straight away."

"I know. I understand that, I do."

"Mum's not coming, though. Sorry. She's just — she's having one of her episodes. That's what Gran always calls them. She just goes into herself, doesn't want to talk, or see anyone. Not even me. I think it's the shock."

"Oh God, I'm so sorry, Sam. I didn't want to cause any trouble. I just — I didn't really have any choice. You understand that, don't you?"

He nods. "It's OK. There isn't any other way you could have done it, not really. It was always going to be a shock, whatever you did. I'd have done the same."

Georgie's grateful for the reassurance, even if it doesn't really allay the guilt. Sam continues. "Anyway, Mum will be OK. Give her a few days and she'll have pulled out of it and she'll want to talk to you, I'm sure of it. It's always the same."

Georgie nods, and folds her napkin in half and half again then smooths it down onto the table. She lifts her eyes to meet her brother's.

Her brother. She hasn't even said it out loud yet, and it still feels like a foreign word rolling around in her mind.

"So, what do we talk about today? To be honest, I don't even know where to start."

"I know what you mean. It feels as though there's so much to say that it's actually easier to say nothing, isn't it?"

Georgie nods. "Exactly. But listen, you said something, the first time we met, about how you sometimes wished I'd never been born."

"Oh, I'm sorry, Georgie, that sounds awful."

"No, it doesn't. I mean, it did, but I've thought about it since and of course you must have felt that way, sometimes. Anyone would. I mean, a missing child is going to take up a lot of emotional space compared to one who's always there, isn't it?"

Sam nods. "Yes, that's exactly it. It's just always felt as though, when Mum was with it, when she was being my mum, I mean, more than half of her was thinking about her missing daughter — about you — and there wasn't much of her left for me. As though she cared about me less, because I was there. And when she *wasn't* with it, when she was having one of her episodes, I might as well not have been there at all." He stops and traces his finger round the rim of his empty glass. "But I didn't mean what I said. Not really. I've spent most of my life wondering whether you were still alive and, if you were, whether we'd be alike. And now I've met you and — well, it's pretty fucking amazing, to be honest, Georgie. It just feels — right, being with you. Does that sound mad?"

Sam's face has flushed in the dim light of the restaurant.

"No, it doesn't sound mad at all." Georgie's voice is soft. "I feel exactly the same way."

For a moment they sit there, neither looking at the other, lost in their own thoughts. Then the moment is broken by a movement at Georgie's elbow. It's the waiter.

They order a bottle of house white and some bread. "I hope Gran will be here soon, I'm starving."

"Me too." Georgie lifts her gaze. "So, tell me about your dad. Our dad. What do you know about him?"

Sam's face hardens for a moment, and then the look is gone. But his voice has gone cold. "We don't talk about him. We never have. Mum refuses and Gran says he's not worth talking about."

"So you don't know anything about him at all, then?"

Sam shakes his head. "Only that it was a one-night-stand thing, and that when he found out she was pregnant he didn't want anything to do with her — with us. He was a right loser, Gran reckons, only seventeen; she says he did a runner because he was scared. But —" He stops, thinks for a moment. "It was weird, though. Because when my sister was snatched — when, you know, you were taken — apparently the police thought it was our father's sister who'd taken you. That's why they stopped looking for anyone else, at least for a while."

"Why did they think that?"

Sam shrugs. "I don't really know any details, just that they thought it was her. I think she was a bit older than him, and a bit crazy and — well, anyway, they never found anything and never proved anything and so I guess the case got dropped. Except for us, it never did. It was never-ending. Mum — well, I don't think she ever stopped believing she'd get you back one day, not really."

"And don't you ever think about trying to find him? Your dad, I mean."

"Find him? God no, never."

"Oh."

Sam's eyes flick up. "What do you mean, oh?"

Georgie's gaze meets his. "Nothing. I just —"

"What?"

"I just think I'd always want to know who my dad was. I mean —" she pauses, aware she's going into territory that Sam's very defensive about — "I never met my dad — the dad I thought was mine, I mean — but I'd have done anything to have known him, if I had the chance. But I didn't have that choice to make because — well, because he was dead before I was even born."

"What, and you think that because mine is alive, or at least as far as we know, that makes him worth knowing?" His voice is sneering, and Georgie wishes she could take it back, go back to the beginning and start again, explain herself better.

"Well, I suppose —"

"No. No way. I've never wanted to meet him, not at all. He wanted nothing to do with us, with me, and that's that. I've had Mum and Gran my whole life and that's all I need. All I've ever needed." He stops and his voice softens again, warmth coming back into his eyes. "Anyway, I've got you now too. I've got a *sister*. Why do I need him?"

Georgie can't help but think about Kate, and she feels a pang. She'd love her sister to be here now, talking to Sam, getting to know him. And she knows that, by pursuing this, by getting to know her other family, the one she's only just found out about, she's alienating the people she loves and who love her. Who have always loved her. But all she can do is hope that, one day, Kate will come round, that she'll understand why Georgie's doing this, and let her back in. She doesn't want to lose her because, even if they're not really sisters by blood, Kate will always be a big sister to her.

"Georgie? Are you OK? You've gone pale."

"Oh, sorry. I was just thinking about — about Kate."

"Your sister?"

Georgie nods.

"Is she not happy about this? About you meeting us?"

"No. No, she's not. She thinks I should have stayed well away and — well, never mind. But I think she'll be OK." She doesn't really have any idea whether Kate will come round, but she can only hope. "Anyway, let's talk about something else."

The wine arrives and Sam pours them both a large glass. Georgie takes a huge gulp then wipes her arm across her mouth. "God, I needed that." She laughs and Sam does the same, slamming the glass down onto the checked tablecloth. "Me too."

They both chuckle, relaxed at last.

"Room for an old woman here?" The raspy voice cuts through Georgie's thoughts and she looks up to find Margaret lowering herself slowly into the seat next to Sam.

"Hi, Gran." Sam leans over and plants a kiss on her cheek and she trains her gaze on Georgie.

"Sorry I'm late. Have I missed much?" She's slightly out of breath from her brief walk across the restaurant and she grabs the wine bottle and fills her glass and takes a large gulp.

"Gran, be careful." Sam looks at Georgie. "Gran doesn't drink much, she's not meant to, it interferes with her heart medication. *Doesn't it*, Gran?" She shoots him a look and he rolls his eyes. "Not that she takes any notice of me."

"I'm just having the one, Sam, don't fuss."

Sam looks back at the already half-empty glass on the table and gives a helpless shrug.

"You two carry on. I'll just sit here and listen."

But Margaret's arrival has thrown Georgie, and the ease with which the conversation was starting to flow disappears as quickly as it had developed. Georgie takes another sip of wine as well, to cover her awkwardness.

"We were just talking about — stuff," Sam says.

"What sort of stuff?"

"You know, family stuff. There's a lot to talk about."

"You're telling me." Margaret pulls a piece of bread from the basket and shoves it in her mouth. The few seconds of silence it affords gives Georgie the time to take a couple of deep breaths to compose herself. She refuses to be intimidated by this woman.

"We were talking about our fathers, actually." Georgie holds her head high and looks right at Margaret. "I was saying I wish I'd known mine, and I wondered whether Sam had ever thought of looking for his dad. After all, he is my dad as well, so I thought . . ." She trails off, the look on the old woman's face suddenly making her feel not so brave.

Margaret drops the piece of bread she was about to push into her mouth and puts her wine glass down with a bang.

"No, he hasn't. He never will either, will you, Sam?" Her voice is almost a hiss and, despite Sam's reaction earlier, Georgie is still surprised at the fury that rages in the old woman's eyes at the mention of their father. Margaret turns her gaze towards Georgie. "And you, young lady. You'd better not have any ideas of swanning in here and thinking it's OK to start looking for him either. It's one thing to meet you. It's put Kimberley right back to square one and I'm not too happy about that, but I can deal with it. But it's another thing entirely to come in here and to make things worse by threatening to start looking for that — that lowlife." She spits the word out, crumbs spraying across the table. "I never want to lay eyes on him again. Never." She drains her glass and pours the rest of the bottle in. Georgie is silent, watching her, and neither she nor Sam says anything as Margaret waves the waiter over and orders another bottle of wine.

For the rest of the meal the conversation is stilted. Georgie tries to be polite, but she's furious about the way Margaret spoke to her. There was no need for that. She just wants to find out more.

It's not until Margaret takes herself off to the toilet after the main course that they both relax.

"Georgie, I'm so sorry. Gran — she doesn't mean to be so — well, you know. Aggressive. She's just been through a lot — we all have, and she's very protective of us."

"I know. I just — I didn't deserve to be spoken to like that."

"No, you didn't, and I will talk to her later. But she never drinks and she's had quite a bit of wine already, so I don't think now is the time to call her out on it. In fact —" he glances at his watch — "I probably ought to be getting her home, let her sleep it off. Mum will kill me if she drinks any more."

"OK." Georgie pushes the leftover food round her plate. She's lost her appetite now anyway.

"I'll speak to her. She'll come round, I promise. But just give her time."

They stop as Margaret comes back to the table and the atmosphere darkens again.

Sam turns towards her. "I think we should get the bill and take you home."

"I don't need to go home. I'd like to stay a bit longer, get to know Georgie a bit better." Her words are a little slurred and Sam's face is furrowed in a frown.

"But you've had too much wine, Gran."

Georgie looks away, trying to seem as though she's not listening.

"I've only had a couple of glasses." She slugs back another mouthful. "Anyway, I thought we were here to talk. And that's what we're doing, talking."

Sam shrugs helplessly and slumps back in his chair. It's clear Margaret's not ready to go yet, and there's no way anyone is going to change her mind.

Georgie leans forward. "Let's order some pudding, then. And coffee?" She looks at Sam.

"Yes, coffee's a good idea."

Margaret rolls her eyes. "I don't want fucking coffee. This is meant to be a celebration, I mean — come on, it's been thirty-seven years since we last saw you, Louisa —"

"It's Georgie, Gran."

"Georgie, Louisa, all the same thing." She takes another gulp, waving her arm around dismissively. "Anyway, it's been a long bloody time, I'm not about to start pussyfooting around now. If we want to get to know each other, then let's get to know each other." She slams her glass down again and some wine splashes over the edge, spreading outwards across the white

302

tablecloth. Georgie glances at Sam. He looks mortified. But he says nothing, instead letting Margaret get out some of the things that have been stored up, waiting to erupt for so many years. Georgie feels a sense of dread creep over her, as though something terrible is about to happen. There's no way this can end well.

If Margaret won't go, then maybe she should. She goes to stand but Margaret's having none of it.

"Wait, wait, where are you going?"

"I just —" Georgie stops, sits down again.

"Come on, let's talk, then. There's so much to talk about. I mean, I bet he hasn't told you about Kim's depression, about how when she was really bad there'd be weeks on end when it was just me and Sam? About how she tried to kill herself once? About the years he spent crying himself to sleep?" She looks at Georgie and then at Sam. "No? Oh well, then there's *lots* to talk about." She drains her glass and refills it, sloshing it over the edge. "And you —" she jabs her finger towards Georgie — "you want to know why we don't talk about his father? Sorry, about *your* father? Well, he was a good-for-nothing waste of space, for one thing. Didn't want to know when Kimberley was pregnant, wanted to know even less when you were taken and Kim was grieving. Just stayed away and left us to cope alone. Probably for the best, really, looking back."

Margaret pauses, takes another mouthful of wine, and for a moment Georgie wonders whether she's going to carry on speaking or whether she's run out of steam. But then she starts again, still as angry. In fact, angrier, her voice now a low hiss.

"And as for that bloody *mother* of yours. Don't know how she's got the gall to call herself that, stupid bloody bitch. I mean, it's bad enough taking someone else's baby, but to *keep* her, bring her up as her own, and never give a *damn* what pain she was causing someone else. Good God —" The words are like bullets now, hitting the tablecloth and bouncing back to hit Georgie right in the heart. "I've been thinking. She deserves to be properly punished for what she did."

"What? Gran, what do you mean?"

Margaret's head swivels towards her grandson, her eyes like slits, before she shifts her gaze to Georgie.

"I'm *saying*, dear, that I'm going to tell the police."

Georgie gasps.

"But Gran! We agreed. You said you wouldn't do this."

Her head swivels back to Sam and she sways a little, almost falling off her chair. "I did, didn't I? But now I've changed my mind. Why should this, this *woman* —" she jerks her hand wildly, almost knocking a wine glass over — "get away with this, with destroying a whole family?" She shakes her head. "No. Something needs to be done." Her words are slurred, and her eyelids are drooping, tired; it's clear she's had far too much to drink. But Georgie can't ignore what the old woman's just said, her words like a juggernaut setting out to destroy.

"Sam? Will she really go to the police?" Georgie's voice is a whisper as Margaret fusses about in her handbag.

Sam shakes his head. "I don't know. I don't think so." He stands and shrugs his coat onto his shoulders. "But I need to get her home now, let her sleep this off. Mum's going to kill me for letting her drink too much anyway." He bends down and helps Margaret to her feet. "Come on, Gran. Let's go."

He turns back to Georgie. "I'm sorry, Georgie. This wasn't how this was meant to go. I'll sort it out, I promise." He throws some notes down on the table, then tugs Margaret by the arm. Georgie watches as the pair of them walk unsteadily across the restaurant towards the door. As it opens and the cold air blasts through, Sam turns back to Georgie and gives a little wave. Georgie raises her hand in reply and realizes it's shaking. And then the door closes behind them and they're gone, leaving Georgie sitting there, alone.

CHAPTER
FIFTEEN

9–10 November 2016

Georgie's head hurts and she squints against the light creeping through a gap in the curtains. She closes her eyes again and rolls over to look at the clock on the bedside table: 8.40. She's slept for hours.

As she sits up, a wave of nausea washes over her and she winces, remembering the wine she drank when she got home last night, and the conversations that had led up to it.

She takes a sip of water and props her head against the pillow, trying to piece together what happened, and where it leaves her now.

First was Margaret's threat to go to the police. She doesn't know yet whether she means it, but if she does, where does that leave them? This wasn't something Georgie had considered when she'd started her search, and now it had all gone wrong, threatening to tear her family apart even more. How can she stop her?

And then there's their father. She listened to what Margaret had to say, but she still can't understand why nobody seems to want to find him. It still feels as though he's the missing piece of the jigsaw.

She rubs her throbbing head and sighs. Maybe Margaret's right. Maybe they are better off without him. Perhaps she should listen. After all, her meddling has done more than enough damage already.

Next to her, her phone beeps, and she jumps. Snatching it up, she squints to read the message.

We need to talk. K

Just that, nothing else. We need to talk. But the wave of relief that washes over Georgie is so immense it threatens to topple her out of bed. Kate's the person she's gone to her whole life whenever she needed comfort, or advice, or just someone to talk to. Not having her there has been agony. But now here she is, holding out a — curt, but to the point — olive branch.

Georgie starts to type a reply.

Yes we do. Are you free today? G x

She puts her phone back on the side and waits.

She can't stop thinking about what she's found out so far about her new family. About Kimberley's fragile mental health, no doubt made worse by losing her child, Margaret's anger, and her determination to go to the police. And she can't stop thinking about Sam, her twin brother. Just being with him, talking to him, feels so right, and yet it feels like a betrayal of Kate even to think that. She needs to talk to her sister. She needs her help. She hopes she replies soon.

She turns her head to Matt's side of the bed. It's empty, but she can hear someone pottering around downstairs. She swings her legs out of bed and shuffles her body into an upright position, her head lurching as she does. She sits for a minute to quell the nausea, then

307

stands and walks towards the stairs. She can hear Matt in the kitchen, whistling along to the radio, and she smiles. At least some things never change.

She walks down the stairs and into the kitchen where Matt's stirring something over the hob and she peers into the pan to see scrambled eggs.

"Yum, enough for me?"

He plants a kiss on the top of her head. "Plenty. How's the head?"

"Ugh, terrible." She smiles up at him. "Sorry about that, it was a — bit of a tough day."

"I guessed that." He grins, lifting the empty bottle to show her. "I assumed you needed this for medicinal purposes."

"Yes, exactly that." She smiles, pulling her dressing gown tighter round her.

"Were you drunk last night, then, Mum?" Clem's peering at her over the top of her book, amusement dancing in her eyes.

"Well, a bit. Did you see me?"

"No, I was late back, went to Lucy's. Dad picked me up about nine. You were snoring your head off when I got home. Thought it was a bit weird."

"Yes, sorry. There's been — there's a lot going on at the moment." She's wondering how much to tell Clem but her daughter has already lost interest and turned back to her book, her mind occupied with other things. She'll leave it for another day. Georgie turns back to Matt, who's spooning an enormous pile of eggs into a bowl.

"Made enough?"

"Hmm, there is rather a lot, isn't there?"

"Don't worry, I'm starving."

They sit down at the table to eat and Georgie's grateful for the normality. The last few days have been so emotionally draining she needs this moment of peace, this oasis of calm, to get her mind back to a good place again. A place where she can prepare herself to go and speak to her mother, and to Kate, and to tell them everything she's discovered. She wonders how much else there is to find out, then pushes the thought away, for now.

Matt doesn't ask her any questions while Clementine is still there, and Georgie's grateful for that too. But when Clem disappears upstairs for a shower she knows she has to tell him what's happened so far. And as the words come out of her mouth, as she paints a picture for Matt, untangling the twists and turns and the shocking revelations of the past, she can't quite believe all this has happened to her, or to her — until now — perfectly normal family. When she finishes she turns to look at him and sees him watching her over the top of his coffee cup, his eyes serious.

He lowers his cup to the table and leans forward, running his hand through his hair.

"Fuck, George."

"I know."

"I mean — your *mum*. I just can't quite put it all together. It doesn't make sense. How could someone so — so *quiet* have done something like that?"

Georgie shrugs. "That's what I want to find out. I mean, I know I've been really angry with her. But now

I just think, what must have happened to make her do something like this? Did she plan to take me from Kimberley? Or was it a spur-of-the-moment thing, something she did while her heart was breaking after Dad died?" She hesitates, lost in thought. "It doesn't matter how angry I am with her, I still think I know her pretty well, and I just can't imagine she would ever plan something like this. Can you?"

Matt shakes his head. He's known Jan for a long time and he simply can't imagine a woman as quiet and overprotective as she's always been walking into a hospital and taking someone else's baby. Something serious must have happened.

"You've got to speak to her."

"For all the good it will do. You should have seen her the other day, Matt. She was like a woman possessed. But you're right, I do need to at least try. But I'm going to talk to Kate first. I think we need to sort things out."

Before all this, Georgie had never been worried about speaking to her sister. Ever. In fact, if anything, she'd always been the first and often the only person she wanted to speak to when something went wrong.

But earlier, as she pulled up outside the familiar house and walked up the path, her whole body was shaking and her heart felt as though it was going to thump right out of her chest. Not only because of what she was about to tell Kate, but because they hadn't spoken since she walked out on her and their mother nearly two weeks before.

Here she is now, and her body is quaking as she tells Kate exactly what she's found out since she saw her last. As the sisters sit there on separate sofas, the silence grows so large it threatens to get bigger than the room, to shatter the ornaments that have been carefully dusted and placed on the shelves.

"I am Louisa Foster," she says, simply, breaking the silence. "I walked into that house and I knew the second I saw Kimberley that she was my mother. And she knew me too. She went white as a sheet. I thought she was going to faint."

Kate stares at the coffee table, running her nail along the outside edge of the wood. She doesn't look up.

"And your brother?" The word comes out slightly choked, as though it's got stuck halfway out. "What was he like?"

"He was — lovely."

Kate looks up now, sharply. "But is he like you? Does he look like you?"

Georgie knows Kate doesn't want to hear the truth, not really, but she can't lie any more. She nods her head. "Not exactly, but — yes, there's something about him that looks like me. He's — we're definitely related."

Kate nods briefly, and looks back down at the coffee table. Georgie's heart hammers against her ribcage.

"It's a mess, Kate."

"You're telling me."

"No, it's worse."

Kate's head snaps up, her forehead creased, waiting. "Worse?"

Georgie swallows. She's been dreading this bit, worried how her sister is going to react when she tells her. "The thing is —" She stops, unsure how to carry on. "The thing is, Kimberley's screwed up. Badly. She's clearly on something most of the time, which makes her seem calm, a bit zombie-like, but it's obvious she's a bag of nerves. But then there's her mother. Margaret." She pauses, looks at Kate. "She's angry, Kate."

"Well, I guess she would be. Anyone would be." Her voice is like glass as she contemplates this woman she's never met.

"She wants to go to the police."

Kate doesn't speak straight away, and Georgie doesn't know what to do with the silence. She'd thought Kate was going to explode, shout and cry and scream, rail against this terrible new development. But instead she sits there, still as a statue, her face a mask, staring at a spot on the wall just behind Georgie's shoulder, until Georgie starts to wonder whether her sister has even heard her. When she does say something, her words are quiet, deadly.

"Aunty Sandy does too."

"Aunty Sandy does what?"

"She wants to tell the police too."

"What? Why?" Georgie's not entirely sure she's heard right.

Kate shakes her head sadly. "She's hurt, George. But she's also furious at the way Mum spoke to her last time she saw her, at the way she's been treating her for the last few months, to be honest. I know she's always been on Mum's side, no matter what, but this time

Mum's gone too far, and Sandy's flipped. Something about what Mum was doing in the garden the other day, that digging, and the swearing at her, calling her a bitch. She says she's had enough of covering for her, of lying for her, and that it's time."

"Time?"

"For her to pay. Her words, not mine."

"God."

"I know."

Something occurs to Georgie then. "So you knew? Before I came here today, that what I told you last time was true? That Mum snatched me?"

Kate nods. "I knew from the minute you showed me that newspaper cutting. I just didn't want to admit it to myself. Because —" She stops, clears her throat. "Well, that would mean you weren't my sister any more and I don't think I could stand that. Losing you."

The sisters sit in silence for a moment, the tick of the clock on the mantelpiece the only sound. Finally, Georgie speaks.

"You'll always be my sister." She looks at Kate. There are tears running down her face and in one swift movement Georgie moves across from the sofa she's sitting on to join Kate on hers, and wraps her arms round her, squeezing her tightly.

"Thank you, Georgie."

Slowly, Kate pulls away from the embrace. "So what are we going to do, then? About these two women who want Mum to pay for what she did? Mum can't go to prison. She's ill."

Georgie nods. "I know. And to be honest, even if they do tell the police, I can't imagine they'd send Mum to prison, not now."

"But what if they do?"

"Oh God, I don't know, Kate." She runs her hands through her hair and clasps them together, her knuckles white. "We've got to stop them, haven't we?"

Kate nods. "The thing is, Aunty Sandy told me something. Something that changes everything."

"Oh?"

Kate nods, thinking back to the day after Sandy had stormed out of her mother's house, when she'd gone to see her to try and put things right. Sandy had still been angry, but now there was hurt in her eyes too. She looked broken apart, scared.

"The thing is, Kate, I've covered for your mother for too long now," Sandy had said. There was a wobble in her voice that Kate had never heard before, an uncertainty her Aunty Sandy had never shown, and it scared her. "I think your mother always thought I had my suspicions about what had happened back then, but she never knew for sure what I knew." She'd paused, pacing back and forth across her tiny living room. "But when Georgie found those papers, and then I saw your mum scrabbling at that patch of earth in her garden, it brought it all flooding back, and I realized I couldn't lie for her any more. It was wrong. Too many people have suffered."

"But what do you know, Sandy?"

Sandy had looked at her as though she didn't recognize her, this woman she'd known since the moment she was born. "I saw her."

314

Kate didn't ask what she meant, who she'd seen. Instead she waited for Sandy to carry on. She needed to know what had happened all those years ago, what had happened that had made Sandy turn against her closest friend all these years later, and so she waited for her to tell her story. She didn't have to wait long.

"Your Mum lost a baby, the day before she took Georgie. And I saw her, that day. Only she doesn't have any idea I saw her." She ran her hand through her short hair and down her face, pulling her mouth into a grimace as she did. "I'd come round to check on her, to make sure she was OK, because she'd been ignoring me since she'd moved down here and she couldn't afford a phone, not in those days. But I was worried about her, and so I drove round to see her. It was quite late when I got there, after your bedtime, so I was surprised when I rang the bell that nobody answered the door. I thought she might be in the bath or putting you to bed or something. I peered through the front window and I saw the lights on, and toys scattered across the living room. I didn't think your mum could have gone far so I decided I'd try the back door, as she usually kept it unlocked, and wait for her to come downstairs. So I — I walked round to the back of the house and as I got near to the garden I could hear crying. I called out but Jan — your mum — didn't hear me. I walked closer. It was pretty dark, but then I saw your mum, bent over at the end of the garden, by the shed — where she was the other day — digging at the ground with her bare hands. She was like a crazy woman, soil flying out behind her and falling in her hair, her arms covered in mud. She was in her nightdress and I wondered what on earth she was doing. She hadn't heard me approach and I didn't want to scare her, so I stopped and waited until she'd finished. I hadn't planned to spy on her. I'd always meant to let her know I was there, make sure she was OK. But as I continued watching, my concern turned to horror and I found I couldn't speak. She scooped up a bundle of blankets, soaked in blood. And then she tipped the contents into the hole in the ground, and covered it up, sobbing wildly. I wanted to reach out and hold her, but I was too shocked, too horrified to move. And when she turned round and headed back to the house, the look on her face terrified me. She looked broken, possessed. And I knew in that instant what had happened here. The worst thing anyone could imagine. She'd lost her baby, and in a moment of madness had buried it in the garden."

She stopped, took a breath. "I'm not proud of myself for leaving then, rather than going to comfort her. But I was so horrified by what I'd seen, I turned and walked away. I got in the car and drove numbly home, without even letting her know I was there.

"It haunted me for months afterwards, years even, what I'd seen that night. But back then when I finally brought myself to go and see her a few days later, to ask if she needed anything, give her the chance to tell me what had happened, I got a shock. She had a baby there. She had Georgie, and she was acting as though it was perfectly normal. She was telling me this baby — this dark-haired, olive-skinned baby — was hers, even

316

though she looked nothing like her, or you. She didn't even look like Ray, your dad. But as I peered into the cot and studied Georgie's face, it all fell into place. After all, everyone had been following the terrible story about the baby who'd been snatched from her cot at Norwich hospital. It was all over the news for days, weeks. And I knew in that instant what had happened — that it was your mum who had taken that baby. I also vowed I'd do anything to protect her from being found out. Whatever I thought of what she'd done, she was my best friend, and I couldn't let her lose the love of her life *and* her children. And so I lied. Well, I omitted the truth, which is the same thing. I went along with her lie and now I know that it allowed her to believe that what she had done wasn't such a terrible thing. It helped her justify it to herself, to the world."

The room was filled with an oppressive silence as the words sank in. Kate had thought she was going to be sick. So that place where her mother was digging the other day was her baby's grave? It was almost impossible to believe.

"So why have you changed your mind now, after all these years?"

"I — I couldn't believe it when Georgie came round the other day asking your mum why she didn't have her birth certificate, and what those newspaper cuttings meant. After all this time I thought it was all over and done with. That it was far in the past and that nobody was hurt, so it need never be mentioned again. But then it made me realize that of course people had been hurt, and were still hurting. And now — well, now

Georgie has found them, it's more real, isn't it? It made me think about what I'd done, how I'd been complicit in these people's pain. And I hated myself for it. But the final straw came when your mum started digging at the ground the other day and then screamed at me, accusing me of all sorts.

"It hurt, Kate. And it made me realize I can't do this any more. We have to tell someone. We have to go to the police. That poor family deserves that, at least."

Kate takes a deep breath now, having finished telling Georgie Sandy's story. She can see that Georgie's face is so pale it's almost translucent. "She buried her *baby? That's* what's buried in that patch of earth, the bit where she was scrabbling around in the dirt? My God, she must have been utterly heart-broken."

"I know."

Georgie frowns. "We —" She stops, unsure whether to say the next words. "We have to go and see if we can uncover the remains, don't we? Give the baby the goodbye it deserves?"

Kate nods stiffly. "I suppose we do. Soon." She shudders, wanting to get the image of it out of her mind. "Poor, poor Mum. I can almost understand why she did it now — why she took you, I mean. Can't you?"

Georgie nods. "Almost."

"Except —"

"Except what?"

"Well, she had me. Wasn't I enough for her? Wasn't I enough to get her through?" Kate's eyes are heavy with pain and she blinks as if trying to wipe it away.

318

"Oh, Kate, I don't suppose it had anything to do with you. I think Aunty Sandy was right. I think Mum was probably drowning in grief, almost swallowed up by it, after losing Dad and then her baby. I mean, she buried the baby in the garden, for goodness' sake, somewhere where she'd have to see it every day and remember what had happened, what she'd done. Someone who was coping, who was in their right mind — well, they wouldn't behave like that, would they, no matter how grief-stricken they were? And it makes sense, doesn't it? It explains so much, about the way she was. About how scared she was of us ever going out of her sight. If she could take a baby and get away with it, then what was to stop someone else taking her babies away? And let's face it, if she'd been caught, that's exactly what would have happened."

Kate nods, slowly, as though processing the ideas. "So where does this leave us? What do we do now?"

Georgie shakes her head. Kate's usually the practical one, the one who has all the answers, and the fact that she's so lost, so unsure of herself right now, makes Georgie feel worse.

"Well, Sam's going to talk to his gran, see if he can convince her not to go to the police. So we need to do the same with Aunty Sandy."

"And we need to speak to Mum, don't we?"

Georgie nods. "We do. But I'm worried that —"

"We're too late?"

Georgie nods, suddenly very aware that she's left her sister alone to cope with this for far too long. "Yes. I'm so sorry, Kate. I'm sorry for leaving you to deal with all

319

this. I — I've just had so much to deal with too. How — how is Mum? I haven't even asked what the doctor said the other day." She doesn't add "when I left you alone", but the words are there, hanging in the air between them.

Kate hesitates for a moment as though trying to slot together the words she needs in the right order.

"She's not well, Georgie. We were right, she has got early-onset Alzheimer's." Three little words that change everything for everyone involved.

"So what does it mean?"

Kate twirls her rings round on her finger, the diamond catching the light on every spin. "It means we'll have to look after her, and when we can't look after her any more, she'll have to go into a home." She takes a deep breath which catches in her throat. "It means that the confusion she's been suffering from, the anger, the living in the past — it's only going to get worse."

"It means she's not going to be able to tell us much, doesn't it?"

Kate nods. "Exactly. Which is precisely why we can't let this get out. We can't put her through any trauma, she'll never cope. But more than that, it would be completely pointless, because it's too late for her to pay for it now. It's too late."

"Oh Kate." Georgie wraps her arms tightly round her sister, feeling the warm softness of her skin next to hers. And slowly, she can feel Kate start to relax, the tension slipping from her body, as she responds to her sister's hug. They stay like that for a short while, locked in the moment, until Georgie pulls away.

"You know what else this means, though, don't you?" Kate shakes her head.

"It means we're still sisters. We always will be, whatever happens. Nobody will ever take that away from us."

"I never doubted it." Kate looks at Georgie. "I want to meet him, George."

The words are so quiet Georgie's not sure she's heard them right, and she leans closer. "What did you say?"

"I want to meet him. I want to meet Sam. Do you think he'll want to meet me?"

"Of course he will, Kate. And he'll love you." The truth is, Georgie has no idea whether Sam is in the right frame of mind to meet Kate yet. But she's certain she can convince him, ask him to come, and she's thrilled Kate wants to meet him.

"I just think it would be good to get to know him. See what a male version of you is like, for a start." Kate smiles weakly.

Georgie nods. "I'll speak to him. I promise."

"Thank you. And I'll speak to Aunty Sandy, OK? Try and change her mind."

"Thank you, Kate."

"Don't thank me. We're in this together. Always have been, always will be. Nobody can ever change that. Right?"

"Right." Georgie turns her head to look at the blurry image of the street outside through the voile blind to hide the tears that have escaped down her cheeks. She knows she's never going to risk losing her family again.

CHAPTER
SIXTEEN

January 2017

There's a room full of people who don't know each other; some Georgie hardly even knows herself yet. And yet they are all her family. And they are all together, here, now.

She sits on one end of her sofa and looks round the room. The silence is almost oppressive yet she doesn't know how to break it. She can feel her shoulders hunching and her hands clenching and unclenching in her lap. She's desperate for this to work, for everyone to get on, to make today count so they can all move on. And sometimes, high expectations can lead to bitter disappointment. She of all people knows that.

She looks over at Kate. She's sitting on the sofa opposite, the one that was once cream but now is so discoloured it's covered by a large dark-red throw. She's sitting right back in her seat, her knee-length skirt hitched up on her thighs, exposing creamy flesh. Every now and then she tugs at the bottom of her skirt but it makes no difference. Her knees are together, her hands on her thighs. She looks drawn, her expression blank, and she isn't meeting anyone's eyes, not even Georgie's; instead her gaze is trained studiously on the edge of the rug where it curls up slightly. Next to her Joe's perched on the arm of the sofa. His hand is pressed on top of hers and every now and then he looks down at her lovingly, but she doesn't notice. She's too afraid to look up.

Georgie flicks her eyes across the room to where Sam is sitting, stiffly, on a straight-backed chair that's been hurriedly dragged over from the dining table. Georgie's trying not to stare but it's hard. She just wants to study his face, to make its contours and lines as familiar to her as if she's known them her entire life.

He's her brother. No, her *twin*. She can't believe she has a twin. It makes her shiver every time she thinks about it.

She's worried Kate will think that it means she's less important to her than Sam, as she's not her twin; they're not really related at all, not by blood. But she hopes that Kate understands that love is about more than blood, and that nothing can ever take away what they have between them. She vows to spend the rest of her life making sure she does, anyway.

She's so pleased they're both here, but so scared about how they're going to get on. Or not.

Sam's fiddling with the spikes in his hair, absent-mindedly pushing them back into place. His left foot is hitched up onto his right knee and he's leaning forward, resting his chin on his hand thoughtfully. He looks up and catches Georgie's eye and when he sees her looking he smiles tightly. Then his eyes slide over to his mother, Kimberley, who's sitting next to him on another hard wooden chair.

Kimberley's grey hair is loose today, softening the hard lines of her face. She looks thinner than she did before, her cheekbones sharp in the cold winter light that pours through the window. She's smiling gently as though she's thinking of some happier time, but her eyes are empty, searching. Every now and then she rubs her head, or scratches her arm, a nervous action that she's not even aware of. She doesn't notice Sam glancing at her every now and then to make sure she's OK. She doesn't really seem to notice anything at all.

Matt and Clementine are sitting next to Georgie, Matt's hand resting gently on Clem's knee. Georgie watches her daughter as she looks crossly round the room, as though she's expecting someone to say something ridiculous at any moment. She probably wishes she was anywhere but here, but Georgie's glad she came. She's glad she's a part of this.

Everyone seems to be waiting for someone else to speak first. The room practically crackles under the strain of anticipation.

Georgie can't stand it any more.

"Tea?" She leans forward and picks up the pot and looks round. There are some nods so she methodically pours tea into the cups arranged haphazardly on the coffee table in front of her. She slops milk into each one and passes them round. The ripples on the top of the cups give away how much her hands are shaking, and she's relieved when everyone has taken one and she can hold her own cup with both hands, warming her freezing fingers. The steam rises up and swims in front of her face until she can almost believe she's in the room by herself.

Sam leans forward and scoops a spoonful of sugar into his cup and the sound of the spoon tinkling against the cup as he stirs is almost deafening in the quiet room. A car drives slowly past outside and disappears up the road, and then the room is totally silent again apart from the gentle sound of seven people breathing.

There are, of course, two people quite obviously missing from this little gathering. One is Jan.

They'd all agreed — well, Kate and Georgie had agreed — that Jan just wasn't well enough to be here today: she's sunk too deeply into her Alzheimer's to help answer any questions, and her presence would only upset everyone, herself included. But there's more to it than that. Having their mother here would have made it too difficult for Kimberley, who's still fragile after everything that's happened. Sam's relieved too, as it means he doesn't have to face her either. He's still too angry, too shocked by it all.

The other missing person is Margaret, and she's not here simply because she's too angry. She doesn't want to meet Georgie's family; she's made it perfectly clear that she doesn't want anything to do with them. Sam admitted it had taken all his skills of persuasion to stop her from going to the police. She was adamant she wanted Jan to pay for what she'd done, for the pain she'd put them through. Georgie can't blame her, she understands why. But she's relieved that, now Kate has talked Sandy out of it too, the threat of the police has passed, for now, at least.

"Mum's been punished enough, don't you think?" Kate had said to Sandy. And, once Sandy had calmed down, she'd agreed. She'd almost lost her best friend. She didn't want to lose her in disgrace.

And so there are seven people here. Seven people who don't know what to say to one another, and so they say nothing at all.

Georgie knows she has to be the first to speak. After all, she's the one who invited them all here. Yet the slightly scruffy living room of her home feels so unfamiliar right at this moment that she's not sure how to behave.

She clears her throat. It's dry and scratchy and she's not sure whether anything will come out at all. "So." She coughs again, giving the words space. "Thank you for coming here today. I know it's going to be hard but I'm very happy you've all agreed to meet each other." She glances at Matt, who nods his head and smiles encouragingly. Kate's looking down at her hands. "I just — I hope we can all make it work, somehow."

Sam must notice how uncomfortable Georgie is in the silence that follows, and steps up to help out. "I'm sure we can." He casts a glance at his mother. Her leg bounces up and down nervously. She turns to meet her son's gaze and, for the first time since they met, Georgie sees the smile on her lips reach her eyes.

Someone coughs and a car alarm goes off somewhere in the street outside.

"Oh, I think that might be mine." Sam jumps to his feet, glad to have something to do for a few minutes. He peers out of the window and clicks the fob on his key ring and the ringing sound stops instantly. The silence sounds louder for the interruption, somehow.

Sam stays standing and turns to look down at them all with interest. He's used to his mother being slightly absent, the drugs taking away part of her personality and never quite returning it fully once they've done their job, so that a little bit of her slips away week by week, month by month, year by year. But the others he barely knows, and it's hard for any of them to know where to start. How must it feel, Georgie wonders, having been an only child in a troubled family all his life, to now have a sister whom he doesn't know at all, plus her sister, who wants to get to know him as well?

It must seem almost unbelievable. And yet it's true.

He notices Georgie looking at him and smiles. Then, unexpectedly, he walks across to the seat next to Kate and sits awkwardly, smiling at her, and then at Joe. Georgie wonders for a moment what he's going to say, but then he holds his hand out stiffly and says, "Hello, I'm Sam."

She watches, breath held, as Kate hesitates for just a moment. Then she takes his hand in hers and shakes it firmly. Joe does the same.

"Hello, Sam. It's lovely to meet you. I'm Kate, Georgie's sister." Relief floods through Georgie's body. This is a start. This is good.

Kate and Sam study each other for a moment, Kate searching Sam's face for familiar features. It's clear to Georgie that Sam has the same arch of the eyebrow, the same curl of the lip, the same flush of the cheek and flick of the hair as her, and yet she has no idea whether

Kate can see it too. Sam seems to be studying Kate just as closely, as though trying to read her mind.

There's so much for them both to take in.

It was never going to be easy, getting everyone together like this, and so far it's been as tense as everyone expected. But Sam's bold move, under the scrutiny of everyone else, has shifted the atmosphere; it's as though a bath plug has been removed, allowing all the tension to seep slowly away and leaving just an overwhelming desire to get to know each other. Georgie wants to hug him but instead she just watches as her brother — she loves saying that — and sister talk to each other. Their gazes hardly leave each other, their faces are animated.

Georgie feels a pang as she watches them, as their initial awkwardness slips slowly into an ease she hadn't expected. She's got to know Sam pretty well over the last few weeks, and she and Kate have slowly come back together again, repairing the rift that was caused by Georgie wanting to find her real family. She's so happy that Sam and Kate both seem to want to get to know each other, after everything they've found out.

Georgie stands and walks across to the chair next to Kimberley that Sam has just vacated and sits down, crossing her left leg over her right knee and turning to her. Kimberley hasn't looked round and Georgie gently places her hand on her leg. Kimberley turns and her eyes meet her daughter's. Georgie wishes she could see behind those dark eyes, inside her head, see what she's thinking, how she's feeling. She wishes she could mend all the hurt.

But no one can.

So all she can do, for now, is talk to her, get to know her and try to let her know how sorry she is for everything that's happened.

And, as they chat, and Georgie is surrounded by the gentle hum of voices, voices that are trying to find a future, she feels an unexpected sense of warmth settle over her.

They all still have a very long way to go to mend all their broken bridges, but now she's sure that, one day, they'll get there.

Part Four

Kimberley

CHAPTER
SEVENTEEN

1979–present

I saw him the second I got on the bus, and sat directly opposite him. The dark-haired man in the denim jacket was the most gorgeous man I'd ever clapped eyes on and, even though it was totally out of character for me, I knew I had to talk to him. I leaned forward, letting my hair fall over my shoulder, which was bare except for a slim strap.

"Hello, I'm Kim." I smiled and tried to look sexy. I didn't think it had worked, though, because he gave me a funny look and then shook his head.

But then he spoke. "Hello, Kim. I'm Ray. Nice to meet you." He stuck out his hand and I shook it. It probably sounds corny, but it felt like lightning had struck when I touched his skin, and I pulled my hand away quickly. He didn't seem to notice and I sat on my hand and tried to look normal again, even though I couldn't really breathe properly. I blinked a couple of times. I was aiming for sexy lash-fluttering but I think I came across as more rabbit in the headlights, because the next thing he said was, "So, why are you here on this bus instead of at school?"

My cheeks felt hot. I was starting to lose my nerve. I couldn't really chat someone up if he thought I was only a silly little schoolgirl, could I?

"I don't go to school. I'm sixteen." I was only fifteen, actually, but I didn't want him to know that, so I stuck my chest out defiantly and hoped it made me look older, in spite of the high pitch of my voice.

He smiled a crooked smile. "Oh right. Sorry. So, what *do* you do then?"

I tucked my hair behind my ear. "Well, nothing, at the minute. I'm looking for a job, though." I tipped my head towards the bus window as if the job was just outside. "Got an interview today, typing." I shrugged, trying to look like I didn't care either way, but the truth was I really wanted this job. I was still living at home with my mum and although we got on OK she was pretty controlling. I'd left school earlier that summer with a couple of O levels, but nothing to write home about. This typing job would help me save up and get a place of my own. At least, that was the plan.

"Wow. Good luck."

"Thanks."

I looked out of the bus window at the red-brick buildings creeping slowly by. I wasn't great at talking to strangers, it made me feel awkward. But there was something about this dark, handsome stranger that had made me want to strike up a conversation, so I had to think of something else to say, to keep him talking. Something funny, something irresistible, so he'd never be able to forget me.

"Are you going to work, then?"

Brilliant, Kim, really original. I felt my face flame again.

"Yeah. It's just in the sweet factory, nothing special." He flicked his eyes over my face and I felt my skin shiver with delight. "I play in a band as well, though. You know, in pubs and that. You should come and see us play some time."

"I'd love to." It came out as a squeal and I coughed to get my voice back under control. "That would be really nice." I didn't say, "if mum will let me." That would *not* have been cool.

Ray nodded, studying me closely. I met his eye defiantly. "OK, well, we'll be at the Crown on Saturday, you know, the pub in town?"

I nodded, although I had no idea where it was, as my heart fluttered around in my chest like an out-of-control wasp. Suddenly Ray lurched towards me as the bus came to a halt, and his face was inches from mine. He pulled back immediately, looking awkward, but I'd caught a sniff of his warm, musky smell, and I breathed it in deeply, trying to keep the memory of his scent in my mind.

"Right, this is my stop." He stood, towering above me, his dark eyes boring into my skin. Then he turned and left without glancing back, and strode off down the street. And as I watched him disappear round the corner and into the gates of the factory, I smiled. I knew, without a doubt, that I'd get to that pub on Saturday night, whatever it took.

The music was loud as I walked through the doors of the Crown with my friend Angie. I lifted my head and tried to look as though I was used to being in places like this, and hoped the make-up I'd applied at the bus stop was enough to make me look at least eighteen.

We made our way to the bar and ordered a vodka and orange each. The barman didn't even give us a second glance as he poured the drinks, and I gripped my glass tightly and took a big gulp to hide my shaking hands.

"Is that him?" Angie pointed at the stage and I turned and looked and there he was. Ray. He was standing under a spotlight and the muscles of his arms looked taut and lean as he strummed his guitar. His skin glistened with a light layer of sweat and his face was deep in concentration.

"Yes. Yes, that's him." I stood, transfixed, and watched him for a few moments. Then the song came to an end and I joined in with the applause as he said his thank yous and made his way from the stage towards the bar. And then he was there, right in front of me, and I stood frozen to the spot.

"You came!" He looked genuinely pleased to see me and I felt myself go hot all over underneath the too-high collar of my shirt. I rubbed my hand over my neck.

"I did." We stood and looked at each other for a moment, then he looked away and turned towards Angie. "And who is this?"

"Oh, sorry. This — er, this is Angie. My friend."

"Nice to meet you, Angie," he said, and flashed her a smile as warm as the sun. She grinned back.

"So, would you like a drink?"

"No, we've got one. Thank you."

We waited while he bought himself a beer and a glass of something brown, it looked like whisky. He tipped his head back and drank it down in one, wiped his hand across his mouth and then took a sip of his pint. "So, we've played a bit already, but we'll be back on again later. Are you going to stay?"

I nodded mutely. This was all so strange and grown-up for me. I couldn't believe I was actually here. Mum would kill me if she found out but at that moment, standing next to this man, I couldn't have cared less. I'd have run away with him, right there and then, if he'd asked me.

He didn't, of course.

As we chatted I found myself relaxing at last. There was something I needed to know, though, so I took a deep breath and asked him.

"So —" I paused, unsure how to word it. "Are you single?" I blurted it out in the end, it seemed the easiest way. My face felt hot at my forwardness, so unlike me.

He didn't even flinch, though. I supposed he must have been used to it. Or just expected it. He shook his head slowly, a slight smile on his face. "No. No, I'm not."

"Oh."

"Are you disappointed to hear that?"

"I —" I didn't know how to answer. Disappointed was not the word I'd have used. Devastated.

Heartbroken. Crushed. They were all more appropriate words. I'd hoped he would say that yes, he was single, of course I had. But I'd also hoped that if he wasn't single, he'd like me enough to lie about it, and at least say that he was. Or that it didn't matter. Because I didn't care about some other woman, some vague thought of a woman who might be waiting for him at home, someone I didn't know and didn't ever want to know. I just wanted him.

Unfortunately, it seemed he did care about this other woman, and now I didn't know what to say.

I put my drink down. "I think I'd better get home." My voice wobbled but I didn't think he noticed.

He grabbed my arm gently. "Don't. Stay a bit longer. It would be nice to get to know you better."

"But — but you're with someone."

He shrugged. "Doesn't mean I can't talk to you, does it? I like talking to people. Doesn't mean I have to run off with you." He smiled and I tried to smile back but it was weak with disappointment. I'd had such high hopes for this evening and now they'd been crushed with just a few words.

And yet I knew I'd still stay. I'd take whatever I could get.

"OK." My voice cracked and I coughed to clear my throat.

And I tried really hard that night. I stayed and we talked and I tried to sound more grown up than I felt among all these older men. But when Ray finally went back on stage to finish his set I turned to Angie.

"Can we go?"

"Oh come on, you can't drag me all the way here and then leave this early." She checked her watch. "It's only 9.30. Let's stay a bit longer."

"But —"

"Come on, Kim. He might not be interested in you, but we're here now. We might as well enjoy ourselves."

I nodded miserably. "OK."

I hardly heard the next few songs, I felt so torn apart. But I danced and put on a brave face and waved my arms to the music anyway. I didn't know what it was about this man that had made me feel this way, but I felt as though he'd ripped out a piece of my heart and that I'd never get it back.

I was desperate for the night to end so I could go home and sob into my pillow, try and get over the rejection. And so I knocked back drink after drink until everything in the pub started to look a little hazy. Ray's set finished and I hoped he'd come back and talk to me again, give me the chance to get to know him a bit better, so I could try and get him to see how much he liked me. But this time, as he came off stage he walked in the opposite direction without even glancing my way. I watched as he strode across the pub and into the arms of another woman — a young, pretty woman with a halo of blonde hair round her face — who he kissed passionately. She smiled happily as he circled his arms round her tiny waist and left them there, resting his chin on her head. She looked up at him then and he looked down at her with such love in his eyes I thought my heart was going to break.

I turned to Angie, tugged her sleeve.

"I need to go."

"Oh come on, just a bit longer."

I shook my head. "No. You stay. I'm going home." And I stood, stumbling out of the pub and home to nurse my broken heart, leaving Angie, Ray and the tiny blonde woman far behind me, as though physical distance could help mend a broken heart.

It didn't work, of course. Over the next few days, weeks, months, Ray was on my mind all the time. He was all I thought about, all day and late into the night as I lay in bed staring at the ceiling, unable to sleep. I was like a lovesick puppy.

I knew Mum was getting fed up with me.

"What's wrong with you, mooning around the place all the time?" she asked. But I couldn't tell her, she'd never understand; she'd tell me to pull myself together, that she'd never let herself be distracted by a man, that I needed to grow up. She'd only ever loved Dad, and when she fell pregnant and he'd left her she'd hardened her heart, closed it up to protect herself. So no, I definitely couldn't talk to her.

"Nothing's wrong, I'm fine."

She might not have believed me but she couldn't prove any different, so she left it.

To my shame, though, I started following Ray around to every concert he played in every pub around Norwich. Well, as many as I could get to, anyway. I told Mum I was out with friends or working late, and she just put my new-found love of going out down to my new job at the typing pool, to having made new friends.

It didn't matter to me whether I had someone to go with. Sometimes I'd spend the entire evening standing at the front, by the stage, watching Ray as he played his bass guitar, lost in the music. Other times I hung around the edge or at the back, sipping a drink. I wanted Ray to notice me, but I didn't want him to think I was stalking him, so I tried to hang back a bit, sometimes.

I knew *she'd* seen me though, Ray's woman. One night she must have noticed me watching them because she caught my eye, whispered something to Ray, who looked towards me, then turned back and shrugged.

I knew I should feel ashamed, that I was making a fool of myself. But I just couldn't help myself. I needed to see him. I'd never been like this about anyone before, and I didn't know how to handle it. It was like a drug. And so I kept going back for more.

I noticed other things too. I noticed Ray started wearing a wedding ring, and then later I noticed his woman looked fatter than usual. She stopped coming to see him very often, and it occurred to me she was pregnant. It was like a dagger to my heart but something made me keep going back anyway. Ray barely even spoke to me any more, hardly even glanced in my direction. But it still made no difference. I kept thinking, "Maybe one day he'll leave her and want me."

Tragic, I realize now, looking back.

Then one day I was at a pub waiting for the band to come on stage. I was with Angie, who still agreed to come along with me sometimes, maybe hoping she'd be able to chat up another member of the band, when I saw Ray's wife arrive, holding a toddler's hand. I glanced at my watch. It was still quite early, only seven o'clock, and I saw Ray's face light up with love as he spotted them across the pub. As I watched from the corner of the bar I felt tears prick my eyes. All I wanted was for him to look at me like that. Only, I finally realized, he never would.

It was time to stop doing this. To stop torturing myself with the hope that I could ever be with him. I vowed this was the last time.

I stayed at the bar that evening, though, long after his wife and daughter had left, nursing vodka and orange after vodka and orange. The pub started to tip on its side a little.

I needed some air. I wobbled as I climbed down from my stool, and gripped the bar for support. I walked slowly outside to the car park, where the cold hit me like a hammer between the eyes and I stumbled, almost falling over.

"Oops, careful." An arm had reached out to catch me and I looked up to see the man attached to it.

"Thanks," I slurred. I looked at him again. "Wait, don't I know you?"

He nodded, his closely shaved head shining like a snooker ball in the fluorescent streetlights. "We went to school together. Barry." He stuck his other arm out and I shook his hand, and without thinking I pulled him closer to me and kissed him full on the lips. They tasted of beer and cigarettes and slightly unclean teeth, but I didn't care. I needed to forget about Ray who didn't want me and find someone who did, and Barry seemed to, responding hungrily, so I dragged him across the car park towards the bins. Barry had always been keen on me, I remembered now, so I knew he wouldn't refuse. And so when he pinned my back against the wall of the pub I made it clear I was up for it and we had cheap, sordid sex, right there and then. It was my first time and it hurt quite a lot, but the pain — and the shame of what I was doing — was numbed by the alcohol, and as he ground against me in the dark I tried to imagine it was Ray and not Barry inside me. When he came I could hardly bear to look him in the eye.

I felt bad for him because it wasn't him I'd needed, it was just someone, to stop me caring about the man inside the pub who didn't want me. I regretted it immediately, but as I pulled my knickers up and he kissed me on the lips I pulled away.

"Thanks. I'm going home."

"Aren't you coming back inside with me?"

He tried to grab my hand, kiss me again, but I couldn't stand him near me and I snatched my hand away, clutched my handbag to my stomach and almost ran away, stumbling along the road to the bus stop, tears pouring down my face. I didn't look back to see whether he was following as the cars flowed past me, almost blinding me with their headlights.

In the weeks that followed I tried to block out what had happened that night. It seemed to be the only way of coping with it. I decided if I didn't think about it, maybe it had never happened. I stopped stalking Ray too, and stayed at home most evenings getting under Mum's feet. She didn't ask why I was suddenly at home all the time. I don't think she really wanted to know the answer.

Then one day, in June 1979, I realized something.

I'd missed my period. I tried not to think about it too much, but when my next one didn't arrive either, I knew.

The doctor confirmed it.

I was pregnant.

I'd almost blocked out the fumble I'd had that night, hazy with alcohol, behind the pub bins. It wasn't my proudest moment, and I'd thought I could file it away somewhere, pretend it had never happened.

But now there was this very clear evidence that it *had* happened, and I didn't know what to do about it.

I wondered if I could hide it. If I wore baggy clothes, stopped going out, maybe I could get away with it and not have to tell anyone, at least, not for a long time. I quit my job, deciding it was important to focus on growing the baby inside me. It didn't matter that its father was someone I'd rather forget about. I loved this baby straight away, and I knew I had to keep it.

But soon it became too hard to hide it, and I knew I had to tell my mother. I was scared. She might have been only small, but when she was angry she was a terrifying bundle of fury.

"I've got something to tell you, Mum. You might want to sit down."

"I most certainly don't want to sit down." She folded her arms and stared at me as my face flushed. "What have you done, young lady? What sort of trouble have you got yourself into?" She stopped and glanced at my belly, where my hand was resting on the small mound, and then her face went white and she did sit down, almost collapsing into the plastic chair next to her.

"Oh no. You've not gone and got yourself up the duff, have you?"

I gave a small, tight nod.

"Oh, you silly, silly girl." She put her head in her hands and shook it slowly, staring at the tabletop. Then she looked back up at me.

"Who?"

"It — it was just this boy. Barry. We met at the pub and we — well, it was only the once, Mum, but, well . . . I made a mistake. I'm sorry."

"A mistake?" she spat. "I should say you've made a mistake. A very, very big one." She shook her head again.

"I'm sorry." It came out as a whisper.

"It's a bit late for that, isn't it?" She glanced back at my belly and then up at me. "So. How far gone are you?"

"Four months. I'm due in November sometime."

"Four months."

I nodded and waited for her to say something else.

"So are you staying here or are you going off with this — Barry?"

"I was hoping I could stay here, with you. That you'd help me, you know, a bit."

"So he's having nothing to do with it, I take it?"

"I — I haven't told him yet."

"Well, you'd better. Even if he wants nothing to do with it he needs to know."

I nodded miserably. She was right, but I was dreading it.

"So, will you help me?"

Finally she nodded and when she spoke again her voice was softer. "Of course I will. But you do realize how bloody stupid you've been, don't you?"

I nodded, the tears threatening to escape. "Yes. I'm sorry."

"It's all right. It's all a bit late for sorries now, anyway." She held her arms out. "Come here, you daft thing." And, gratefully, I walked into her arms and we held each other for a few minutes. Relief flooded through me as the tears finally came. Everything was going to be all right.

Mum threatened to go and find Barry and "give him a piece of her mind", but I managed to stop her — mainly by refusing to tell her where he lived — and, apart from that, the next few months passed by pretty smoothly. I slowly stopped thinking about Ray as much, and, although I sometimes wished I could go to the pub and see him again, I knew I had to stay away. There was no point. He was married and had a child. And besides, if he didn't want me before, he was never going to want me now, like this.

I went to see Barry once, alone. I knocked on his door and when he opened it I felt sick at telling him the news. But, as I expected, he wasn't interested.

"It's fine. I don't need your help anyway. I just thought you should know." I ignored the look of disgust on his face and, as I walked away and back home, my head held high, I felt nothing but relief. I could do this on my own. We'd be all right. I didn't need anyone else.

The months passed and my belly grew, and I got ready for the baby's arrival. I found myself getting excited, imagining pushing it down the road in its pram. I knew I'd feel so proud, despite everything. I bought a cot and set it up next to my own bed. I bought nappies and formula milk and Babygros and a teddy bear. I was ready.

Then one day I was reading the paper when a story caught my eye.

LOCAL MAN KILLED

It wasn't the words so much as the photo next to it that caught my attention and I cried out in horror. It was Ray. I read the story quickly, desperate for the details, desperate to find that I'd misunderstood, that it wasn't Ray who had died.

But it was, and as I got to the end of the story I thought I was going to be sick.

I hadn't meant much to him — I hadn't meant anything, really. But he'd meant a lot to me. He was the reason I'd got pregnant, in a way. I was trying to make him jealous, to take my mind off the fact he never wanted me.

And now he was dead.

I felt stupid, grieving for someone I hardly knew, and of course that meant there wasn't anyone I could talk to about it. I just had to smother the pain and get on with it. And I did a good job, up to a point. I considered for one stupid moment going to his funeral, but I couldn't. I couldn't see his wife and I didn't want her to see me either. So I stayed away, though it was hard.

Mum put my moods down to my hormones and the fact I was bigger than a whale, and tried to cheer me up. But the only thing that got me out of bed and through each day after I read about his death was the life growing inside me. I had to be strong, for him or her.

I didn't once give a thought to what his wife and child might have been going through. I suppose I just didn't care.

And then something happened that I had no chance of ever getting over.

It started on 23 November, 1979. I'd been in hospital for a few hours with doctors monitoring me when suddenly, and without much warning, I went into labour. The pain over those next few hours was worse than anything I could ever have expected, and when it was finally over and my beautiful baby boy was born I couldn't imagine ever having to do that again. Only I did have to, just a few minutes later. Because there was another baby in there, and she needed to come out.

I was having twins.

I was in too much pain to register the shock, but the moment I was handed these two little bundles wrapped in hospital blankets was the moment I finally felt happy again for the first time in months. It was as though these two tiny people had healed the hole in my heart, and given me a reason to live my life again. I was exhausted that day, though, and kept dozing, on and off. The twins — I called them Samuel and Louisa — spent lots of time in a room at the end of the corridor with all the other babies, but the rest of the time they slept in matching cribs at the end of my bed where I could just sit and watch them. If I'd loved them any more, I'd have burst.

The day after they were born I woke up from a short doze to find the maternity ward buzzing. It was visiting time. Mum was due soon, she couldn't wait to meet her grandchildren, but I needed a cigarette before she got there so I dragged my sore body out of bed and grabbed the fag packet from my bag. The twins were sound asleep; they'd be OK for a few minutes while I slipped out. I stood at the door to my room and scanned the faces of the people in the corridor. There was a woman in front of me, sitting on one of the benches, her hand on a pushchair with an older child in it. The woman looked vaguely familiar, but her face was so stricken with grief I didn't feel I could stop and study her for long to work out how or if I knew her. I couldn't bear to think about what might have happened to make her so desperately sad, and so I turned away from her and scurried along the corridor, away from my babies, and away from her and her sadness.

As I stood by the fire exit, sucking tobacco into my lungs, I thought about how much my life had changed. The smoke made me feel light-headed. My thoughts kept wandering to Ray, to how much I missed him, and I kept trying to drag them back, to think about something else that didn't hurt so much. I wondered whether I should be letting Barry know about the twins. I doubted he'd care much, and I couldn't bear the thought of someone not loving them as much as I did. My heart swelled with love just picturing their tiny, perfect faces.

I took one final drag and watched an ambulance pull into the driveway and its doors fly open. I wondered briefly what emergency they were attending. Then I crushed the stub out on the railing and dropped it down five floors to the ground and made my way back inside, desperate to get back to my babies. I walked quickly back through the doors, back down the corridor, and was almost at the door of my room when I heard my name being called. I turned my head and there was Mum, walking towards me, a smile almost splitting her face in half. It was so rare to see her smile like that it made me smile too.

"Kimberley." She pulled me towards her and sniffed me. "Have you been smoking?"

I nodded and she looked at me for a moment. "Oh well, I suppose you're a mum now, I can hardly tell you off, can I?"

I grinned. "I'll remind you of that."

She smiled at me and pushed my hair gently from my face. "I know I don't say it very often, but I am proud of you, you know."

"I know."

She cupped my cheek with her hand for a moment and I felt like a little girl again. I wanted to stay like that forever. "Right, are you going to let me cuddle my grandchildren, then?"

"If they're awake." We turned and walked the few yards to my room. I wish I'd known as we took those steps that that moment was the very last time I'd ever feel happy, because then I could have tried to hold on to it forever. But it was too late.

I knew from the minute we walked into the room that something was terribly wrong.

There were still two cribs at the end of my bed. But there was only one baby. The other crib was empty, the sheet stretched smoothly over the mattress as though nobody had ever been there. As though my little girl had never existed. It was as though the world stood still for a moment as I took it in, and tried to work out what was going on. Beside me, Mum was still talking, but I didn't hear a word she said. My eyes flicked left and right and I took in the whole room in a matter of seconds. My baby wasn't there. My head whirled and I grabbed the door frame.

"Where is she?" I whipped my head round and Mum must have seen the panic in my eyes because she gripped my arm and said, "What's happened? What's the matter?"

"My baby . . . Louisa . . ." I pointed to the empty crib and felt Mum's hand stiffen.

"It'll be OK, try not to panic. I'm sure it's fine, one of the nurses will have her." She raced away then and left me standing there alone while she spoke to a midwife. They were talking for a while, looking round, dashing off, talking to colleagues. But it didn't matter, because all the time I knew.

I knew she wasn't with a nurse.

I knew she wasn't with a doctor.

I knew she'd gone.

I just knew.

My legs collapsed beneath me and I fell to the floor in the doorway. I felt hands under my arms lifting me and helping me to the bed and I heard voices around me, getting louder, the pitch rising as realization dawned.

I lay on that bed for what could have been seconds but could also have been hours while bodies, faces, people floated around me; voices came at me, soft and kind, but I couldn't hear what they were saying. At some point I must have moved and picked up Samuel because he was by my side asleep or feeding while all around me panic ensued. I stared at my baby boy's face, at the cute little snub of his nose and his shock of dark hair peeking out from under his tiny woolly hat, and I tried to focus on nothing but that, to block out everything else that was happening. I needed to dampen down the sense of panic that kept threatening to engulf me, and the only way I knew to do that was to go inside myself, and stay away from the outside world.

I can't honestly tell you how the events of that day unfolded after the moment that I realized my baby girl was missing. I know the police arrived because they came to talk to me, to ask me some questions. Nurses fussed around and Mum looked strained, her face lined and pale. For the first time in my life she looked old.

At some point I was taken home and tucked up in bed, baby Samuel asleep in his crib next to me. When he cried I fed him, and sometimes I woke up from a fevered sleep to find Mum holding him, his lips sucking greedily from a bottle. But mostly I tried not to sleep. I tried not to take my eyes off my precious boy in case I lost him too.

And all the time I kept asking myself, how could I have done it? How could I have left them there, even for a few minutes, without me? If I hadn't gone for that cigarette, if I'd just stayed there in that room with them, then none of this would have happened.

Days passed in flashes of grief, when I'd wake screaming, or find myself on the bathroom floor, sobbing uncontrollably, until Mum led me gently back to bed. Other days I'd have long periods of calm, when I felt nothing and just sat, perfectly still, utterly numb, staring into space. I think Mum found the shouting and screaming easier to deal with; she knew what it meant, and she knew how to help. But when I was gone, vacant, away from myself, she struggled, unsure how to get through to me. I was too far gone even to try to help her.

I spoke to journalists, I gave statements to the police. They asked me if I had any idea who might have done this but I couldn't think of anyone and that made me feel even worse, as though I was letting Louisa down. I felt bad when I gave them Barry's name, but I knew he had nothing to hide, so it was best to tell the truth.

If you'd asked me a few days ago, I'd probably have said that I knew from the moment I saw Louisa's empty crib that I was never going to see her again. But the truth was, I always had a flame of hope. It slowly diminished until, by the end, it was almost completely extinguished. But deep, deep down somewhere in my heart, it was always there, burning gently.

It's been a tough ride for me and my boy, and there have been times when I didn't think I was going to make it. But every time I've hit rock bottom I've had to drag myself up and out of it, for him.

And now here we are — and here she is, standing in front of me in my very own kitchen: the girl that everyone else gave up on so many years ago.

My girl. My Louisa.

Finally, for the first time in thirty-seven long, painful years, the flame is burning brightly again, and maybe I can believe that, at last, everything is going to be OK.

Acknowledgements

This book would never even have come to be if it hadn't been for the person who gave me the inspiration in the first place. Lisa Beith, my lovely sister-in-law; the words you uttered after darling Megan died never left my mind and it's those words that, many years later, helped shape the idea for this book. So for that, I thank you. I hope I've done justice to how you truly felt.

Many people helped me with the research for this book and I'd like to thank them from the bottom of my heart for giving up their time and knowledge. Firstly, a lovely midwife called Jackie Auger who, amazingly, not only worked in the Norfolk and Norwich maternity hospital during the 1970s but could even remember which floor everything was on! The details you provided were invaluable, and any mistakes are, clearly, mine — plus a bit of creative freedom, of course. Another midwife, Emily Balch, also helped me understand exactly what could and couldn't happen during a late miscarriage and, although I asked her some rather disturbing and upsetting questions, she provided me with excellent answers to which I do hope I've done justice. I also need to thank Gary Oborne, who provided some great details about police procedures during the seventies and, even though much of the detail didn't get used in the end, I hope that knowing it helped make the whole thing more authentic.

My mum, Pam Swatman, also helped me with lots of the everyday detail from the time. Thanks Mum.

I spent quite a long time researching dementia and Alzheimer's and found many useful books and papers on the subject, not least *Keeper*, a book about memory, identity, isolation, Wordsworth and cake by Andrea Gillies.

There are no doubt many people I've forgotten to thank, and for that, I'm sorry. But your help is always appreciated.

I also, of course, need to thank the brilliant Judith Murray. Again, you helped me shape this story into what it is now, and you never stopped believing I could do it. It's amazing to have someone as great as you in my corner. Everyone at Greene and Heaton is a joy to work with.

Thanks also to Victoria Hughes-Williams at Pan Macmillan for your ninja editing skills. It wouldn't be half the book it is without your brilliant ideas. Thanks to the rest of the team at Pan Macmillan too, not least Jess, Abbie and Jayne.

And finally, friends and family. I'll never be forgiven if I don't mention my lovely little brother Mark here, and the truth is, he's always supported me in everything I've done, and especially this book-writing business. Mark, you're the best.

Thanks also to my usual early readers, Serena and Zoe, who give me honest feedback and make great cups of tea.

And thanks, as always, to my frankly amazing husband Tom, and brilliant boys, Jack and Harry. It's all for you.

BEFORE YOU GO

Clare Swatman

Some people stare love in the face for years before they find it. Zoe and Ed fumbled their way into adulthood, both on different paths — but always in the same direction. Years later, having navigated dead-end jobs and chaotic house shares, romance finally blossoms. Their future together looks set ... Then the unthinkable happens. One morning, on his way to work, Ed is knocked off his bike and dies. Now Zoe must find a way to survive. But she's not ready to let go of her memories. How can she forget all of the happy times, their first kiss, everything they'd built together? Zoe decides she has to tell Ed all the things she never said. But now it's too late. Or is it?

TANGERINE

Christine Mangan

The last person Alice Shipley expected to see when she arrived in Tangier with her new husband was Lucy Mason. After the horrific accident at Bennington, the two friends — once inseparable roommates — haven't spoken in over a year. But Lucy is standing there, trying to make things right. Perhaps Alice should be happy. She has not adjusted to life in Morocco, too afraid to venture out into the bustling medinas and oppressive heat. Lucy, always fearless and independent, helps Alice emerge from her flat and explore the country. But soon a familiar feeling starts to overtake Alice — she feels controlled and stifled by Lucy at every turn. Then Alice's husband, John, goes missing, and she starts to question everything around her . . .